There must *[be a woman like]*
this in every man's past,

Lee thought. A woman like Erin Fleming.

A woman who, after months of separation, could still overwhelm his senses. A woman who haunted his dreams and seemed to find a place in his mind at the oddest times of the day. A woman who could still fill him with incomparable desire.

A woman who reminded him of fire—hot and mysterious and inviting—and burned him if he got too close.

Dear Reader,

Once again, you've come to the right place if you're looking for that seductive mix of romance and excitement that is quintessentially Intimate Moments. Start the month with *The Lady in Red*—by reader favorite Linda Turner. Your heart will be in your throat as rival homicide reporters Blake Nickels and Sabrina Jones see their relationship change from professional to personal—with a killer on their trail all the while. And don't miss the conclusion of the HOLIDAY HONEYMOONS miniseries, Merline Lovelace's *The 14th...and Forever*. You'll wish for a holiday—and a HOLIDAY HONEYMOON—every month of the year.

The rest of the month is fabulous, too, with new books from Rebecca Daniels: *Mind Over Marriage;* Marilyn Tracy: *Almost Perfect*, the launch book in her ALMOST, TEXAS miniseries; and Allie Harrison: *Crime of the Heart*. And welcome new author Charlotte Walker, as she debuts with *Yesterday's Bride*. Every one of these books is full of passion, and sometimes peril—don't miss a single one.

And be sure to come back next month, when the romance and excitement continue, right here in Silhouette Intimate Moments.

Enjoy!

Leslie J. Wainger
Senior Editor and Editorial Coordinator

Please address questions and book requests to:
Silhouette Reader Service
U.S.: 3010 Walden Ave., P.O. Box 1325, Buffalo, NY 14269
Canadian: P.O. Box 609, Fort Erie, Ont. L2A 5X3

CRIME
OF THE
HEART

ALLIE
HARRISON

Published by Silhouette Books

America's Publisher of Contemporary Romance

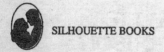 SILHOUETTE BOOKS

ISBN 0-373-07767-X

CRIME OF THE HEART

Copyright © 1997 by Allison Harris

Printed in U.S.A.

Books by Allie Harrison

Silhouette Intimate Moments

Crime of the Heart #767

Silhouette Shadows

Dream a Deadly Dream #20
Dead Reckoning #40

ALLIE HARRISON

has been writing since she was in school but never really took it seriously until she joined her local RWA chapter six years ago. She now works to divide her time between her husband, their two small children, reading the latest hot romance and creating her own intriguing stories.

She lives in a small town in southern Illinois and believes everyone should follow their dream and never give up.

To Wayne and Ben and Rachel
With love always

And to Ginny S. and Linda J.
For the inspiration and support
Thank you

Prologue

Liam McGrey was aware of two things upon opening his eyes.

The pain in his head and the pain in his leg.

His head simply pounded. His leg felt more as though it was on fire. He closed his eyes again, hoping to get lost in the mystical, painless place from which he'd just come. But he couldn't. He had to stay and face the pain.

Opening his eyes a second time, his breath caught and his heart skipped a beat at the sight of the woman who sat in the chair beside his bed. By the sounds coming to him from the open door and the smell of antiseptic in the air, he realized where he was, and so didn't take his gaze off the woman before him to look around.

She was staring at him, her green eyes looking large and round and puffy.

"You're awake," she said.

"What are you doing here, Erin?" he asked at the same time, his throat dry and scratchy, making the words painful.

"I couldn't not come," she replied.

"Why? You wanted to rub some salt into my wounds?" he bit out.

She sighed heavily. "Lee, please—" she began, leaning closer but staying in the chair.

"Please what?" he asked, ignoring the pain in his leg. The pain in his soul suddenly seemed deeper, fresher. "Please accept you with open arms? Please let you hold my hand so that in a few weeks when I'm out of here, you're gone, too? Just get out of here, Erin."

"Lee—"

"Leaving shouldn't be any harder for you now than it was two weeks ago," he snapped.

"I told you my reasons for having to go," she said, her words coming out in a rush.

"Oh, yes, I remember your reasons well. You couldn't live with my being gone so much. You couldn't live with my being in danger. You couldn't live with my line of work. You couldn't live with the worry that someday I *just might get shot*. Well, I'm sorry to point it out to you, but that day's come, hasn't it? And here I am. And here you are. And I don't want you here. I don't *need* you here. So get out." Lee realized for the first time that he was shouting at her, his voice echoing through the bland room.

"Mr. McGrey, you need to remain calm and rest."

Lee looked toward the door, blinking against the pain and taking in the woman in white. Hell, just what he needed—another woman telling him what to do. Well, he could give orders, too. He was, after all, contributing to her paycheck. "Get her out of here," he said.

The nurse looked at Erin. "Perhaps it would be best if you left now."

Lee closed his eyes and refused to look at Erin, but he could feel the heat of her stare. Finally, he heard her footsteps on the tiled floor as she left.

The nurse, however, didn't leave. She came closer. He opened his eyes to find her checking the IV that was stuck in his arm. Then she took his wrist to check his pulse.

"She's been sitting beside you since you were brought in yesterday," she said quietly.

"I don't care," he muttered. "She didn't want to stay beside me before. I don't want her beside me now."

"Would you like me to give you something for pain, Mr. McGrey?" the nurse asked.

"No," he replied after a moment. "It doesn't hurt that much."

The nurse left a few moments later, first checking to make sure the bandage on his thigh was clean and dry.

After she had gone, Lee thought about his lie. *It doesn't hurt that much.* The truth was it hurt like hell. Not only in his leg, and not only in his head.

But Liam knew damn good and well that no painkiller was ever going to ease the ache he felt in his heart.

Chapter 1

Eight months later

Lee answered the door and stared into the eyes of the woman standing on the other side. There must be a woman like this in every man's past, he thought to himself. A woman like Erin Flemming.

A woman, who after months of separation, could still overwhelm his senses. A woman he could taste and smell. A woman whose face and smile he could see when he closed his eyes. A woman who haunted his dreams and seemed to find a place in his mind at the oddest times of the day. A woman who, after months of not seeing her, of not hearing from her, could still fill him with incomparable want.

A woman who reminded him of fire—hot and mysterious and inviting—and burned him if he got too close.

Erin Flemming now stood on the other side of Lee's

threshold, looking even better than she did in his memories.

He hadn't seen or heard from her since the day in the hospital. Mentally he uttered an oath and did his best to keep the emotion from his face. "Erin," he said through a throat that suddenly felt so tight he would have sworn there was someone trying to strangle him. "What are you doing here?" he tried again.

Her hair was still a lovely auburn, still wavy in its own wild way and looking as soft as he remembered. Only now it was shorter, falling to just below her shoulders in a style that was much more sculpted and fit in well with her tailored suit.

Memories flooded his mind. Memories of the way she looked with her hair fanned around her on his pillow as she lay beneath him, the way her laugh floated away on the breeze as they fed ducks in the park and the way her emerald eyes sparkled in the moonlight as they walked hand in hand along the shores of Lake Michigan.

Hell, Lee could picture it all so clearly. He closed his eyes briefly, not wanting to see any of it at all. For with the memories came the sharp, familiar pain of her desertion.

Lee did his best to ignore that pain, just as he'd learned to do for the pain in his leg.

"I need to talk to you, Lee," she replied. "And I was afraid to call you."

He pushed aside the sound of his name on her lips. The way she said it, the words seemed to reach in and take hold of his heart. It was the breathy, needful tone in her voice he had to fight to ignore.

"What do you need to talk to me about?" he muttered, doing his best to keep his gaze fixed on her face and not let it travel down her body to her shapely legs. "Did you suddenly discover you'd forgotten something when you moved out?''

Get this over quick, he thought. The sooner he shut the door, the sooner he could collapse in the nearest chair and try to stop the pounding of his heart. The sudden throbbing in his bad leg, too. *God, it must be going to rain,* he told himself.

Lee took a deep breath, trying to bring his body under some semblance of control. But all he managed to do was inhale a strong whiff of her perfume. It was the same one it had taken eight months to wash out of his bedding...out of his whole damned house.

''Can I come in?'' she asked.

For a long moment, he didn't respond. Once Erin stepped through his door, somehow, someway, she would be back in his life. And he didn't want her there. He had worked too hard to get her out of his system, to convince himself that he didn't need her...or anyone.

He could say no. It was his house. And it was just one word. It should be easy. *No.*

So why couldn't he say it? Instead, he motioned her inside. The moment she stepped through the door, the house felt different to him, warmer, more like home. Even his own house betrayed him.

''Would you like some coffee or something?'' he asked, running a hand through his hair.

Erin watched his movements, and Lee thought he saw something reflected in her eyes, some hint of sadness, as if his actions or appearance had brought back some unwanted memory for her. Well, good, he thought bitterly. She deserved it.

''Coffee would be great,'' she said.

Lee turned toward the kitchen, not wanting to feel her eyes on him any longer, not wanting to see the way she seemed to be drinking him in. Still, he felt her closeness as she followed him.

He had been up most of the night trying to exercise away the pain in his leg and fighting the urge to take something for it. He didn't understand why his leg hurt the worst at night—it should have hurt more after his exercise therapy. When he'd last looked at the clock, it had been a quarter to three in the morning. And it had been some time after that before he was finally able to fall asleep.

Erin's knock on his front door had awakened him after no more than three or four hours of fitful sleep. He glanced at the digital clock on the stove. Ten after eight. He felt like hell and imagined he looked even worse.

"You're still limping," she observed.

Lee grimaced. His leg stood out worse than a sunburned nose, and despite all the therapy, he often felt just shy of having to resort to the damned cane he'd used after coming off the crutches.

"Yes, well, I suppose it's going to take awhile before I'm as good as new. But don't worry, I've got lots of time," he muttered, without turning toward her.

"I heard you were still on leave," she said.

"I wonder who told you that," he muttered, knowing full well his ex-partner, Tom, had probably told her.

Erin didn't answer.

Lee ignored the dirty dishes piled in the sink and pushed several pieces of junk mail from the counter in order to make room for the coffeemaker. "Sorry about the mess. I wasn't expecting anyone, and the cleaning lady isn't due back until early next week."

Even with his back to her, he could still feel the heat of her stare. He forced his hands to stop trembling as he scooped coffee into the filter.

No other woman had ever had this effect on him, and

he was annoyed that Erin still held the strange physical power over him that she always had.

Lee laughed to himself when he recalled that he once had actually planned to spend the rest of his life with her. He'd come home after a two-week stakeout with a ring in his pocket...and found her suitcases packed in the foyer. It had taken twelve months for him to reach that point in his life where he was willing to commit himself to one woman forever. And with merely a snap of the lock on a suitcase, Erin had closed that door in his heart before it was ever really opened. Lee had vowed never again to be that vulnerable.

Lee let the coffeemaker do its thing and turned to face Erin. "So what did you need to talk to me about?" he asked, trying to ignore the pain in his bad leg, and the way his emotions were tearing his insides apart. A part of him wanted to pull her to him, to feel what he'd been missing in his life for the past nine months.

But another part wanted to rattle her.

"I'm in trouble," she blurted out, wringing her hands together. She sounded as though she had no idea where to begin. And Lee thought he saw fear in her eyes.

He kept his feet firmly planted to keep from moving closer and taking her in his arms. "What kind of trouble?"

"I..." She started pacing back and forth in his kitchen.

"Sit down, Erin," he ordered, trying to remember if he'd ever seen her so upset. Her job as a reporter with the *Chicago Earlybird* had gone well because she didn't let herself get emotionally involved. She asked questions and searched for answers with a calm certainty and strength that had attracted him to her the first time she interviewed him about a case.

He knew she'd recently accepted an award for her investigative report on medical hazardous waste that was being dumped a short distance from one of the largest grade schools in Chicago. He'd seen her picture on the front page of the *Earlybird*, where she'd been labeled the paper's best new asset. In the picture, some nice-looking stranger was holding her hand.

Lee forced away the memory.

Erin sat down on a nearby kitchen chair, still twisting her hands.

"Now take a deep breath," he instructed.

She did. Lee didn't think it helped much.

"What kind of trouble are you in?" he asked again.

She bit her bottom lip. It was a nervous habit, Lee remembered.

"Take another deep breath and let it out slowly," he persisted, hoping she would relax. She was starting to worry him. He'd never seen her behave like this.

Lee found two clean mugs. Remembering that Erin liked two spoons of sugar in her coffee, he pulled out the sugar bowl and a spoon and took them to the table before filling the mugs.

Erin's breath sounded loud in the quiet room. Out of the corner of his eye, he glimpsed her sitting at the table. How many times had she sat at that same table with him? Lee tried to close his mind to such memories.

He brought her the coffee and sat down across from her, not daring to sit any closer. Out of habit, he propped his bad leg up on the chair next to him. It did little to ease the pain he felt.

"Be straight with me now, Erin. No games. Calm down and tell me what kind of trouble you've gotten yourself into," he said.

He wanted quick, precise answers. Nothing more. He didn't want her to talk about anything else or show him any more unwanted concern. Letting her into his house was bad enough. He damn sure wasn't going to let her into his personal life. Again.

And if she told him her trouble was something trivial, like being unable to find all her tax information or balance her checkbook, he was liable to show her to the door with no second thoughts.

Erin wrapped her fingers around her mug as if to warm herself and he tried not to look at her hands. Gentle, soft hands that only served to remind him how she had once touched him....

"I need your help," she said, getting right to the point. "Your protection."

"What for?" he snapped, feeling disappointed and just a little relieved at the same time.

"I'm in trouble," she repeated.

"You said that before. What kind of trouble?" he asked again, wondering how many times he was going to have to ask. He could have laughed, just imagining what kind of trouble she had gotten herself into. Hell, she was the most straitlaced person he'd ever known. She was frighteningly honest and would never harm another soul. Even though she could be a cut-to-the-quick reporter in her search for the truth, she was always up-front about it.

"I saw a murder—and now I think somebody's after me. Someone keeps calling, but when I pick up the phone, I only hear breathing. And I have the feeling I'm being followed. Actually, I'm pretty sure I'm being followed."

Lee's heart started to pound, the pain in his leg gone and forgotten. He'd spent his life protecting people, and the fact that someone had put a look of fear into Erin's eyes sent a sudden surge of anger through his body. "Tell me everything. You're sure it's not just an old boyfriend wanting you back?" he blurted out, unable to hold the barbed question back.

"I told you. I saw a murder," she replied evenly.

"Maybe you should contact the police," he said bluntly.

Her beautiful green eyes widened, looking like sparkling pools of water. "You are the police."

"Not right now."

She ignored his comment. "Besides, I did contact them. They're investigating the murder, but they haven't found any evidence. And since no one has physically approached me, they can't help me."

"Why me? Couldn't you find anyone else in the whole state of Illinois to run to?" he asked, keeping his voice and his gaze hard.

Suddenly, she was crying. Tears poured down her cheeks. Lee stared at them for a long moment.

"I didn't know where else to go. I came to you for help," she said between sobs. "I'm sorry I hurt you. I'm sorry about your leg. I'm sorry about everything, all right? But I can't change any of it. I would if I could, but I can't."

Lee couldn't stop staring at her, finding it hard to believe she was the same woman who had looked him straight in the eye—with dry eyes, too—and told him she couldn't live with the worry that something would happen to him.

"I know you can't," he said, not knowing what else to say. Taking a large gulp of coffee, he burned his mouth as he tried to swallow past the bitterness in his throat. *She'd* left him! Without even a backward look. Now she sat there, crying as though he was the one to blame.

He should throw her out right now, Lee thought. Tell her to forget it, as she once so easily had forgotten about him. Tell her to find someone else. Hire a professional bodyguard. She could even go to Tom, his old partner.

He should just walk away. The way she had nearly three-quarters of a year before. Only that time, she had walked; he would have to limp. His mug hit the table with a loud thunk that echoed through the room.

No, he couldn't throw her out. Not like he wanted to.

His leg couldn't manage it. And even if it could, he still couldn't do it. But that didn't mean he had to be the one to protect her. There were other people who were qualified to do that.

"I'm sorry, Erin," he said quietly. "You'll have to find someone else. I'm on the disabled list." It was the truth. So why did it feel as though he was hunting for excuses?

She blinked at him as though his words surprised her.

"I'll pay you anything you want, Lee," she said.

He put up a hand, bringing her words to a halt. "Don't," he said. "Don't make offers like that, Erin." He realized she had no idea how her words and her tears affected him. He wondered what she would do if he took her up on the offer, saying she had to pay him with something other than money.

Her eyes widened and she appeared to have stopped breathing. For a long moment, Lee had the strange sensation that she knew exactly what he'd been thinking. "Okay," she began, "but—"

"No buts. I couldn't take the job even if I wanted to." He waited a few anxious seconds after he uttered the words—the first untruth he'd ever spoken to her—to see if he'd be struck by lightning. He wasn't, of course, but the lie only added to the bitterness within him.

The truth was he could take the job. Tom had been calling him for weeks, trying to get him back to headquarters. Yes, the leg hurt him, but he could get around. He could sit at a desk and work a phone.

"If you want, I'll give you the names of a few guys who can probably help you. Or I could call Tom for you. I'm sure he'd help you."

"I don't trust anyone else," she flung at him. She'd managed to control the sobs, but the tears were still heavy in her eyes.

Lee stared down at his coffee, no longer able to bear

the haunted, fearful look in her eyes and lie to her. "I'm sorry, Erin," he said slowly.

"I see," she said just as slowly, letting him know that she saw right through his lie. She took a deep breath. "I, um, suppose there isn't anything I can do to change your mind, is there?"

She could give him what his body so desperately wanted—hers, he thought. But that was more than he was willing to let her pay. He cleared his throat.

"You saw a murder?" he asked, trying to sound neutral, but not having much luck.

"Yes, down at Pier 37."

"Let me call Tom—" he began.

"No," she interrupted. "I want you to hear the story first."

"Tom could be here in fifteen minutes."

She was going to cry again. He could see it coming.

"I don't want Tom! I came to you. Do you hate me so much that you won't at least listen to me?" she asked.

The question threw him. No, he didn't *hate* her. That was exactly why he didn't want to listen to her story. But at the same time, he didn't exactly *like* her, either. Maybe it was best to say he *wanted* her.

She took another deep breath, trying to regain her self-control. "The house hasn't changed much, Lee," she said, saying his name as though she had trouble forcing it out. "But you have. You don't smile. You haven't smiled since you opened the door. And you don't listen, either."

"I don't have much to smile about these days," he snapped. It was probably closer to months, he realized. "And as for the listening part, I'll listen. After that, I'm calling Tom. Technically, he's still my partner."

"But he got promoted," she pointed out, confirming his suspicion that she must have talked to Tom.

"Yes, he got promoted," he replied just to satisfy her.

"But our partnership has never officially been terminated." He took another drink of his coffee, knowing it would have to do. It was too early for anything stronger. "Let's start at the beginning. You're still living at your dad's house?" He already knew the answer.

"His old place outside of Wilmette? It's right on the lake, remember?"

Of course he remembered. "Tell me everything you saw, everything that happened," he prompted.

"A man by the name of Felix Jenkins sent me a note at the newspaper office and asked me to meet him. He said he knew of something big that was going down, something he felt he needed to tell me. So I met him last Tuesday night at Pier 37—"

"At night?" he interrupted. "Not a smart move, Erin."

"It was all he would agree to. Said he'd been doing some work down on the docks. I knew it was dangerous, but if a person seems to have an important story, sometimes I meet on his terms. Anyway—" she spoke quickly before he could say any more about the danger she'd put herself in "—he wouldn't let me write anything down or use a tape recorder. He said he wanted to be certain of my ability to protect my sources. But all he got the chance to do was mention something about some robbery that was being planned and tell me the name of a possible lead before—"

"What name?" Lee broke in to ask.

"Forest Burke."

"Isn't he an art dealer or something?" The name sounded oddly familiar to Lee.

"Yes, a collector and connoisseur," Erin answered.

"Okay, go on. Before what?" Lee tamped down his lingering anger that she had brought this problem to him and not someone else. He was becoming more and more curious as her story unfolded.

"Before he thought he heard something," she continued. "I hid behind some crates. And all of a sudden, this other man popped out of nowhere. He seemed to come right out of the darkness without a sound. He strangled Jenkins with a cord or a wire or something. I don't know. I couldn't see exactly what he had in his hands."

"There was just the one man?" Lee asked.

"That's all I could see." Erin was still holding her cup, but she hadn't moved since beginning her lengthy explanation.

"What happened then?" he asked.

"The man dragged Jenkins's body to the edge of the pier and dumped it into a small boat moored there. Then he climbed in, started the motor and left," she explained.

"What did you do?" Lee couldn't help but ask.

"As soon as he left, I got the hell out of there. I was terrified. I remember thinking every shadow was another man waiting to grab me. I called 911 from the phone in my car."

"But you didn't stay at the scene?"

"I know it was probably stupid of me to leave, but I was afraid the man would be back. So I went to the police station. I work a lot with two detectives, Burger and Reece, getting inside information."

"I've heard of them," Lee said. "They're with the Sixty-third."

"That's right. I told them what happened, what I saw, and they went down there to help out with what little investigation there was. But they said the pier was completely empty. There wasn't any sign of foul play or a struggle. I told them Jenkins didn't get much of a chance to struggle. Since they didn't have a body, there wasn't much they could do. But they said they'd keep the investigation open."

"And you don't know anything more about this Jenkins

guy?'' Lee asked, feeling as though he was suddenly standing in mud up to his knees.

"Nothing."

"When you got the phone calls, what did the caller say?''

"Nothing. I had the feeling someone was just checking up on me. Maybe to scare me, make me nervous.''

"If the killer didn't see you, why are you certain these calls have something to do with Jenkins's murder?''

"Maybe with the murder or maybe just with the information Jenkins gave me. I don't know which. Jenkins had my business card. When I first met him, he was hesitant to tell me anything at all. I told him I didn't have all night. If he made up his mind and wanted to talk, he could call me. I gave him my business card. All the killer would have to do was check his pockets.

"But the calls didn't start until after I put Burke's name into a computer to do some checking. I'd hit one too many dead ends when it came to finding anything on Jenkins, so I thought I'd try Burke. I even called his secretary.''

"What kind of checking?'' Lee asked.

"Just the usual. I put his name into the computer and didn't get much—birth date, address, phone number, that kind of thing. Then, like I said, I called his secretary to see if I could schedule an interview, but he declined, saying Burke was too busy at this time,'' she explained.

"Did you find anything to link Jenkins's story with Burke?'' Lee asked.

"No.''

"When did all this happen?'' Lee asked.

"I saw Jenkins late Tuesday night. The morning following his murder I started putting names into the computer at the paper.

"Then yesterday when I went to the grocery store,'' she went on, "I thought I noticed someone following me. I don't feel safe staying alone in the house anymore. I was thinking about checking into a hotel somewhere. I even thought of leaving town and going to New York or something.''

But then she must have thought of him, Lee realized. Gee, he felt so lucky.

Her gaze touched him, just as he thought she could have touched him before and gotten anything she wanted. She shivered suddenly. Lee fought the urge to take her in his arms and warm her.

"Are you certain you were being followed, that it wasn't just your imagination? Sometimes when you've been under a lot of stress—"

"I'm an investigative reporter, trained to notice things. I know when I'm being followed, Liam! I know when I'm being watched!''

"Fine. So you're certain you're in danger?" he persisted, finally accepting the fact that he cared enough about her to not want anything to happen to her. He also had to acknowledge that he couldn't walk away from a challenge like this, at least not without searching for a few answers first. Instinct told him she *was* probably in danger, and it left a cold feeling in his gut. There were just too many coincidences.

"Yes," she said.

"You've dealt with threats before when it came to your job," he couldn't help but observe.

"Yes, but nothing like this. And I've never seen anyone get murdered before, either.''

"Do the police have your name? Did you give it to the 911 dispatch?" he asked.

"Yes, and both Reece and Burger know that I witnessed Jenkins's murder. I'm sure it all got put into a report somewhere. That means anyone could have seen my name.''

The kitchen was completely silent for a long moment.

"That's not all," she said slowly.

Hell, he didn't like the way she said those three little words. That cold feeling in his gut was suddenly replaced by a burning fear. He wasn't going to like this, not at all. He'd felt this same way on seeing her suitcases in the foyer nine months ago. All she'd said then was "Lee, I have to talk to you," and he'd known something was wrong. It wasn't so much her words; it was the slow, even way she'd said them.

That's not all.

Lee waited, unable to stop the burning sensation from filtering through him.

"Someone tried to run me down in the parking garage of the newspaper office last night."

Lee didn't want to think about this, either. God, why did she have to come to him with this? Why did she have to involve him? "Did you see who was driving the car?" he asked, hardly able to get the words past his parched throat.

"Just that it was a man," she replied.

"The same one from the pier?"

She shrugged, shifting her shoulders in such a way that her suit jacket tightened over her breasts. Lee's mouth went suddenly dry, but he didn't take a drink of his coffee. He couldn't move.

"It happened so fast, I hardly had time to get out of the way. I called the police, but all I was able to give them was a brief description of a red car. Do you have any idea how many red cars there are in Chicago?" she asked.

Lee didn't.

"I'm some reporter, huh?" she asked with a bitter chuckle. "I didn't even get a look at the license plate. After that, I decided to take a leave of absence until things cooled down. So here I am. The only problem is, I don't think anything's going to cool down. At least not while I'm alive."

She said all this with an odd sort of calm in her voice. Still, her eyes gave her away. He could see the terror in them.

"Is there anything else I should know about?" he asked, hoping there wasn't.

Erin shook her head. "I know this all sounds farfetched, but I have a really bad feeling about this thing. And you always said I should trust my instincts."

"I did, didn't I?" he agreed, remembering full well his advice to her. Then curiosity compelled him to go on. "If we were to assume no one knows you saw the murder, can you think of any reasons at all why someone would be calling you or following you?" he asked after a long moment, telling himself that it was just another question. It didn't mean he was going back to work, that he was taking on the job of protecting her.

Her eyes narrowing, she looked at him, hard. "I think someone's worried about what kind of information I might have dug up on Forest Burke, or maybe the information I might dig up if I keep trying."

He should look away, he knew. He should show her the door and be done with her. Spend the next hundred years convincing himself that his body really didn't ache for her. Tell her to find someone else. Anyone else. But he didn't move. He just asked another question. There was no harm in just one more question. "Who knows where you live?" He wasn't sure he wanted to know the answer to that question. "A lover, friends, colleagues, clients you've done stories about, enemies you've made along the way?"

"Jack Brennan, the editor at the paper," she began. "And my partner, Jerry Hartford. He's my photographer. And I suppose almost anyone could get my address out of my personnel file even though the records are supposed to be confidential.''

''Your phone number and address are still unlisted, though, right?'' Lee asked.

''Yes. But that doesn't mean someone couldn't follow me home from work.''

Lee met her gaze, only to find her looking at him with hope in her emerald eyes.

''That's all?'' he asked. ''That's everything?''

''Yes,'' she promised.

Lee knew that he'd have more questions for her later, after he put some names into a computer to check them out.

Hell, no, he thought. There would be no later. He wasn't doing this. He was not stepping in to rescue her. Yes, he was worried about her. Yes, he wanted her. Yes, he cared about her. But protecting her and getting her through this meant getting involved with her. And he wasn't getting involved with her. Not again. Not ever. He wasn't getting any closer to her than he was now.

It just wasn't going to happen. No matter how much his body tried to convince him otherwise.

But it was happening.

Erin said she trusted you, he said to himself. And the truth was, he trusted only himself. No one else. If he handed this job over to anyone else and something happened to Erin, he would never be able to forgive himself. That was why it was happening.

So he had no choice. None.

He might as well admit the truth to himself. He'd have to talk to Tom about the details, but there was no longer any doubt about it. He simply couldn't trust Erin's safety to anyone else.

So he'd help her. What then? Erin would be his *concern*, his *responsibility*. What nasty words when they were tacked onto his former lover. When they were tacked onto the woman he desired more than anything else in his whole life. The woman who seemed to have the ability to turn his life upside down with just a look.

Questions flew through his mind. He questioned his ability to keep her safe. He questioned his ability to keep his distance while he worked to keep her safe.

Hell, then there was the question of his leg. He couldn't run, and at the rate he was going, he might never run again. He couldn't chase down a stalker. He couldn't come rushing in to save Erin if circumstances called for it.

He still had friends down at headquarters, he still had his job and he still had Tom as his partner. All he had to do was go back to it. The problem was—and this was the biggest question of all—was he ready to? And then there was the question of what he called his "protection mode." Would it come back to him after so many months of not needing it, of not using it? Like an athlete who hadn't worked out in years, how long would it take him to feel up to par when it came to acting as an officer of the law again?

"I've been out of it for a long time, Erin," he said.

"I don't care," she asserted. "You were one of the best cops in the whole Twenty-seventh Precinct, and you know it."

"Not anymore. All that changed when I got my leg nearly blown off," he returned simply.

She flinched at his words, but held her ground. "I think it would take a hell of a lot more than something like that to change the Liam McGrey I knew," she argued.

He should have realized she'd put up a fight. How many times had he told her she should have been in a courtroom instead of behind a typewriter?

"It's a sense you have," she went on. "It's part of you.

It was what you were, and what you still are. And it has nothing to do with your leg.''

She said it in a way that almost had him believing it. Almost.

At least he believed it enough to say, ''All right. I'll talk to Tom and see what I can find out. That's all I can promise for now.''

She smiled at him, a smile so full of gratitude Lee was momentarily ashamed of his own reluctance. ''Thank you, Lee,'' she said. Again she used that breathy tone he forced himself to ignore. ''What do we do first?''

''First, you're going to stay here for a while, until I can find a safer place for you. And you're to tell no one, and I mean absolutely no one, where you are. Do you understand?''

''Yes,'' she replied, ''but I need some things from the house.''

''What things?'' he asked. ''Whatever you need, I can buy.''

''But you want to look at all the information I've gathered on Forest Burke, don't you?'' she insisted. ''I haven't even put most of it into the computer yet. I don't really have much, just newspaper clippings and notes, but it's all hidden at the house. Besides, I wanted to put some of it into your computer network and see what I can come up with.''

He almost told her to forget about it and if anyone was going to check out Burke, it was going to be him. He tried to tell himself he didn't want or need her help. But he knew perfectly well he wouldn't be able to accomplish as much without all her background research.

''Fine,'' he finally agreed. ''Write down everything you need, where it is, and I'll go get it.''

''I'll go with you,'' she offered.

''No.''

"I don't want to stay here alone, Lee. What if someone followed me to your house?" she asked.

Lee could hear the fear in her voice. He let out a heavy sigh. He could understand that fear, but how in the name of heaven was he supposed to keep her safe when all she did was argue with him and resist everything he said?

"Erin, if you want me to protect you, then you have to do everything I tell you," he said, fighting to keep his voice relatively calm.

"I know that, but I don't want to be alone, all right?" she replied. "Besides, this information is all I have on Burke and it took me a day and a half to gather it. It's hidden all over the house."

"Why?" Lee asked.

"Because if anyone comes looking for it, they won't be able to find everything in one place, that's why. So there's less chance of losing it all," Erin answered patiently.

Lee grew uneasy as he listened to her explanation. Didn't she realize if someone came to her house, the hidden information would be the last thing she'd have to worry about, considering the way she was nearly run down in the parking garage? As usual, she was putting the story first.

But the fact was, he didn't like leaving her alone any more than he liked taking her with him.

"All right," he agreed slowly. "But you better listen to me every step of the way, or so help me, you'll be out looking for another bodyguard. Understand?"

"Completely."

A few moments later, he opened the front door and stepped out after checking to be sure there was no one watching or waiting. Erin stayed close behind him. "We'll take my car and put yours in the garage where it won't be seen from the street."

"Okay," she agreed.

They stepped off his covered porch.

Only then did Lee notice that it was starting to rain. He muttered an oath under his breath, wondering if things could get any worse.

They could, he discovered as Erin reached from behind him to take his hand in hers. The warmth of her touch was everything he expected, filling him with unmistakable heat. His heart actually skipped a beat, and Lee was certain it was because she had somehow found a way to grasp his heart just as she had his hand.

She held on to him.

And Lee found he couldn't let her go. All the way to his car, he tried to convince himself he was only holding her hand because keeping her safe was now his job. All the way to his car he kept trying to convince himself that her touch meant nothing.

Absolutely nothing.

Chapter 2

The ride to Erin's father's house in Wilmette was un-eventful, at least to anyone who might be watching from the outside. To Lee, it was just a continuation of all the rushing memories. He hadn't done much driving in the past eight months, but not because of his leg—his left leg was the one that had been shot up and he didn't need it to drive. He simply didn't feel much like going out. Twice-a-week therapy sessions at the rehab center and trips now and then to the grocery store were enough.

Now, not only was he driving, but Erin was in the front seat next to him, her soft, musky scent filling the car, her closeness invading him. Still, it was an invasion he wanted to welcome, an invasion he wanted to embrace and hold to himself in hopes it would fill the void that had been in him for so long now. If only he knew it wouldn't bring more pain and despair. If only he thought he could trust her. Which he couldn't.

Erin was quiet beside him. And he wondered if she was

being overwhelmed with an equal amount of emotion. Or if she was feeling anything at all.

Lee told himself he didn't care what she was feeling, and he tried to concentrate on the road. He drove carefully, constantly checking in the rearview mirror to make sure no one was following them. He reminded himself that protecting her was now his first priority. He tried his best to think of the job ahead and forget about the past. But, hell, it wasn't easy.

He glanced at the rearview mirror and noticed a green sedan. Making a quick left at the next yellow light, he lost the sedan when the light turned red. From then on, it was a trip of turns, taking much longer than it should have, but he felt a lot more secure. He was almost one hundred percent certain they weren't followed.

Lee parked the car around the back of the large house where it couldn't be seen from the end of the drive, then reluctantly climbed out and looked around. Hell, he didn't want to be here. At least the rain had stopped and turned into mist.

He noticed the trees were just beginning to bud, a sign that spring was really coming. Through the leafless trees, he could see the boat dock and the guest house. The sight of the guest house caused his breath to catch in his throat. He and Erin had made love there for the first time that night so long ago....

So why did Lee suddenly feel as though it had been only yesterday, the pain still so raw and deep and fresh? They'd just started dating. It was another six months before he asked her to move in with him and another four months before she agreed.

Lee wanted more than anything to ask Erin if she thought of them whenever she looked at that stone building. But the words wouldn't come to him. Besides, he didn't think he could handle it if she said no.

His heart heavy, he turned to look at the main house. Not overly massive, it was an attractive house of Colonial design and made of the same stone as the guest house. Large enough to show that the family who owned it had the money to live comfortably, but not so large that it lost the feel of home. He and Erin had spent their only Christmas when they were living together here with her father and her three brothers and their families. It seemed like a lifetime ago.

At the same time, as with the night spent in the guest house, it seemed like yesterday.

He had to clear his throat before he could speak. "Can I have your key?" he asked. He noticed that Erin hesitated slightly, her gaze drawn to the lake, or was it perhaps the guest house? He looked away, forcing himself not to think about that possibility. Instead, Lee forced his legs to carry him through the mist toward the wide back porch.

"Sure," she replied, following him and digging a set of keys out of her purse.

Together they reached the porch and climbed the few steps to the top. Lee slid the key into the lock and froze as the door slipped quietly open, revealing the kitchen within.

Silence, heavy and thick in the moist air, settled all around them. Lee glanced at Erin, only to find she stood as frozen as he. He could almost see the color fade from her face, leaving her pale with fear, her green eyes shadowed by apprehension. She didn't even appear to be breathing.

A moment later, all his senses sharpened, on the alert and ready for anything. He prepared her for the worst. He strained to hear any sounds. He heard only silence.

"Are you sure you locked the door?" he whispered.

"I think so. I know I shut it at least."

"Stay close to me." There was only a shuffle of move-

ment as Lee handed her back her keys and slipped out the
gun he carried in a shoulder holster under his arm—the
same gun that had sat on the top of his chest of drawers
these past eight months. Cautiously, he slipped noiselessly
into the kitchen.

The eerie silence remained, seeming to entomb them
both once they were inside. But the kitchen was empty.
From the doorway leading down the hall, Lee had a clear
view of the living room. It was empty, too.

But it was a mess.

Cushions from the sofa, love seat and two chairs were
ripped open and thrown about, pieces of their stuffing scattered everywhere. Papers, books and magazines lay all
over the floor while lamps, pictures and knickknacks had
been knocked over and broken. An end table was
overturned.

Beside him, Erin gasped, the sound loud in the stillness.

Slowly, they made their way down the hall to the living
room. Lee looked around, ready for anything, watching for
any movement that would tell him if anyone was still in
the house. But there was no one.

Erin could only stare at the mess before her as they
entered the living room.

Out of the corner of his eye, Lee saw her reaching down
to pick up a broken crystal figurine. "Don't," he warned.

She stopped just as she was about to touch it.

"Don't touch anything until after the police come."
Then he saw what she'd been reaching for. It was the small
crystal Cupid with his bow and arrow that Lee had given
her on the first Valentine's Day they'd shared.

Forcing the memory back behind the heavy door he pic-
tured in his mind, Lee walked into the center of the room.
He took in the smashed computer on the floor near the
desk. Destroying that piece of equipment had been easy.

One nice sweep and everything had been cleared off the beautiful antique cherry desk.

He looked back at Erin and wished he hadn't. She was frozen, colorless, looking rather sick. Still standing next to the little broken figurine of Cupid, she hugged her arms tightly across her chest as though she must be freezing to death.

God, he wished he could protect her from this. He wished he could just snap his fingers and make it all disappear. More than anything, he wished he could take her into his arms. Instead, he said, "We have to call the police, Erin."

"Yes," she said, her voice sounding so small. He could see she was fighting to maintain some semblance of composure. "You're right. There's a phone in the kitchen on the wall. The one in here doesn't look as though it would work." She turned stiffly toward the kitchen, after giving the phone on the floor nothing more than a quick glance. Its cord had been torn from the wall.

"I remember," he said, moving right behind her. "I'll call them. Then we should wait for the police outside. It looks like whoever did this has gone, but I'm not taking any chances."

"All right," she agreed.

She agreed too easily, he thought. He liked it better when she argued with him, when she put her foot down and demanded that things be done her way.

Careful not to touch anything, Lee used his jacket to hold the phone and his handkerchief to punch the buttons to dial 911, even though he was pretty certain that whoever had destroyed the living room hadn't taken the time to make any calls.

Erin watched Lee while he spoke into the phone. Everything about him left her feeling torn. Everything about him was familiar, yet excitingly new. She wanted to fall into his arms. At the same time, she wanted to run in the other direction. She wanted him to hold her and tell her everything was going to be all right. But she felt his job made him a dangerous man. And at this moment, Erin didn't think she could handle the worry and fear that came with his occupation, even if he was helping her.

He swept his fingers through his hair, just as he always did when he was frustrated, and the dark, wavy locks fell in all directions. She couldn't help remembering how soft it was. It was so soft she never could keep from touching it when she moved past him....

All she had to do was lean toward him and she'd be in his arms. Again. How many times had she longed to be there? She couldn't even guess. In the past eight months, and even before then, she had discovered that being in his arms was the only safe, warm place in this world to be.

Erin had tried to find other safe, warm places. She had returned to what had always been her home—at least until she shared a home with Lee. She had dated a few other men in the past few months. She had let them hold her hand and she had let one or two kiss her. There had even been that time a month and a half ago...

She shuddered and fought to shut out the memory only to realize she suddenly was leaning closer to Lee. And she also fought the desperate urge to cry again. She hadn't cried since the day in the hospital when Lee had kicked her out. She hadn't even cried when her evening with Dex Carter had ended in nothing but humiliation. And she found it hard to believe she'd broken down and cried in his kitchen earlier. She promised herself she wouldn't cry now. She wouldn't let Lee see how much she was hurting. Not again. Not anymore.

Until now, it had been easy to keep from crying.

But she'd never had to face anything like this. Never had she felt so violated. In the course of her job, she learned of others who'd been threatened and sent hate mail. Three years ago, the celebrity reporter had actually quit *Earlybird* because of a stalker whose threats and actions became too hard to take. There were crazy people everywhere, and dealing with them was a hazard of the job when you put yourself in the limelight.

Now, Erin had to deal with it. And there wasn't anyone she trusted more to help her than Lee. After the first crank phone call, she had thought of contacting him. Now here he was standing before her, even though she knew he didn't want to be. She knew he'd only taken the job to keep from feeling guilty. She, however, no longer cared about his reasons. He was here, with her.

Standing so close, she could smell the clean, male scent of him. She could feel his warmth, a warmth that was drawing her into his arms.

Erin took a deliberate step backward, away from Lee. She knew he wouldn't want her in his arms. How could he possibly want her so close to him? He could barely stand to look into her eyes. And right then, she felt too shattered, too lost, too alone, to handle the rejection when he shoved her away from him.

To her amazement, Lee reached out and took her hand. His touch sent something close to an electrical shock racing through her. His hand was warm, almost hot against the coldness that had settled inside her at the invasion of her home.

"Come on," he said, his voice sounding husky. "We'll wait outside."

He pulled her through the back door and into the heavy mist.

In that single touch of his hand, Erin felt grounded again. She felt as though she finally belonged somewhere. Even if it was only for this brief moment in time...with only the warmth of his palm against hers. She would have to grasp this moment and make it last a lifetime. Because he would never give her more than that. Because she could never take more than that, even if he did. The sleepless nights worrying about Lee out on the streets, trying to stop dangerous criminals, were still fresh in her mind, like a cut that refused to heal. Those lonely nights had on occasion lasted for weeks. She didn't want those nights again, no matter how good his touch felt.

Standing next to his car, he finally let her go so she could climb in and wait out of the damp. Yet as soon as he released her hand, the coldness took hold of her again.

Erin tried to ignore it. She tried to convince herself that this feeling wasn't anything like the cold loneliness of those nights when Lee was out making the world a safer place. As he closed the car door for her, she avoided meeting his gaze, knowing that if he looked into her eyes, he would know exactly how vulnerable she'd become. He'd never seen her like that before, and she'd be damned before she let him see her in such a weak state now. The crying had been enough. No more.

Lee made his way around to the driver's side and climbed in beside her. His presence, his very essence, seemed to take up whatever room was left in the car.

"Are you ever going to tell me what happened to your leg, how the shooting happened?" Erin asked, needing to talk to him. Needing to hear his voice. Needing to talk about something other than the condition of her home or what was happening to her. "You said you got it nearly blown off? I mean, I know you were shot, but I never heard the details," she added, trying to keep her voice light, trying to ignore the tug at her heart at the thought of the pain he must have endured. Knowing, too, that he hadn't wanted her around. That he hadn't wanted to share his pain with her. He still didn't want her. She should be glad. So why wasn't she?

"The police should be here any minute," he replied, intentionally changing the subject and letting her know that he wasn't going to share any of it with her.

Erin almost had to bite her tongue to keep from asking more questions, digging for answers as her job and instincts forced her to do. She'd get the story out of him sooner or later. That's what made her so good at her job— her ability to get the answers she wanted. An approaching siren told her now wasn't the time to try.

The police soon arrived, and Erin felt she was being invaded once again. First by an unknown intruder, then by a swarm of men in uniform who swept through the house with fingerprint powder.

Erin and Lee followed the police back into the house, answering their questions as best as they could. They told the approximate time they arrived and what they found. Just inside the kitchen, they stopped.

"Are you okay?" Lee asked her gently.

Erin had to swallow before she could answer. "Yes," she lied. "It's just easier pretending this is happening to someone else." Then she couldn't stop herself and reached out to grasp Lee's hand again. The two of them stood in the kitchen, hands linked, and watched the cops do their job.

Several of the uniformed men knew Lee and greeted him, asking if he was back at work. He shrugged them off and turned the conversation back to the ransacked rooms.

"You want to be a part of this, don't you?" Erin asked Lee softly. "You'd like to take over this investigation, wouldn't you?" She met his gaze and found that she didn't need an answer, it was so clearly written in his eyes.

"Yes," he admitted. "I only wish this wasn't happening to you."

But Lee wasn't in charge. And all he could do was offer what little comfort his hand linked with Erin's could give.

Any closer than that and he feared he'd take her in his arms and try to sweep her away from the mess so she wouldn't feel any more pain. Besides, searching for evidence at the crime scene in a break-in like this wasn't his specialty.

A young officer with blond hair approached them, carrying a clipboard. "Ms. Flemming?"

"Yes?" Erin didn't move away from Lee.

"I'm Officer Ollin. I'll need you to walk through the house with me so we can take an inventory of whatever's missing," he said.

Erin knew this was the procedure. Just another necessary step in the investigation to find out who might have done this. Still, Erin didn't want to let go of Lee's hand. She wanted him close to her.

But she had to face the fact that he was only here because he'd agreed to protect her. Nothing more. It was only a job. And it didn't include protecting her from the pain of what lay ahead. On legs that felt like rubber, she left Lee and followed Officer Ollin.

But her thoughts weren't on answering Officer Ollin's questions about the vandalism or whatever might be missing. They were on the man she'd just left. Her hand was still warm from holding his. Fighting the urge to go running back to him, she licked her parched lips and made an effort to pay attention.

"Do you know if anything's missing?" Ollin asked.

"It's kind of hard to tell in all this mess," she muttered.

"I know, but if you could try, it would help us out. If you really don't notice anything missing, this is no longer a robbery. It's breaking and entering and destruction of property."

"I realize that." Erin stared at the destruction all around her, seeing so much more than broken glass and sofa stuffing. She saw holidays and Sundays spent on the sofa watching football with her family. Tears stung her eyes again, and Erin did her best to keep them at bay. She took a deep breath and tried to look at the scene with her reporter's eye and not let it touch her personally. But it was impossible. No matter how much she forced herself to see past the lifetime of memories smashed on the floor, her gaze continued to be drawn to the broken crystal figure of Cupid. Erin had kept it with her, putting it near her computer now that she was no longer sharing Lee's bed. She could see from where she stood that the chubby legs were broken off as was the arrow in his bow.

"I don't see my tape recorder," she murmured, trying to keep her voice from shaking.

Officer Ollin made a note on the clipboard.

"The answering machine is gone, too," Erin told him. "And I don't see my disks," she added, checking out the smashed computer on the floor.

"What was on them?" Ollin asked.

"Nothing. They were all new. I hadn't used them yet." She absently wiped her hand across her face and was surprised to find her cheek moist with what must have been tears. Quickly she swiped them away.

Erin spent the next half hour going through the house, feeling as empty and hollow as a ghost. With Officer Ollin beside her, she tried to spot anything else that was missing. They moved upstairs, where Erin discovered her bedroom wasn't in quite the same shambles, but had clearly been searched.

When she reached the bottom of the stairs, she saw Lee working with a uniformed officer he called Stan. They were doing something to one of the drawers on the desk. It seemed as though Lee knew she was not far from the doorway, despite the fact that she hadn't said a word since coming down. He looked up at her, meeting her gaze. They could get lost, she thought. Just the two of them. They could get lost in the look that passed between them and the rest of the world could fade away, taking the pain and frustration and fear and insecurity with it, leaving only the two of them.

Then Lee turned back to the desk and the spell was broken. The rest of the world wasn't about to disappear, no matter how much Erin wished it could.

Another officer approached and addressed Ollin. "We checked out the grounds and the guest house and the dock. There's no evidence that the intruders were anywhere but in the house," he said.

"All right," Ollin said, leading Erin back into the living room. "Let's get things wrapped up."

Finally able to get away from him, Erin crossed the room, trying to ignore the debris that crunched under her steps, and sank into what had been her father's easy chair. Crossing her arms over her chest, she absently tried to rub some warmth into herself. The house that had always been home to her now felt so different, so alien, so cold. Even the week after her father had left to retire in Florida, the house hadn't felt so cold and empty. By sitting in her father's old chair, Erin hoped that something so familiar would give her comfort. Closing her eyes, she thought she had never felt so alone in her life.

"Drink this."

She looked up to meet Lee's heated gaze once again. He held out a mug.

"Hot chocolate," he said when she didn't respond. "I found it in the kitchen. I couldn't see any instant coffee. Ollin said I could touch things in the kitchen so I made you a cup," he explained, the fire of his gaze seeming to be the only warmth in the room. "There isn't much food out there, Erin. Have you been eating anything at all?"

"I picked up a few things on my last trip to the grocery store. Don't worry, Lee, I'm smart enough not to starve," she snapped. Things were starting to get to her, she realized. She knew she should try to shake them away, but she didn't seem to have any strength left to stand up and face them head-on. She felt suddenly drained from everything that had happened in the past few days. And since she couldn't take any of it out on the person ultimately responsible, she took it out on the next best thing—Liam McGrey.

"I never said you weren't," he said, his voice sounding as unruffled and calm as Lake Michigan on a beautiful summer day.

And why shouldn't he be calm? None of this was happening to him. He wasn't getting crank phone calls. No one was chasing him down in a parking garage. No one was ransacking his domain. He probably didn't give a damn about that poor little Cupid over there on the floor.

"Drink this," he said again, pushing the mug at her.

She thought for a fraction of a second about refusing him, just to see what he would do, just to give him a taste of what it was like when things in your life didn't go as expected. But she knew he was persistent and almost always got whatever he wanted merely because he went after it.

Oh, yes, she remembered he could be very persistent when there was something he wanted. And he would do whatever it took to get what he wanted, too. Like the time he wanted her to wear a little black dress to a New Year's Eve dance instead of the red dress she'd put on. He'd kissed her until they were both hotter than fire, and then easily peeled off that little red dress. He'd made love to her. Wild, passionate love that she felt she'd never know again. They'd ended up late for the dance, but she was wearing the black outfit because the red one was in a wrinkled heap on the floor near the bed.

Damn, why did she have to remember this? And why

couldn't he have been as persistent when it had come to her leaving him? Yes, he'd asked her to talk to him, but he had never really asked her to stay. Why couldn't he have been just a bit more persistent when it came to his job? She hated his having to leave her for days on end when he was protecting someone else, when he couldn't even call her and let her know he was all right. Why?

Because he hadn't cared whether she'd stayed or not....

She took the mug from him, holding it tightly so he wouldn't notice how her hands were shaking.

"Why doesn't your father sell this place or at least rent out the guest house or something?" Lee asked. "It's an awful lot for you to take care of all by yourself, isn't it?"

"Because it would be too painful to get rid of everything here, I guess. Like all this furniture and the things he kept of my mother after she died. He took some of it with him when he went to live in Florida, but he left a lot. Besides, he still spends most of the hottest part of the summer up here, as do all three of my brothers. Arnie just bought a new sailboat so he could teach his kids how to sail next summer," she replied before taking a soothing swallow of warm chocolate. It did taste good going down.

Lee let his thoughts drift to her brother, Arnie, even though his gaze never left her. Arnie had been the wild, fun-loving one, with two little kids at the time Erin had left Lee. Two little boys who seemed as rambunctious as their father, with the sparkling emerald eyes so common in the Flemming family. How much had they changed in the months he and Erin were apart?

God, it had been almost a year, he thought. Or it would be in June. A year lost. How could time go so slowly and yet so fast at the same time?

Hell, he was only thirty-one. But he'd somehow lost nearly a year. And he felt as though he had somehow lost much more than just time. He couldn't even remember doing much, except for exercising his leg. He'd done a great deal of that.

"Still, the house is pretty big for just one person and the guest house is sitting empty for a good part of the year," Lee persisted, pushing the thoughts of her family out of his mind, a family that had welcomed him as one of their own. Talk of family made this too personal. And he wasn't going to get personal. Personal meant getting close. Lee had no intention of getting close. If he did, she might worry about him, and he didn't want that, he thought sarcastically.

Even if it was hard to look at her and keep from getting hit right where it became personal.

"I pay two sisters, Martha and Gertie Madison, to come in once a week to clean and dust. During the summer, I pay the Harrington boys to do the yard work. And my father has been known to rent the guest house out to friends and associates from time to time. Besides, there haven't been any problems until now," she added. "Until I started with this story…"

Officer Ollin came by just in time to hear the latter part of Erin's explanation. "When were the Madison sisters here last?" he asked.

"On Monday," Erin told him.

"Did you see them, or talk to them at all?" the officer continued.

"Yes and yes," she replied, taking another long swallow of chocolate.

"So you think this has something to do with a story you're working on for the newspaper, and it's not just a random break-in?" Ollin persisted.

"It's possible," Lee returned.

Ollin was writing everything down. Nodding slowly, he didn't look up as he asked the next question. "What story?"

"Actually, it's not really a story yet. I was just checking out a man by the name of Forest Burke," Erin offered.

Ollin went on writing. "Checking him out how?" He briefly looked up.

Erin shrugged lightly. "I put his name in my computer and I called his office. That's as far as I got." She looked as though she'd been put through the wringer once or twice. And Lee felt for her, even though he tried not to. He knew she was doing her best to stay strong—or at least to appear strong—in her efforts to handle this latest offense. But he could see in her eyes it was a battle she was losing little by little.

He wanted to get this business over with. He wanted to get her out of the house. And he didn't know how much longer she could put on a good front. But Ollin's questions continued, and Erin answered all of them, explaining everything from the murder she witnessed to coming to Lee for help. Ollin just wrote in his notes and gave nothing more than an empathetic expression—one that said, "Well, we'll do all we can, but gee, I don't really know for sure if it will help you."

"So you think this Forest Burke doesn't want you sticking your reporter's nose into his business?" Ollin asked. "And that's why someone broke in here and smashed your computer?"

"I don't know. It's just a guess," Erin replied, sounding tired. "Maybe even just a gut feeling," she added under her breath.

"Are we about finished?" Lee asked, wanting more than ever to get her out of there.

Whoever was following Erin could be watching them all, and Lee wanted to get her someplace warm and safe, wanted to protect her and shelter her from danger. And he told himself there was nothing personal about it, that he would want to protect anyone who was threatened. Right? Right.

Officer Ollin took Lee's subtle hint. "I think so. What's your opinion of the print you and Stan got off the desk, McGrey?"

"It's smudged quite a bit, but hopefully your people can do something with it," Lee said. Erin said nothing, listening quietly and trying not to get her hopes up too high.

"The rest of the place was pretty well wiped clean. I know it isn't much, but we have to take what little we have to go on and see where it leads. Can I reach you here, Ms. Flemming?" Ollin asked. "In case I need to ask you any more questions."

"She'll be at my place," Lee answered for her. "Here's my card. It has my home phone number as well as my beeper number on it." He handed Ollin his business card.

Ollin glanced at it before slipping it into his pocket. "We'll let you know what we find, if anything." He took a moment to hand Erin one of his own cards. "And if you remember anything else that might help us or notice anything else missing that needs to be added to the inventory, please call me. You can reach me at this number at any time, day or night."

"Thank you," Erin muttered, holding her mug of chocolate in one hand and taking the card in the other. She didn't get up to see him out.

A short time later, the police were gone, leaving a strange emptiness in their wake. Lee looked around only briefly, then looked at Erin, who still sat in her father's chair. God, she looked so small, so fragile, so stunned.

True, she'd left him, but it was because she couldn't handle the loneliness when he was gone and she couldn't handle the worry over the danger that came with his job. True, she'd torn his world apart by leaving, but it was for reasons he could understand. And she didn't deserve this.

Absently, Lee flexed his foot, hoping to stretch the ache out of his leg.

Erin took a final drink out of the mug, then set it on the table beside her. It was one of the few pieces of furniture that had been left untouched. Her gaze never left the ransacked room.

"God, look at this mess," she muttered with a long, drawn-out sigh.

"Where's your research?" Lee asked, hoping that a distraction would put a little spirit back into her. The Erin before him now was someone he'd never seen before, someone he didn't know. She seemed too distracted, too defeated, too different from the woman who'd lived with him, who'd never let anything stop her, who went after a hot tip with gusto. She'd never let her emotions deter her from doing her job as a reporter.

She looked up at him and chuckled bitterly. "Thanks to all this, I completely forgot about my notes. What if whoever did all this found them?"

"Where did you hide it?" Lee asked, not wanting to answer her question.

"Most of it's in the oven," she replied absently. "There's more taped to the inside of the lid on the rolltop desk. The only way you can reach it is to close the top nearly all the way. You'll have to feel for it then. The rest was on the stolen disks."

"I thought you said the disks were empty."

"The ones on the desk, next to the computer, were," she replied without looking at him. "The two that were hidden inside that broken lamp over there weren't." She pointed to the smashed lamp on the floor near the sofa.

"Why didn't you say something before? Why didn't you tell Ollin?" Lee asked.

"There were too many cops here," she said. "I know that's not much of an explanation, but I told you before you're the only one I trust. Besides, I was kind of hoping the lamp was merely broken, that whoever did this swept it off the table and didn't notice the disks. But they did.''

Lee watched her for a long moment, looking for the familiar spark she always had when her mind was on a story. But for the life of him, he couldn't see any trace of it now.

Lee was worried about her. When he and Erin had lived together, and even before then, when they had only been dating, he'd seen her face many things—threats of bodily harm and other physical dangers that went along with the life of a gutsy reporter. But he'd never seen her like this before. Or was there something else that he didn't know about, something he couldn't see?

He wished he could help her. But he had to face the fact he couldn't, wouldn't, not without getting close to her, not without putting his own emotions, his very heart—again—on the chopping block for her. And he wouldn't take that chance.

What was it she'd said when she left? That she couldn't bear the idea of opening the door in the middle of the night to find someone standing there, waiting to tell her he wasn't ever coming home again? He couldn't remember her exact words, but that was pretty damned close.

Turning away, Lee tried to force the thought aside as he headed back to the desk. Because the top of the desk had been cleared, it was easy to pull down the lid, leaving just enough room to squeeze his arm inside. Reaching up, he felt for the envelope that was taped there and pulled it free. Rolling the lid back up, he left the large brown envelope lying on the desk and went to the kitchen, leaving Erin straightening the sofa cushions.

Lee found a second brown envelope taped inside the oven. Returning to the living room, he stopped just inside the doorway and watched Erin, his heart in his throat, threatening to choke him.

She was on her knees, holding that silly, broken Cupid as though it was the most precious thing on earth. But what grabbed him most was the fact that there were tears coursing down her cheeks. She was crying again.

Lee had only seen her cry three times. The first time was the night in the guest house when he'd made love to her for the first time. She'd been almost twenty-one and a virgin. He thought he'd hurt her and that was the reason for the tears. "I've hurt you," he'd said, his voice rough, his throat tight. "I'm so sorry. I never wanted to hurt you."

But she'd only held him tighter, seeming to wrap her entire body around him. "Please don't stop, Lee. Don't let me go. Don't stop loving me...."

The second time, he'd seen the tears only in her eyes. If they ever reached her cheeks, she'd already gone out of the room and down the corridor of the hospital after he told her to get out.

The third time, of course, had been in his kitchen hardly more than two hours ago. All three times he could understand.

Now, in the middle of her father's living room there were full-fledged tears on her face, and Lee felt a stabbing pain in his chest at seeing them. Mostly because he couldn't understand her crying over that Cupid. Not when so many other irreplaceable things lay in pieces about the floor.

For a moment, he couldn't move, even though he would have liked to back out of the room and leave her to her crying alone. But his brain couldn't seem to send the message to his feet.

Erin stared down at the broken Cupid, a tiny crystal figure that had appeared on Lee's nightstand the same night Erin had moved in with him. It had remained next to the bed they shared, always with its arrow pointed toward the two of them. Erin hadn't been gone two hours when Lee had noticed the figure was gone, too.

Silently and swiftly, she slipped the Cupid into the pocket of her jacket.

Lee blinked and tried to force a much-needed breath into the tightness of his chest. Hell, he wished he hadn't seen her do that. He wished he never had to know just how much that stupid piece of broken glass meant to her. But he did. And it made keeping his distance from her all that much harder.

Now he was afraid to move at all, afraid that the only direction he could make his uncooperative legs go was toward her until he was close enough to sweep her into his arms.

She still didn't know he was there, that he was watching her as she absently stacked a few magazines and newspapers that littered the area around her. When he cleared his throat to get her attention, she started slightly, looking up at him. Just as quickly, she turned away and wiped the traces of tears from her cheeks. Lee pretended not to notice.

"Sorry," he muttered. "I didn't mean to scare you."

"It's all right," she said. "I guess all of this has just made me jumpy."

Her voice was a little shaky, but Lee pretended he didn't notice it, either. "I found your stuff. Is this all of it?"

"Yes," she replied. Finished with her stacking, she pushed herself to her feet.

"I could have come for this by myself, Erin."

"I came to you for protection, Lee. That's all. I don't need you to be my gofer." She paused. "I have to face this. I can't just close my eyes and hope it all disappears."

"I know," he said, wishing she was wrong. "Do you

want to stay here and clean up the rest of this?'' he asked, setting the second envelope on the desk on top of the first. ''I could help you if you want.''

For a long moment, she didn't reply. He turned back around to find her gently placing a framed photograph of her mother on the mantel. The glass was broken, but the frame and the photo were still intact. Erin looked more lost than ever. Slowly, she lifted her gaze to meet his, and again he took in the tears filling her eyes, making them look like large green pools.

''Please just take me home, Liam. I just want to go home.''

The fact that she'd called him Liam, when everyone else he knew just called him Lee, didn't register until later, after he got over the pleading, lost expression on her face—as well as the fact that she still referred to his house as home.

Chapter 3

After Erin had gathered together some clothes, Lee took her home just as she asked. His home, even though it hadn't really felt much like home to him without her these past months. It was just a stopping place, a place where he could prop up his leg and rest for a while until he ventured back out into the world or to his next therapy session.

Still, it was home, the only one he knew. Heading there now, he had to concentrate on his driving. It was raining again and large drops were splattering the windshield. Instead of watching Erin, he kept a watchful eye on the rearview mirror, checking for anyone who might be following them. When he did glance her way, he found her staring straight ahead, looking as pale and lost as before.

Lee gripped the steering wheel until his knuckles turned white to keep from slamming his palm against it. He needed to do something to release the surge of hot anger that was racing through him. Anger at the vicious creep who was doing this to Erin. At the same time, Lee felt an icy cold, as though the damp chill of the air had somehow settled deep within him where nothing could reach it and warm him. He recognized it as the icy cold of terror. For Erin. A terror he hadn't known since the bullets whizzed into his leg, shattering his life and changing him forever. Like the terror he'd felt as he lay there waiting, unable to move, knowing the thug with the gun was going to come close enough to finish him off.

He gripped the steering wheel even harder to keep from reaching out and taking Erin's hand. But whether it was to comfort her or himself, he no longer knew.

Uncertainty as to what he should do next grabbed hold of him, mixing with the feelings of fear and rage. And to top it all off, he had a healthy dose of desire.

Not just the casual desire a man might experience when seeing a pretty woman on the street. No, this was something verging on the brink of hot, primal need. The same need that drove primitive man thousands of years ago to drag the object of their lust into the nearest cave and ravish her. Yet there was also the urge to take her in his arms and give her the comfort he knew she needed. And it was getting harder and harder to fight it. He seemed to need to hold her as much as she needed him to hold her. And why the urge should overwhelm him now, he didn't know. Nor did he know how to ignore it or resist it.

"It's been a long day. Let's get something to eat," he said, trying to take his mind off this need of her.

For a long moment, Erin didn't answer, and Lee wondered if she was so wrapped up in her own thoughts that she hadn't heard him. Hell, she looked so far away, he thought for a moment he was going to have to reach out and touch her after all, just to get her attention.

"I don't really feel like eating," she muttered finally, without looking at him.

Lee could feel her pulling away from him, distancing herself from the rest of the world in order to make herself feel more secure. He'd seen countless other victims do the same thing. With her brief response and toneless voice, she'd managed to add another row of bricks to the wall between them.

He should be glad, he told himself. He should just let her drift farther and farther away. If he couldn't reach her, then he'd be safe from her. So why didn't he let her go?

"Okay," he said, forcing his voice lighter, wishing more than anything he could get his hands on the guy doing this to her so he could tear him to pieces. "You have until we get home to decide what you want."

He glanced at her again, suddenly glad she was staring straight ahead. He didn't want to see that lost look in her lovely eyes. Even thinking about it seemed to burn a hole right through his soul.

Telling himself again that he wasn't going to get close to her, that he wasn't going to let her get close enough to him to capture his heart, he found it was already happening despite the wall she was putting up. Just seeing her like this was doing it to him. And he couldn't stop it, no matter how hard he tried, no matter how much he wished he could.

For a long time after she'd left, he wanted only to have her back in his life. But then, he'd sworn never to need her again, and had spent months convincing himself of that. And now she was close enough for him to smell her and feel the warmth of her body. But he didn't want her like this. Despite the way she'd hurt him, he didn't want her to be hurt or feel such fear.

He'd seen the way she slipped the Cupid into her pocket. And she'd called him Liam. He thought she might as well have used that broken figurine to slice away a large chunk of his heart.

Lee forced himself to stop this train of thought. It was getting him nowhere. "Tell me what he looked like," he said, trying to keep his tone neutral, trying to make this nothing but business.

"Who?" Erin asked.

He felt her glance over at him, but he didn't take his eyes off the road to meet her gaze.

"The guy who killed your informant. What was his name, Jenkins?"

"Yes," she replied, sounding stronger.

Maybe this was what she needed all along, he decided. To talk about the case, keep her mind on the "job." "So what did the killer look like? How well did you see him?"

"I saw him about as well as can be expected on a dark night. He was tall and muscular with dark hair. And I think he had a pockmarked face," she said.

Millions of people could answer to that description, Lee thought. "And you gave the description to Burger and Reece?" he asked.

"Of course I did. I even spent an evening searching through several mug books, but never found him."

"Was there anything at all distinctive about him?" Lee persisted, trying not to sound too happy now that he was drawing her out of her shell. "Perhaps something he was wearing?"

"I don't know. It happened so quickly, and it's funny what details hit you, what sticks with you. I remember he was wearing a suit and tie, looking more like some kind of businessman. And at the same time, I can't tell you much about his hair—if it was long or short, whatever. I just recall it was dark. I can still picture the way he seemed to come right out of the darkness. I was so scared, Lee. I didn't know what to do," she explained.

Lee could just imagine her hiding behind the crates, unable to keep from watching despite the horror of the scene.

He realized he was holding her hand, but couldn't remember moving to take it. He wouldn't think about having her hand in his. He would think about the case, keep her talking about the matter at hand.

"Where do you suppose he took Jenkins?" he asked. Although he had a pretty good idea.

"Somewhere out in the lake where he could dump him and never have to worry about anyone finding him, I imagine," she replied. Lee was thinking the same thing. "But my word saying it happened isn't enough evidence to bring in divers. Besides, where would they start? I don't even know for certain Jenkins's body was dumped in the lake."

"So tell me what you know about this Forest Burke," Lee said.

"Well, no one has ever been able to pin anything on him. He has no criminal record. He's immaculate. Before he was killed, Jenkins mentioned stolen art, and Burke has been known to have these huge art auctions. But there's never any evidence left behind to show anything illegal ever takes place," she explained. "I know that none of this means Burke was behind any of my problems, but I think it was too much of a coincidence that as soon as Burke's name was mentioned, terrible things started happening to me. Jenkins must have known Burke. I'm not sure exactly how yet. But I think Burke made sure Jenkins's body would never be found so there'd be nothing to lead anyone to suspect Burke."

It made sense to Lee, but they had no proof about any of it.

Erin stopped talking as though she'd said all she had to say. Lee sensed she'd put the wall back up again.

He pulled into his driveway, feeling more drained than ever. He'd like to take one of the pills in his medicine cabinet that would kill the pain in his leg for the next twenty-four hours. But it wasn't that pain he wanted to get rid of. No, this pain was closer to his soul, and it was getting worse every time he looked at the woman beside him.

Shutting off the engine, he didn't let go of her hand. She felt so cold.

"We're going to figure this one out, Erin," he said softly. Whether it was to convince her or himself, he really had no idea. But he knew they had to start somewhere. "We're going to find the answers to all the questions and we're going to get through this."

She turned to look at him, her eyes large and moist and dark green against her pale face.

"You said you trusted me," he went on. "Do you still?"

"Yes," she replied firmly. "Yes, Liam, I do. So what's next?"

He ignored the fact that she called him Liam. Again.

Trying to warm her hand, he tightened his grasp. "First thing we're going to do is have something to eat. One thing physical therapy has taught me is that you have to keep up your strength. Then we're going to contact Tom. I want to make sure it's Burke behind all of this and not just someone you crossed while doing a story. Then we're going to do whatever it takes to stop it, understand?" What he considered his "police mode" was in full swing, seemingly having returned when he hadn't even noticed, and Lee fought the urge to smile.

"That sounds so easy. But it won't be, because I know how hard it was just to find a few pieces of personal information on a man as private and rich as Forest Burke," she returned softly, not looking at him but at the raindrops splashing on the windshield with a noisy rhythm.

"I know," he said just as softly, trying not to think how good it felt to be close to her, holding her hand. "But we have no other choice. Let's go in," he said after a moment.

He let go of her hand and reached over the seat into the back. He grabbed the small bag of clothes and personal things she'd tossed together before leaving her father's house. Stuffed inside were the two envelopes holding all the information she'd gathered on Forest Burke. It didn't seem like much.

But one thing Lee had learned in all his years as a cop was that it didn't take much to ruffle someone's feathers enough to make him do something about it.

Lee got out first and looked up and down the street to make sure no one was watching before leading Erin quickly up the porch steps and into the house. Once inside, behind locked doors, he wondered if she'd feel any safer. She was safer. No one had followed them, and no one except Officer Ollin knew she was with him.

Raindrops spotted the jacket of her suit, and it took all his willpower not to wipe away the one that had landed on her cheek, which she didn't seem to notice. He turned away before he could no longer control the urge to touch her and headed toward the kitchen, taking her bag with him.

Erin was quiet, following him silently until her high heels left the carpet and started clicking on the tiled floor in the kitchen.

Lee set down her bag just inside the kitchen door. "How about some soup?" he asked, opening the pantry cabinet. "I also have a bag of ready-made salad in the fridge."

"That sounds great," Erin replied. "Do you mind if I go wash my face?"

"Go ahead."

Erin left. The fact that he'd been the one asking questions left Lee worried about her. Where was the gutsy reporter who used to ask a million questions? he wondered. Maybe she'd be more herself once she had a little food in her stomach. He knew he'd feel better. He dumped a can of soup into a pan and turned on the flame. The soup wasn't yet warm by the time he had two salads in bowls on the counter. How convenient life could be, he thought, glancing at the instructions on the back of the salad bag. *Pour into bowl. Top with favorite dressing. Mix.* Too bad other things in life weren't so easy.

The truth was, nothing important was ever easy. Nor did it help to delay the inevitable, Lee knew, reaching into Erin's bag for the two envelopes of notes. It was time to get started. Tossing them on the table, he moved to the phone. From down the hall, he could hear the faint sound of water running in the bathroom.

His hand on the receiver, he stopped, knowing full well what making this call meant. It meant he was back on the job; he just hadn't made it to the office yet. For a long, still moment, he could think of nothing else except what it would be like to be back at work. He knew Tom had been promoted a little more than two months ago. But Lee hadn't gone into the precinct since he'd been shot, although he had attended an awards banquet, walking with the help of crutches. He'd been given a medal for putting himself in the line of fire to protect a witness—not that he'd had a lot of choice in the matter.

Lee took a chance that Tom would be in and punched in the number. Then he sat down and propped up his leg.

"Hello, Tommy boy," Lee said once he had Tom on the phone.

"Lee? Is that you, old man? How've you been? And when the hell are you coming back?" Tom asked in his friendly, familiar, fun-loving tone, a tone it seemed Lee missed more and more every day. "I figured you must have dropped off the face of the earth."

Lee smiled, feeling better than he had all day. "Not quite. Although sometimes this damned leg of mine hurts so bad I wish I could."

"I told you when you were lying on that table you should have let the doc cut it off."

Lee laughed. "I offered him a thousand dollars if he would, but he refused."

"Just a thousand? Hell, no wonder. Everyone knows that doctors won't even look at you for a thousand bucks. You should have offered him at least fifty grand."

Lee laughed again, feeling even more relaxed. "Oh, right, as if I keep that much stashed under my bed."

Erin came back from the bathroom. Lee met her warm gaze, but didn't pause in his conversation with Tom.

"Well, I heard that the rich witness you were watching over paid you big bucks for taking the bullet that was meant for him," Tom joked.

"Oh, yeah, now I remember. He did," Lee said, trying to keep from laughing. "But I didn't want it, so I gave it to charity."

"Charity who?" Tom asked.

"She didn't tell me her last name. With all that money changing hands, who remembers to ask names?" Lee tried to sound serious, but found it was impossible. "Besides, she knew you. She said you were her best customer, visiting her every week. What's that lovely wife of yours going to say when she hears about this?"

Erin grinned at the side of the conversation she was hearing before she moved to the stove to stir the now-boiling soup. Then she turned off the heat.

"Don't tell her. She'll make me sleep on the sofa for a week," Tom replied, trying to sound just as serious.

"Hey, that's a great sofa."

"Not anymore," Tom said. "Victoria traded in that great sofa that you almost became permanently attached to for every Cubs game for some art deco furniture. It looks great, but you can't sit on it. Torry won't let you. And even if she did, it's the most uncomfortable piece of work you've ever planted your backside on." He paused. "So what's up, my man? How are you, really? Still busy with therapy, because if you're not, you know you've always got your desk just waiting here for you?"

Lee didn't reply for a long moment as he let Tom's words cut through him. Talk of a desk job always hit a raw nerve. "Yeah, I'm still going to therapy, and I don't know if I'm ready for a desk yet," he muttered finally. "Listen, I need a favor, though." Lee looked out the back door at the rain and not at Erin, who still stood by the stove. He could feel her looking at him.

"If you want to borrow my wife, you can forget it," Tom bantered lightly.

It was enough to lighten the mood created by Tom's job offer. Lee smiled, glad to have it. "Oh, damn, that's what I needed, too. No, really, what I need is some information. Anything you might have on the art connoisseur, Forest Burke."

Tom didn't reply right away, and Lee thought he heard an intake of breath coming across the line.

"Are you sure about that, Lee? Are you sure that's the guy you want?" Tom asked slowly, completely serious now.

"Why do you ask?"

"Listen, why don't you come by my office later this afternoon? I could serve tea or something." Tom tried to joke, but it didn't come off very well. "We could talk about old times and catch up on things. You game?" Tom offered.

It took Lee only a second to realize that Tom didn't want to talk about Forest Burke on the phone. "Sure," Lee agreed quickly. "I was planning on coming by anyway. I'm going to need your help in protecting a witness."

"That'll be great," Tom agreed. "Can you keep this witness safe until then? Or are you having any problems?"

"No problems. I think we'll be all right," said Lee.

"I'd better go now, buddy. But listen, old man, you be careful out there. You're not as young as you used to be."

Was that a warning Lee heard in Tom's voice? Yes, he thought so. Lee and Tom had been partners for years before the shooting. Lee always felt he knew Tom inside and out. He knew what Tom was thinking. And right now, even after weeks of no communication at all, Lee was able to pick up on Tom's hidden message.

"I will," he promised.

Tom's next words stopped Lee in his tracks. "And take care of that pretty witness, too."

Lee was so shocked that Tom would know, he nearly blurted out Erin's name in question.

"You're wondering how I knew," Tom broke in before Lee could say a word. "Alex Kaffel at the FBI called me."

Lee let out a heavy sigh, keeping the oath he uttered under his breath. "Why would he call you on this?" he asked, closing his eyes for a brief moment.

"It looks like the FBI is investigating something that ties in with your witness. So they're watching her, too."

"Just what I need," Lee muttered.

"Hey," Tom returned. "I know you and Kaffel have had your differences, but don't you think it's better to work together on this? Besides, isn't our main objective keeping the witness safe?"

"Yes," Lee had to agree.

"Yes is right and you well know it," said Tom bluntly. "You can blame Kaffel all you want for causing you to almost lose a witness, but it was a long time ago and nothing you do now is going to change what happened. Now I've got to go. Torry's dropping by to see me, said she's got something important to tell me."

"Good luck," Lee said, suddenly able to think no further than the fact that when Erin had told him she had something important to tell him, it was that she couldn't handle the loneliness and the worry anymore. He hoped Torry wasn't going to tell Tom anything quite so grim. He didn't wish that on anyone.

"You, too." Tom took a deep breath that Lee could hear. "I'll see you later. If you're not here, I'll figure you're in big trouble, and I'll send out a team to find and rescue you."

"We'll both be there. I don't think it's a good idea to leave my witness alone."

Lee hung up, his hand resting on the receiver for a long moment.

The call was made. Finished. He'd done it. And it hadn't even hurt. Not really. It hadn't even been as scary as he thought it would be. Lee took a deep breath, realizing for the first time that he'd been holding it.

So Tom already knew about Erin, probably knew about the break-in at her house if Kaffel had called him. Lee figured Tom had probably already tapped into his computer and learned about everything. That was fine, he thought. Then they wouldn't have so much to explain once he and Erin got to the police station.

Lee ran his fingers through his hair. Looking out at the rain, he sat perfectly still for a long moment. The room was filled with the tempting aroma of the soup. And with Erin. He could feel her presence and he wished he didn't.

This time yesterday, he'd been in the swimming pool working his leg at a physical therapy session. His therapist had admitted she was puzzled by the lack of progress in his treatment. Yesterday, she had even accused him of not wanting his leg to get better, saying the healing had to happen in his mind as well as his body. Lee had continued exercising and told her to go to hell. He was doing his best. But he was suddenly tired of all the hard work. He had to face the fact that his leg might never be as good as it was before.

Lee kept watching the rain and thinking. The cleansing rain helped the flowers to bloom and the leaves to burst forth on the trees. It also made his leg ache more. But for some reason, he unexpectedly didn't feel so bad. This was something he could handle.

Feeling more optimistic, he rose from the chair to find Erin spooning out the soup.

"Hungry now?" he asked, moving closer, but not too close.

"Yes, now that I've smelled it."

"Good. Let's eat, then we'll go downtown to see Tom."

Erin helped him carry the bowls to the table. "You know," she said, stirring her soup to cool it once they both were seated, "this is really strange, but ever since this all started, it's as if I haven't been able to think clearly. Since these things are happening directly to me, I can't seem to see things with what I call my reporter's eye. I keep thinking there should be a witness to the crime that I need to try to interview."

"But you're the witness," Lee returned.

"Yes, I know. I feel confused and I don't know what direction to take. I never thought of myself as being such a coward, but I'd like just to get in my car and keep driving until there's a thousand miles between me and the guy I saw kill Jenkins, if that's what it takes to get through all of this with my life and my sanity."

Lee looked at her and offered her a quick smile. "It's all right to feel that way. It's just your way of reacting to a situation you've never really had to face before. It's a lot like how I felt when I got shot. I knew my chances of getting out of there alive were slim, and suddenly that's all I could think about—surviving. Only problem was, I couldn't seem to remember which direction I needed to go to reach the door and escape. Nor could I remember just where the guy I was there to protect was, either.''

For a long moment, all Erin could do was stare at him. In the past twenty seconds, he had just revealed more about himself than he had all day. And brief as it was, that smile, the first genuine one he'd given her since he opened his door to her that morning, seemed to wrap around her heart, making it hard for her to catch her breath.

But just as quick, the smile was gone, and the door that led into Liam McGrey was closed again. He was back to business. He was once more a cop just doing his job.

Lee dumped out the contents of the first envelope on the table and looked at the notes and photographs that lay scattered in front of his soup bowl. ''So let's see what you've got on Burke.''

''I've gone over this for what seems like a million times. And I haven't seen anything new. What exactly do we look for?'' she asked.

''Anything that links him to Jenkins, so we know for certain there's a connection,'' he replied, shuffling papers around.

''I don't think there's anything here that can do that. Most of what I have are photographs—and nothing really personal, either. Lots of press photos from various magazine and newspaper articles, you know, all public relations stuff. I did manage to get the addresses of his many homes and offices.''

''I didn't think there would be any easy answers here,'' Lee muttered. He was trying to examine the information before him, but the fact that he'd let slip that bit about his feelings when he was shot left him hot and dizzy. He'd never told anyone how his own confusion was what had terrified him the most. He purposely kept his gaze on the photos, even though he could clearly see that—apart from now knowing what Forest Burke looked like—there was little helpful information to be learned from them.

He didn't look at Erin. He absolutely couldn't let her see into his eyes, the window to his empty soul, not after telling her about the shooting. He couldn't let her see how empty he was, how much he needed her to fill that hollow place within him. That need to have her back in his life had become so strong, so powerful now that it just lay beneath the surface, waiting for her to uncover it.

And he *wouldn't* let her. Instead, he emptied out the second envelope and looked at even more useless information, searching for answers he knew weren't there, but hoped would miraculously appear. He had to find those answers and he had to find them fast. Before Erin got the chance to look into the window of his soul.

"What was on the disks?" he asked after sifting through a lot of paper that told him Burke was a very private man—rich, but private.

"A list of people who work for him," she replied.

"Did you ever get a chance to check it out?" He still didn't look at her, but he could feel again the heat of her gaze. He could feel the nearness of her presence. He could smell the sweet, alluring woman scent of her under the smell of soup.

Picking up a magazine photograph of Burke, dressed in a tuxedo, Lee tried to concentrate on it.

"No," Erin replied softly. "And I was trying to dig up more information on Burke that I didn't really read the list."

Her breath touched him. "What else was on the disks?" He forced himself to concentrate on the picture, but he saw nothing in it but a man in a black tuxedo. The woman beside Lee was what was real.

"His itinerary for the past three months, except for the past two to three weeks," she said.

Now Lee couldn't help but look up at her. He could very easily get caught up in looking, but her words were enough to help him keep his thoughts on the business at hand. "I hope you got a chance to look at it."

"I saw enough of it to safely tell you that after a show and an auction in Paris two months ago, he's been here in the States, staying nearly the whole time at his house in Jamesbrook, a few hours south of Chicago," she explained.

Lee could see the way she was looking at him. She was trying to read him, trying to peer deeply into his eyes. He quickly avoided her gaze. "Jamesbrook?"

"It's his hometown. He was born there. His parents are buried there. It was the first house he had built after acquiring a bit of wealth. He gave it to his parents. But they're both dead now."

"Is he still there?" Lee asked.

"I don't know. He could have gone anywhere in the past week."

Lee looked at the information scattered about the table. So much and yet so little, he thought. "Maybe Tom will have something to link all this to Jenkins's murder."

"What if he doesn't?" Erin asked.

"I don't know," he replied slowly, still without looking at her. "We'll worry about that if and when we get to it."

A short time later, when Lee and Erin stepped out of the elevator on their way to Tom Weatherby's office, he fought to push aside his other worries, as well.

God, he thought, the precinct smelled the same. The carpet had been replaced, but nothing else seemed to have changed. He felt a welcome familiarity. They stepped off the elevator into the inviting brightness of a large open area. The outside walls were glass, letting in the afternoon sun. It was a busy place with the sound of phones ringing, uniformed officers going about their duty and the distant hum of conversations. Two men in suits passed by, one of them stopping short and greeting Lee. "Hey, Lee, welcome back. Are you finally coming back to work or is this just a visit?"

"Good to see you, too, Henshaw. A little of both, I guess," Lee admitted through a tight throat.

"How's the leg?" Henshaw asked absently.

"Couldn't be better," Lee lied, wishing he hadn't been reminded of it just now. He never slowed his pace, striding across the room while trying not to focus on anything specific. There were just so many little things about this place that he didn't want to admit he missed. And he had to move past it all in order to reach the Specialists Division where he knew he would find Tom.

Headquarters had been something of a home away from home to him. And if he allowed the memories to flood in, they'd be bombarding him now just as they had earlier when Erin stood outside his door. And right at this moment, he didn't think he could handle it. There was a strange pounding in his head, and it took him a long moment to realize it was the sound of his own heartbeat thudding in his ears.

"Nervous?" Erin asked quietly beside him.

"I haven't been here since the shooting," he muttered without thinking.

"But you still see Tom, don't you?" she asked.

She reached out and took his hand reassuringly. That action caused him to pause in his steps. It was just a slight movement on her part, hardly more than a touch of her fingers and palm. Still, she could very well have taken his heart in her hand just then. He glanced at her, wondering if there was ever anything he was going to be able to keep from her. Probably not, which was all the more reason to clear this mess up and get her out of his life for good.

"Occasionally, but we don't meet here. Usually it's for

lunch somewhere. Or he comes over to the house. I've been to his place a few times, too," Lee replied. "But it's been a number of weeks since I've seen him." Erin didn't let go of his hand.

They followed the hallway to the Specialists Division, where trained officers specialized in different areas of the law—hostage situations, crimes involving children and witness protection, which was Lee's area of expertise. When they stopped at the doorway to Tom's office, he came toward them, a genuine smile on his face. Tom Weatherby was just the opposite of Lee. Where Lee could be dark and brooding and just a bit intimidating, Tom was cheerful, sunny and outgoing. His emotions were clearly written on his face. His sandy hair was cropped short, his gray eyes sparkling. His dark suit was beautifully tailored and fitted him perfectly, accenting his muscular body in all the right places.

Even though they had worked closely together as partners, Lee could never wear a suit like Tom and look so sharp. He almost always wore jeans and his leather jacket, just as he was now. Lee let go of Erin to grasp Tom's extended hand.

"Hey, Lee," Tom said, in the happy voice Lee remembered so well, "you look great. I'm glad you're here. And you, too, Erin. It's good to see you again," he added, turning his attention to her.

Erin smiled at him and offered her own hand. But Tom wasn't satisfied with that. Standing just outside his open door, he drew Erin into a big bear hug. The action drew a chuckle from Erin and an unfamiliar wave of something akin to jealousy in Lee.

No, Lee realized, it wasn't jealousy. It was longing. He would like to be able to pull Erin to him so easily, so comfortably, without worrying about her rejecting him, without worrying about what might happen afterward when he let her go, without putting his own heart at risk. He would like to have his best friend and partner back, too. Seeing Tom hold Erin for that brief moment only served to remind him of all the things he'd let slip away in the past few months. All the things that might never be the same again. Because if the leg never healed, what would the future hold for him? He swallowed hard against the thought and cleared his throat.

"Come on in," Tom invited with a sweep of his arm. Ushering them into his corner office, one that Lee guessed went with his promotion, Tom continued with his questions. "So how are you both? Everything holding up all right?" His words were weighted with apprehension. Lee thought it was probably because Tom already knew all about their troubles. He closed the door to his office. "Can I offer you some coffee or something?"

"No, thanks," Lee replied for both of them. He didn't answer Tom's first questions. He wasn't quite ready to tell Tom everything that was happening to Erin. He was still trying to get used to being in Tom's new office. Still observing the man before him, the one who had been his best friend ever since their training together. That would never change, but Lee felt he had to take his time here. He wanted to see just how much Tom knew before he started telling Erin's story. "How are you doing, Tom?" Lee asked, more out of courtesy than curiosity before they got started.

Tom gave them a wide grin. "Just fine today." He looked from Lee to Erin. "Torry told me a little while ago that I'm going to be a father."

Tom's words caught Lee off guard. So that had been the "something important" Torry had told Tom. Lee fought down a wave of regret that spoke of broken dreams and lost hopes. He couldn't afford to think about kids right

now. Every time he had in the past, they'd always had
sparkling green eyes like Erin.

"That's great. Congratulations," Lee forced out.

Erin's echoed congratulations sounded more heartfelt
than Lee's, and he could sense her smiling without having
to look at her.

"Yeah, isn't that something else?" Tom remarked,
fairly beaming. "After years of trying, it finally happens
when we decide to give up."

"I'm trying to picture you as a dad," Lee lied.

"So can you?" Tom asked.

"No." Lee grinned, starting to feel at ease.

"Oh, well, I'm sure you didn't come here to listen to
the news about me. Tell me what's going on with you."
Tom looked knowingly at Erin.

Erin and Lee each took a seat in front of the large desk
near the windows. Lee gave the office one last glance,
trying to put out of his mind everything Tom had accomplished. He was moving up in the department, he had a
happy marriage and now he was starting a family. It was
even harder to put out of his mind what he himself could
have accomplished if he'd never been shot, if Erin hadn't
left him.

If he had never let her leave....

The eight months since the shooting had flown by in-
credibly quickly. But at the same time, Lee felt he'd somehow lost much more than a mere eight months.

How did Tom and Torry make it when he and Erin
couldn't?

He looked at Tom, only to find his friend watching him
closely. "What do you think, Lee?" Tom asked quietly,
looking around his office and weighing Lee's reaction.

"Great office," Lee replied. "Are you going to share it
with me when I come back?"

"When *are* you coming back?" Tom asked pointedly.

"I'm not sure if I'm ready. I'm only here for Erin right now."

"That's what I figured," Tom said.

Still, Lee saw something in his friend's eyes, something that told him Tom was thinking more than he was saying. "What are you up to, Tommy boy."

"I was just thinking I wouldn't let you out of this office until I have your official say-so that you're coming back. We need you back, Lee. Just as much as I think you need to be back."

"What makes you so sure about that?" Lee couldn't help but ask.

"The only way you're ever going to get over your fear of falling off the horse is to get right back on, and you've wasted too much time already waiting to do that."

Lee didn't take a chance on opening his mouth again. Tom was just too close to home with his assertion. Lee couldn't help but admit to himself that yes, he was terrified to come back. He'd let his guard down and gotten himself shot. He could have gotten the witness killed, too. And he was terrified of it happening a second time.

Still, if Lee didn't know better, he'd think Tom was doing this on purpose to force some sort of reaction or response from him, perhaps get him to admit his fear. Well, he wasn't about to give Tom what he wanted. As evenly as he could, he looked at Tom and replied, "We're here to talk about Erin. So why don't we get down to business. We can discuss my bright future some other time."

"What are you going to do if you don't come back? Spend all your time arguing with your therapist?" Tom asked.

The words seemed to hang in the air for a long moment.

"What've you been doing? Keeping tabs on me?" Lee challenged, doing his best to keep his voice even. He didn't give Tom the chance to reply. "I said we'll talk about my future later, all right?" He let the words out through gritted teeth.

"If you insist," Tom said slowly, just slowly enough to let Lee know he wasn't about to drop the subject. Then after a moment, he turned his attention to Erin. "I understand you've had some problems, Erin."

Lee let out a heated chuckle. "That's putting it rather lightly, Tom. Why don't you tell me what else Kaffel told you?"

"It really bothers you that he called me, doesn't it?" Tom asked.

"No, it bothers me that if he would call you, no telling who else he might call. It makes it a bit harder to keep Erin safe."

Erin said nothing, letting Tom answer the questions, letting the conversation go on between Tom and Lee. It surprised Lee that she wasn't asking her own questions, but he supposed she was still experiencing a certain amount of confusion and it was probably easier for her to sit back and watch the two of them try to get a handle on things.

"Here's what I know," Tom began, getting right to the point. "And I didn't get this just from Kaffel. The FBI has been investigating Forest Burke for some time now. I think they even planned to question you, Erin, once you tried to gather information on him. And especially after it came across the wire that you were nearly run down in the parking garage. They wanted to know why you were interested in him. They even investigated your report of witnessing a murder. When I learned Erin was the eyewitness, I almost called you, Lee. Then Kaffel calls me about a break-in at Jackson Flemming's house. Both your names were in the police report. That's how I knew she was with you. Lee, I was just about to call you when you beat me to the punch."

"Why is the FBI investigating Burke to begin with?" Lee asked.

"There's been a series of art thefts," Tom replied.

"From museums?" Lee queried. "Yesterday, I thought I heard something on the radio about some stolen artworks, but I was at therapy and wasn't really listening to it." He'd been trying to shut out his therapist and he must have shut out everything else, too.

"No. Private collectors. There was a major theft in New York two days ago," Tom explained. "A painting worth over a million dollars called *The Cornucopia* was stolen out of the home of a man named Benjamin Montgomery."

"A million dollars?" Lee repeated. "What kind of security did this Benjamin Montgomery have?"

"Enough to protect it. Whoever's responsible is doing a good job of it, throwing red herrings all over the place, creating diversions and cracking security systems like you wouldn't believe," Tom said.

"And the FBI thinks Burke is behind these?" Erin asked, speaking for the first time.

"The FBI has discovered that at least one piece of recovered art changed hands through one of Burke's auctions. And Burke certainly has the means and the connections to deal with the art. But the Bureau has no proof, no positive leads that connect Burke himself with the crimes. And whoever did take these artworks has hidden them well. There's no trace of them anywhere."

For a moment no one spoke.

"We got a print off Erin's desk. Have they matched it with anyone?" Lee asked.

"As a matter of fact, I contacted an Officer Ollin on that myself. Ollin's team was able to match that print to a man by the name of Jimmy Doreli. Ever heard of him?"

Both Erin and Lee said they hadn't.

"Ollin faxed all the information he had, including this

picture. It seems our man here has been arrested for—
would you believe?—tax evasion.''

He handed the copy of the mug shot to Lee first, who
looked at it long enough to memorize the man's features.
Then Lee passed it to Erin.

"This is him! This looks like the man who I saw grab
Jenkins," Erin exclaimed.

Total silence followed her words.

"Are you sure?" Lee finally asked.

"I'm positive."

Tom picked up his phone and dialed, speaking quickly.
"I need an APB put out on one Jimmy Doreli. He's
wanted in connection with a murder." Tom didn't add that
there still wasn't a body. He merely went on to give Doreli's description off the sheet he was holding. "If he's out
there, we'll find him," Tom said to Erin when he'd put
down the receiver.

"What we need to know now is if he's connected to
Burke," Lee said.

"Well, let's see what we get." Tom turned to the computer on the corner of his desk.

Lee watched him. Inside, he felt the excitement of the
job returning. It was like a rush of heat flowing through
him. It felt good to be doing something helpful, something
important. It wasn't quite the same as sitting in a safe
house watching out the windows, but it was important
nonetheless. That feeling of importance had drawn him
into police training to begin with.

He felt the warmth of Erin's gaze. Turning toward her,
he found her watching him with awareness sparkling in
the depth of her bright green eyes.

God, she knew, he realized. She knew just what he was
thinking, what he was feeling. After being apart for eight
long months, how could she possibly read him so well?

Lee couldn't begin to answer that question. He might as

well stick to the vital matter at hand, like how to keep Erin safe. He deliberately looked away and watched Tom.

"Nothing here yet," Tom muttered, punching more computer keys. "Let's try something else."

Again, Lee could feel Erin watching him. The tiny hairs on the back of his neck stood up, and he grew warm, suddenly needing to take off his leather jacket.

"You know, it's really good to see you two again," Tom said, his eyes on the computer screen. "After this is all over, maybe we could get together, the two of you and Torry and me. We could have dinner or take in a movie, celebrate our upcoming parenthood. It would be just like old times. What do you say?"

"I don't think so," Lee answered, not even wanting to think about the old times anymore. He felt badly out of shape and didn't care to be reminded of how things used to be.

"That would be fine," Erin said at the same time.

Lee couldn't help but look her way. Their gazes clashed like steel, seeming to send sparks into the air around them. Lee suddenly felt as though he was burning up. They were challenging each other now in a fiery confrontation that both of them were facing head-on. He couldn't run away from it. He could see she was going to defy him. He just knew it.

So it came as no surprise when she did. "We'll see, Tom," she said. "But I think that sounds like a great idea. We'd love to see Torry."

Well, it wasn't quite an act of defiance, but it was close enough for Lee. He would have loved to grab her just then and shake some sense into her. They couldn't go out together. He couldn't. He wouldn't.

He would have loved to jump over the desk and shake some sense into Tom for even making the suggestion.

But he let it go for now, needing to put his own problems aside until this was over. He forced himself to remember his first priority—to keep Erin safe. After that, he could limp away and leave the past behind. Looking up, he found Tom staring at him strangely.

"Find anything, Tom?" he asked, trying to get down to business and forget about going out all together—just like the old days. He'd worked too hard getting past those good old days.

Tom looked at the computer screen. "Maybe I just did," he said slowly.

"What?" Lee and Erin spoke out at the same time. Lee threw her another heated glance. Then Tom had both their attention.

"According to Doreli's record, he's been arrested for tax evasion, as I said. But his bail was paid by none other than Forest Burke."

Lee sat back in his chair and let out a heavy sigh. Knowing for certain who was behind all of this somehow made it easier to face. Looking at Erin, he noticed she was taking the information with a sense of relief, too. At least he thought she was until she reached out and took his hand again.

Her touch was cold. He gave her hand a squeeze in an effort to warm her. It didn't help much, but he didn't let her go.

"What do I do, Tom?" she asked.

Lee could hear the way she was fighting to keep her voice strong.

"We're going to start with some police protection," Tom replied. "I may have put out an APB on Doreli, but that doesn't guarantee he'll be caught any time soon."

"Do you think she's safe with me?" Lee asked. He meant safe at his place as opposed to a safe house or perhaps a hotel.

Tom's answer caught him off guard. "Do you?"

"I just wanted to know if you feel my house is safe enough or if I should take her somewhere else," Lee replied, unable to keep the edge out of his voice.

"Have you noticed anyone following you?" Tom asked.

"I've been careful," Lee replied.

"Does anyone know she's with you?" Tom asked next.

"Just Ollin and Kaffel. And you."

"With police surveillance, I would think it's probably safe enough. But it wouldn't be a bad idea to have somewhere else in mind in case you have to leave," Tom suggested.

"Fine," Lee said shortly.

"I'll see to it that a couple of men in an unmarked car are assigned to watch your house. I'll also put a team at the end of your street. And unless you have any objections," Tom added, "I'm going to keep in contact with Kaffel and let him know what's going on so don't be surprised if the FBI ends up watching, too."

"Do you really think all this is necessary?" Lee asked. True, he wanted to do everything to keep Erin safe, but the fewer people who knew where she was, the better.

Tom nodded, his expression reassuring. "Yes, absolutely. It's what we do, remember. It's our job to protect witnesses, and right now, I'm calling the shots. Besides, I'd feel better. And you know as well as I do that I can do it this way or I can do it behind your back."

Lee fought back a grin. Yes, the man before him hadn't changed a bit. He was still a sly fox in a dark suit who played by whatever rules it took to win.

"Do what you want, then," Lee returned.

"Thank you."

"You're welcome."

Erin stood up suddenly. "Will you both excuse me for a moment?" Both men stood. "The ladies' room is still where it used to be, right?" she asked Tom.

"Yes," he replied, motioning. "Just down the hall past the elevators."

A second later, she was gone.

Before Lee could say anything, Tom picked up his phone again and got a hold of Alex Kaffel at the FBI to let him know what was going on.

"Kaffel said he would see what he could do about getting FBI surveillance, too, but he doesn't want to take any men off Burke," Tom explained once he'd hung up.

"That's fine," Lee replied. "I'd feel better working with our guys anyway." The room was quiet for a long moment. "Those were some pretty sly moves," he finally said. "Asking us to go out with you and Torry, offering me half your office in front of Erin." His voice was even, only its huskiness revealing the touch of anger he was trying to hide.

Tom grinned. "For over six months, you've been capable of coming back to work, and all you've done is weasel your way out of talking to me, or at least having to hear what it was that I wanted to say to you when it came to the job. I knew if I said something in front of her, it wouldn't be so easy for you to ignore me."

Lee leaned back in his chair and relaxed for the first time. Of course it wasn't easy. It was impossible. He nearly laughed, letting his lingering anger slip away, thinking he should have known Tom would try something like this.

"And yes, to answer your earlier question, I do keep tabs on you. You're the best friend I've ever had. In my opinion, you're one of the best cops in this department— aside from myself, of course. I can't help worrying about you, now can I?"

There was a lump in Lee's throat and he couldn't reply. Yes, Tom could be a sly fox in a tailored suit, but he was also painfully honest. God, how could Lee have forgotten that little detail about his best friend?

He shouldn't have come back here, Lee realized. It was just another painful rung on the long ladder of memories Erin Flemming was forcing him to climb. It was just another reason to either strangle Erin or get her out of his life, whichever was easiest or came first.

"Listen," Tom continued when Lee refused to say anything, "if you need me for anything—and I do mean anything at all—I'll be here for you. You've always known that. I just wish I could do more now."

"So much points to Burke, but all of it is circumstantial. And even if there was something strong enough to warrant an arrest, a sharp lawyer would make sure we couldn't hold him for very long. After that, Burke would cover his tracks and be out of the country before you could say 'Prussian blue paint.' And then the FBI would be on our butts for screwing up their investigation." He paused and rubbed his temple absently. It was the first sign that showed he was worried about all of this. "God, the thought makes me sick."

"Lee," he added, "if anyone can keep Erin safe, it's you."

This time, Lee forced himself to his feet. "Enough already. I'll keep her safe. But I want to know about Burke."

"What about Burke?"

"Whatever you've got on him. Whatever you can access from the FBI."

"I can't do that—"

"Yes, you can," Lee insisted, trying his best to keep his voice calm.

Tom looked hard into his eyes. "Your job is to keep her safe, Lee. That's it. Your job is not, and I repeat, not to go after Burke. You got that?"

"I still need to know exactly who and what I'm up

against here. All Erin had on Burke was a bunch of public relations stuff that didn't tell me anything more than the fact that the man likes expensive Southwestern clothes.''

Tom raised an eyebrow. "Southwestern?"

"Just like a rattlesnake," Lee said absently.

Tom punched some keys on his computer and checked the screen. "I'm afraid I can't access more than that. His record is clean."

"That's because he's got men like Doreli doing all his dirty work." Lee wasn't able to hide his frustration.

Tom turned on his printer. "Here's the most recent picture I can get." He passed it to Lee, who stared at it for a long moment so he'd be able to recognize Burke in a crowd if it came to that.

"But that's not all," Tom added.

"What else is there?" Lee asked, even though he already knew what was coming.

"I have to officially reinstate you. I have to take you off the disability list. If I don't and there's trouble, if there's any shooting, if Erin gets hurt, if any innocent bystanders get hurt…" Tom let the sentence slide away.

But Lee already knew the rest. If anything happened before Lee was officially back on the force, it could blow his chance at any future career. He could be ruined. Lee took a deep breath, knowing that circumstances had made his decision for him.

"Do it," he said.

"My pleasure." Tom grinned.

"You don't have to be so happy about it."

"Are you kidding? As soon as you're gone, I'm having your desk moved in here."

Lee let out a frustrated huff. "Go to hell," he muttered. Tom only laughed.

Chapter 4

Erin returned just in time to hear Tom say, "And work with my men and the FBI if you see them, all right? Instead of against them."

She looked at Lee, only to find him grinning. His grin didn't quite reach his eyes, however. What startled her most was the tension she felt in the air. It was as thick and dense as a storm cloud.

"I'll try, but I can't make any promises," Lee said.

"That's what I was afraid of," Tom muttered. "Look, I've assigned Johnson and Maggs to your case. They're probably downstairs already and should follow you home." Tom spoke to both of them. Looking at Lee, he added, "So don't decide to have a little fun and lose them. They're there to help protect you."

"I'll try," Lee said again.

"They're good cops."

"I know," Lee agreed.

Erin only nodded, feeling herself relax, feeling safer

than she had in the past few days. "Thank you, Tom.
You've helped us out more than you can possibly know."

"You're welcome, Erin." He looked back to Lee. "I
suppose I don't have to tell you the rules, right? You still
remember them?"

"Rules?" For a moment, Lee pretended he didn't have
the foggiest idea what Tom was talking about.

"Oh, that's right," Tom retorted, his tone caustic. "You
don't live by any rules. Well, let me tell you anyway.
There's really just one main rule you have to remember,
old man. Keep in touch. That means if something goes
wrong and you get separated from my men, call me. If you
have any questions or learn anything new, call me. If you
have to leave or you think Doreli is close or knows where
you are, call me.

"Don't—I mean *do not*—try to go up against these guys
alone, Lee. I mean it. Call for help."

"I got it, boss," Lee replied, giving him a mocking
salute.

Tom only smiled. "I think I like the sound of that—you
calling me boss."

"Forget it, *partner*." Lee tried to hide the amusement
in his voice and failed. Not that it mattered.

All three headed for the elevator. Tom gave Erin a hug
goodbye and shook Lee's hand, giving him a hard look as
they waited for it to come.

"Be careful out there, Lee," Tom said, with no hint of
amusement in his voice or his expression. "Take care of
the both of you. Sure you have the address of the safe
house?"

"It's engraved in my brain," Lee muttered.

"If you have any problems, you can even come back
here," Tom added.

"What?" joked Lee. "And sleep on that lumpy-looking
sofa you have in your office? Forget it."

Tom just grinned.

"You can sleep on the floor, then, and I'll be glad to take the sofa," Erin offered with a smile.

Lee let her remark pass.

"And you take care of Torry," Erin added as she and Lee stepped into the elevator.

The doors closed. And neither Lee nor Erin saw Tom give one of his men a small slip of paper. Neither did they hear him assign another team to watch over the two who had just left and make sure nothing happened to them. No matter what the cost.

"So what was that between the two of you?" Erin asked as they descended. "Did Tom ask you to come back permanently and you turned it down, or what?"

"No comment," Lee said.

"Oh, come on, Lee. Tell me what went on while I was gone."

"I've been reinstated, Erin, my job being to keep you safe. I'm once again officially back at work, only it's not quite what I expected. It's not a desk job," he said without looking at her. He expected more questions from Ace Reporter Erin Flemming. Questions about how he felt, questions about whether his leg was still hurting, questions about just what he planned to do next.

"All right," she agreed easily, surprising him with the way she dropped that topic. Then she moved on to a worse one. "Why didn't you want to go out with Tom and Torry after this is over?"

Lee clenched his hands at his sides to keep from punching the elevator door. Why couldn't the elevator stop? he wondered. Or why couldn't someone get on with them so they weren't alone and she wouldn't be free to ask stupid questions he didn't feel he needed to answer?

"My life is my own now," he finally replied, realizing he'd been holding his breath.

"Oh?"

God, was she actually at a loss for words? Again? Lee nearly laughed at the very idea. He should probably mark this day on his calendar.

"That means we're not a couple anymore," he said instead of laughing. He went on talking as though she were a small child. "I'm working to keep you safe, because it's my job and I'm going to do my job just as I would to keep anyone else safe. You left me. Remember?" he prodded.

"As though I could ever forget," she muttered.

The elevator reached the lobby at that moment. The doors opened, and Erin didn't waste any time getting off and moving away from him.

Again, Lee knew he should be glad that she wanted to distance herself from him.

So why wasn't he?

Catching up with her, he grabbed her by the arm and stopped her from moving any farther away. "Don't do that again," he ordered, trying to convince himself he was just trying to protect her. This had nothing to do with wanting to keep her near him. "Don't leave my side. Don't go off ahead of me by yourself. Doreli could have been waiting right near the elevator and there wouldn't have been any way I could have reached you in time to stop him from doing something to you." He paused, still grasping her arm. The dark of his eyes met hers in a flash of green fire. "I'll do my job and protect you whether either of us wants it or not. But starting now, you've got to do as I say. You've got to be my shadow. No more running off on your own. Understand?"

"Fine," she snapped, refusing to say anything more or do anything other than stand before him and meet his gaze.

A long moment passed and he was certain she would argue or even defy him and walk ahead of him. Most people would let go of things that threatened their lives. But not her. When they'd been together, he had seen the way she worked. She seemed to grab onto a story as if she was grabbing a tiger by the tail. She had such determination, such strength when it came to getting her stories. It was what he loved about her.

What he *still* loved about her....

No! He closed his eyes. He refused to still love her. Not after all this time, all these months. He just wouldn't. He didn't want to feel that uncontrollable emotion ever again in his life. He'd have better luck bailing out a sinking ocean liner with nothing more than a measuring cup than he would surviving her love a second time.

Hell, he was over her. He was back to work, making that giant step to get on with his life.

Yes, dammit, he was. And he felt good about it, too. He should probably thank her for getting him to this point.

So why did he want to do more than just his job when it came to Erin Flemming? Why did he want to catch the guy who was doing this to her and string him up before sticking him with hot knives?

She's been gone for nine months! the voice screamed in his head. Yes, but she'd lived with him for eleven months before that, the other side of him argued. And they'd dated for almost a year before that. But now those eleven months together seemed more important than the months apart. Those long, lonely months without her were wiped out in an instant when she stood outside his front door that morning. Now all he could dwell on was the time he'd spent with her before.

On the drive home, Lee recognized not one car, but two following them. He thought he even recognized Henshaw in the second car, but he couldn't be sure. He had to fight the urge to try to lose the two tails just to see how good they were.

Erin didn't say anything to him, didn't even look over
at him. Again, he told himself he should be glad. Just
drive. Just protect her. Just do his job. That was all he had
to do. Think of it as nothing more than a job, no different
from hundreds of others he'd done. But he couldn't. This
was Erin.

"Hungry?" he asked once they arrived home. He didn't
bother to check on the whereabouts of the two cars following them. He knew the procedure. He knew they were
close.

"No," she said shortly. "But if you are, go ahead and
eat. You don't have to play host to me. Where's my bag?"

"In the kitchen." He led her in and reached for it, but
Erin managed to get her hands on it first.

"Does it matter where I lie down, Liam?" she asked,
holding her bag tightly. Refusing to let him carry it for
her. There was something in the way she continued to say
his full name. It sounded a lot like the way his mother
used to say it when she was mad at something he did.

Lee led Erin upstairs to the first bedroom. "You can
have this room," he said. "It's closest to the bathroom."
It was also farthest from his room—the room that used to
be theirs.

Erin was staring at the quilt on the bed. It was a hand-
stitched quilt. They had won it playing bingo at a church
picnic shortly after Erin had moved in with him. They'd
slept under it together, and after she left him, Lee had
moved it onto this bed because he hadn't been able to get
her scent out of it.

"Are you sure you don't want something to eat?" he
asked, feeling hungry himself.

"I've had a rough day. I think I'd just like to lie down
for a while," she replied, dropping her bag beside the bed.

"Well, I think I'll put a frozen pizza into the oven. You
can crash while it's cooking." He turned to leave, but not

before glimpsing her tenderly reach out and brush her fingertips along the smooth softness of the quilt.

Moving down the hall, Lee took a deep breath. All right, she was here. It was time to go into his protector mode and do his job.

Erin listened to him leave, one footstep heavier than the other. Her hand was still on the quilt. She wanted to ask him why it was here, but she had a pretty good idea. It reminded him of her, and he didn't want to be reminded.

She was suddenly so tired—tired of being afraid, tired of trying to stay clear of Lee. The quilt on the bed only confirmed how much he didn't want her around. Most of all, she was tired of fighting her desire to be with him once more. Everything about him drew her to him. Yes, she'd missed him. She just hadn't realized how much until she was close to him again.

Opening her bag, she let out a frustrated sigh. There on top was the Cupid, where she'd put it when she'd taken it out of her pocket to pack. It stared up with the lifeless eyes of a figurine. It was the expression that spoke for it, an expression that seemed to speak of love. Without further thought, Erin pulled it out of the bag and put it on the nightstand. Because the chubby legs were broken, it could no longer stand. So Erin laid it down so that if the arrow hadn't been broken, it would be pointing at her when she was in bed.

Supper turned out to be a quiet affair. After a short nap, Erin went downstairs and ate a piece of pizza to keep Lee happy. But she didn't feel like talking to him, and she let him know it by the short way she answered his questions.

Since they'd come home there had been a stronger wall than ever between them. It had started in the lobby, she realized, when he'd bluntly told her this was nothing but a job to him.

Erin was beginning to think she'd made a mistake com-

ing to Lee. She should have gone right to Tom. But she
hadn't, she thought as she slowly chewed her pizza. And
even knowing what she knew now, knowing how Lee
would think of her—as nothing more than a job—she
knew she'd come to him again. He might not want her,
but Erin trusted him more than anyone else.

Some time later, with the tension still thick between
them, Erin thought of that trust. As she lay on the quilt
she had shared with Lee so many months ago, she was
comforted by her feeling of trust. Finally feeling safe, she
managed to sleep comfortably for the first time in nights.

Lee, however, wasn't asleep. He sat at the kitchen table,
looking out the sliding-glass back door at the darkness.
Rain was slamming up against the glass in huge drops. His
leg ached. He had cleared the table of the remains of the
horribly quiet supper he'd shared with Erin, but the aroma
of pizza remained. She'd insisted on helping him, and Lee
had finally let her. But they continued to dodge one another between the sink and the table in the process. Now
he sat at the table with only an untouched cup of coffee
and a folded newspaper. It hadn't told him much more than
he already knew. There was the usual assortment of mur-
ders and robberies, car thefts and political scandals, all
wrapped up nicely with a section of recipes on how to fix
potatoes a hundred different ways.

This was the hardest part of the job. The waiting for
something to happen. The something could be anything
from Doreli finding out where they were and coming after
Erin to Burke making a mistake that could get him
arrested.

Or the something could be between Lee and Erin.

"No," he muttered out loud, taking a drink of coffee
as though he was trying to wash down the thought. Nothing was going to happen between him and Erin. He
wouldn't let it.

Lee set down his cup with a heavy clunk and got up roughly, thanks to his frustration and the stiffness that had settled in his leg. He noticed the time; it was just after ten. Hours had passed with Erin upstairs, while he was doing nothing more than sitting down here reading the day's news and staring at the darkness, waiting for something to happen. No wonder his leg felt like hell. He hadn't exercised it at all today. Well, he could take care of that with no problem. He could even go in and watch the television while he was doing it.

First, he wanted to check on Erin. He hadn't heard a sound out of her since she'd gone up after helping him clean the kitchen.

Silently, slowly, he climbed the stairs. He needed to see her. He tried to tell himself he was only checking on her because it was his job. He also told himself there was absolutely nothing wrong with doing that. Yet the truth was he wasn't even sure what he expected or hoped to do once he reached her. Perhaps that was why seeing her in the bedroom caught him off guard.

Erin was asleep on top of the quilt. Her shoes were off and beside the bed. In the dim light, Lee could see she'd unbuttoned the jacket to her suit, revealing a soft, lacy camisole underneath.

Just seeing it sent fire through his veins. Lee recognized the sensation. It was a familiar fire he hadn't felt in almost a year, a fire he had never expected to feel again, at least with Erin. He could imagine himself peeling away her jacket before sliding the straps of the camisole down her shoulders. He didn't have to imagine how soft she would be. He could well remember.

Carefully, he slipped into the room and covered her with the end of the quilt. He suddenly realized he was holding his breath. Erin's chest moved slightly as she breathed. She lay on her side with her hand under her face, looking small and innocent, just as she always had when she slept beside him. Lee remembered all the times he'd wake up earlier than her, only to watch her sleep, then slowly waken her with kisses and make love to her against the soft music of the early-morning birds.

Unable to look at her anymore, he glanced away, only to stop short at the sight of the broken little Cupid resting on the bedside table. True, the arrow was gone, but if it had been there, it would be pointed at the bed. Pointed at Erin. Pointed at him, too.

Lee suddenly felt as though someone had started a fire under his feet. How in the hell was he supposed to do his job and protect her when he couldn't even control himself when he got close to her?

In her sleep, Erin shifted slightly and sighed, the sound only reminding him of her soft cries and moans when he touched her, when he kissed her. Taking one more look at her, Lee forced himself away. Again. At the doorway, he turned and whispered into the silent room, "What am I going to do with you, Erin?"

He surely knew what he wanted to do with her. But he wouldn't. He'd rather cut off his good leg. For what he wanted to do was touch her. And touching her meant letting her touch him.

Never again.

To keep from doing just that, he clenched his hands and stuffed them into the pockets of his jeans.

And he stepped into the darkened hallway without looking back.

He would keep it all business, he promised himself. He would. He would simply talk about Burke anytime he had to talk to her. He'd start off in the morning by calling Tom and finding out if there was any news. That sounded fine and dandy. A good plan.

Entering his bedroom, Lee stopped, looking around. The

memories were stronger in this room. So strong that for a moment, he couldn't catch his breath.

The memories were haunting him like spirits, reaching out to grab him in the darkness. Telling him how Erin had slept in this room with him, covered with the quilt. He even thought he could smell her perfume. And he hadn't smelled it here for months. He blinked against shadows he saw on the dresser, which for a moment he thought were all the things she used to keep there—her jewelry box, her perfume bottles.

When he blinked again, they disappeared.

But her presence in the house was enough to bring back memories of her in his room.

Well, he didn't need her here.

He didn't even want her here.

So why was he still burning inside?

Filled with frustration from something he was unwilling to face, Lee snatched up his pillow and swept the blanket from the bed. He would sleep on the couch downstairs. It would probably be the best thing anyway. If someone had followed them home and tried to come in after Erin, he would be better equipped to handle it if he was already down there.

He wasn't even tired, so maybe he'd just sit for a while, exercise his leg and set up some sort of a plan for the two of them. He could put the plan into action in the morning.

Yes, he knew where he had to start in the morning. For the rest of this night, he had to keep her safe.

But could he keep her safe from himself?

Someone was in the house. He was a mere phantom in the dark kitchen. Lee could see him, moving like a shadow into the living room, toward the stairs.

Silently, ghostlike, the strange dark figure headed up the stairs. Lee tried to follow, but he could hardly walk. Every step was just one step deeper into the hell of pain. Lee's heart was hammering, his chest so tight he could barely breathe. The air felt cold against the sweat that broke out on his brow. He saw the dark figure reach the top of the stairs.

Erin was up there, just at the top of the stairs. And this was Lee's worst nightmare—that he couldn't get there in time to save her. The shadowy figure who had glided up the stairs ahead of him might have already reached her and could be killing her right now, and Lee was still strug-gling at the bottom. The top looked so far away. He finally fell to his knees and tried to crawl the rest of the way up.

As he reached the top, feeling so exhausted he wanted to collapse, and fighting against the pain shooting up his leg, Erin's scream reached him. The shrill terror of it pierced his heart and caused it to freeze in midbeat.

Oh, God, he was too late.

She had trusted him and he had let her down. For the rest of his life, he would never be able to forgive himself.

Using the door frame to pull himself up and into the room at the top of the stairs, he stared numbly through the darkness at the empty bed. Erin was gone. The bed didn't even appear to be slept in. The quilt was gone, too. The phantom was nowhere to be seen. And yet, Lee could feel him, could feel his ghostly presence close at hand.

Lee was hot. At the same time, he felt cold, so damned cold that he was shivering and gritting his teeth to keep them quiet, pressing his jaws together so tightly that they ached.

Another scream echoed through the house, piercing him through the darkness like a cold dagger. This time it was coming from his room. What had been their *room, Lee and Erin's.*

Using the wall of the hall for support, Lee made his way to that room, terror gripping him in a cold vise that was tightening in his belly, making him feel sick, making him want to slide to the floor right there in the hall so he didn't have to face any of this. Lee had the strange, frightening feeling that when he got the chance to look upon the face of the ghostly figure, he would find it to be the man who had shot him all those months ago. At the same time, he knew deep down just what he was going to have to look at—Erin's beautiful but lifeless face.

He couldn't give up. He had a job to do. Forcing air into his lungs, fighting himself, dragging the pain, he pushed himself forward toward that last bedroom.

Erin was in his bed, tangled in the quilt. Lee had no idea how she had even come to be in this room. That phantom, a mere image of a man in black, his features hidden in the shadows, was on the other side of the bed. Lee tried to grab Erin to pull her to safety in his arms. But the faceless figure was too fast, pulling her away from Lee so that she slipped from him like the wind of a dying storm. Her hand was reaching out to Lee, but it was the look on her face that stopped him cold. It was a look of trust, a look that told him she still believed he could and would save her. For just a split second, he thought he'd be able to reach her, to save her just as she trusted him to. He even felt the warmth of her fingers touch his. Before they slipped away into the darkness. Before she slipped away...

Lee jumped up, waking with a start. Only to find his room empty of any phantom figure or Erin. The house was quiet.

He sank heavily onto his bed again and glanced at his watch. He uttered a soft oath, seeing that it was just after three in the morning and he probably hadn't had more than a complete hour of sleep. And that had been filled with the most terrifying nightmare of his life. Between exercising, checking out every noise in the house, fearing that it was someone or something trying to get in, and coming up the stairs to check on Erin, he felt as though he had hardly closed his eyes.

And now he was back in his room again. His leg simply couldn't handle the stairs one more time during the night, when he was already past the point of exhaustion. He decided right then and there that after it was all over and he and Erin were safe, he was going to sell the damn house. He'd start fresh, with no reminders of Erin or his life with her, with not one stair to climb.

Getting up as quickly as his leg would allow, Lee quietly moved down the hall to check on Erin. Again. Maybe it would have been better if he'd put her in the room directly across from his own. It would definitely have been easier on him.

In the darkness, he could see her shape on the bed. She had changed position and was now on her stomach. In the quiet, he thought he could hear her breathing. She was fine.

Lee, on the other hand, was finally getting his own breathing back to normal, and he could feel his heartbeat slowing. He swore under his breath, and it sounded loud in the still house. He needed some sleep if he was going to be worth anything in the morning.

Back in his room, he let himself simply fall onto the bed and closed his eyes, trying not to think of Erin, just a few steps down the hall. At the same time, he tried to put the faceless man of his dream out of his mind.

Listening and taking a few deep breaths to relax, he heard nothing. Only calm, restful silence. The rain must have stopped. That would help ease the pain in his leg a little. He hoped.

The ringing phone startled him awake. Opening his eyes, he had to close them again against the morning sun pouring in through the windows. Surprised that he had slept at all after the dream he'd had, he found he'd slept the last few hours before dawn in the same position. Feeling far from rested, he felt only stiff and cramped the moment he tried to move. To add to his discomfort, a headache was trying to take root just behind his eyes. The sound of the phone on the bedside table just helped that ache to grow.

"Hello," he croaked after blindly grabbing the receiver.

"Hey, Lee, how was your night?" Tom asked.

"Horrible," he muttered, pulling himself into a sitting position, doing his best to wake up and ignore his stiff body. This was a lot like waking from one nightmare into the painful reality of another. "How was yours?"

"If I told you, Torry would have my hide and never be able to look you in the eye again," quipped Tom.

It figures, thought Lee. "What's up?" he asked.

Lee stopped short then, seeing Erin standing in the doorway, listening. Worse, she was gazing at him with sleepy eyes and a disheveled look about the rest of her. It reminded him of how he used to wake her up, of the way she looked when he woke her. Wishing he could turn away, he found it was impossible. She was still wearing her suit, but she had never buttoned the jacket. She leaned against the doorjamb, the jacket hanging open, revealing the lacy little thing she wore underneath. Even from here, he could see she wore nothing else under it. Closing his eyes briefly, he tried to concentrate on Tom's words.

"Not much. I just thought I'd touch base and let you know I talked to Kaffel after the seven-thirty shift change and there's nothing new to report."

Lee couldn't help but stare at Erin, taking in the way she looked so warm, so soft in all the right places. Still. And he couldn't help but think that everything about him went totally out of control when he saw her this way.

Only the dark circles marred her beauty. Lee wished he could erase them, but he didn't have the foggiest idea how.

If he did, he'd probably work on the shadows he suspected were under his own eyes.

"Are you still there, Lee?" Tom asked.

"Yeah." He tried to focus on his friend's words.

"Listen, Alex Kaffel said he wants to talk to you."

That was almost enough to persuade Lee to tear his gaze from Erin. Almost, but not quite. "What for?"

"He didn't say. If I had to guess, I'd say he wants your word that you'll stay out of his investigation of Burke. I'd be happy hearing the same thing," Tom said.

"You know I can't do that," Lee countered.

"At least you're honest about it," Tom replied. "But think of Erin. If you try anything when it comes to Burke, you'll only be placing her in more danger."

"And sitting around doing nothing makes us little more than sitting ducks," Lee retorted.

"Lee, the man is trying to do his job, and you should be doing yours—which is just keeping Erin safe."

Lee was staring at Erin at the moment, and if Tom knew what Lee wanted to do to her, he would know how really unsafe she was. Lee took a heavy breath, trying to bring his desire for her under some sort of control. "Tom, tell Kaffel I don't want to talk to him, but that I'll do my best to stay out of his way. And don't worry, I'll do whatever it takes to keep her safe."

"I guess I can't hope for any more than that."

"That's right," Lee agreed.

"Well, give me a call at noon and check in, all right?"

"Yeah," Lee said again, still looking at Erin.

Slowly, he hung up the phone, never taking his eyes from hers.

"What is it?" she asked, her voice husky from sleep, making him wish he could pull her to him. He didn't move. He knew better.

Lee took a deep breath. "Nothing much. Just Tom keeping tabs. Everything's fine. He's even talked with Kaffel already.''

''Are you sure that's all?'' Her question made her sound more like the reporter searching for answers.

''Yes, I'm sure.'' Lee got up, only to find that some time during the night, some time between checking on the house and Erin and all the leg exercises, he had taken off his jeans. All he was wearing now was a pair of dark red briefs. He looked up to find Erin watching him closely, taking it all in, staring at him as if she had never seen the color before, or what was underneath. He tried to ignore the heat that moved up his belly to his face. Quickly, telling himself it really meant nothing, he snatched clean clothes from his chest of drawers, but all the while, he felt the heat of her gaze on him.

Erin cleared her throat. ''You hate the fact that Tom is working with Kaffel on this, don't you?'' she asked.

Erin's change of subject meant that seeing him without his pants had affected her as much as it did him. ''I respect Alex Kaffel as an FBI agent,'' he answered absently, holding his clothes in front of him. They didn't offer much cover.

''That's no answer,'' she chided, not moving from the doorway, now fully playing the role of a reporter in her search for all the answers.

''Nor is now the time for answers.'' He turned his back on her and headed into his bathroom off the master bedroom. Forget that they had once shared it long ago. She could use the bath down the hall.

He shut the door against the never-ending heat of her gaze. But the door between them didn't stop the heat that filled him. It didn't stop him from picturing her with that warm, sleepy look on her face. And neither did the quick, cold shower he stepped under a minute later.

Erin watched him go and stared at the closed door for

a long moment. There was nothing more aggravating than the feeling of being dismissed, she thought. She could go after him, demand the answers he refused to give her. Isn't that what she always did when she was on the trail of a story?

Yes, it was. Except that this wasn't just any story. These weren't like the idle threats she'd dealt with in the past. Not anymore. This was her life. And this man wasn't just another person to interview for a story she was working on. This was Lee.

Which was all the more reason she should go after the answers. Which was also why she couldn't cross the threshold and step into the bedroom. Erin knew she would be crossing the point of no return if she entered his room, and she wasn't sure she was ready to do that yet. Besides, she was certain if she did cross over to the bathroom, Lee would just give her a good shove back again.

She heard the faint spray of the shower go on. And she imagined Lee standing under it. Naked, slick, muscular, perfect, his dark hair turning even darker and shining with wetness, his rugged, handsome features softening under the water. She could even recall how the faint dark hair of his chest narrowed down into a V to meet the hair at his—

Erin had to literally shake her head to clear away the vision. This was her life, she reminded herself. So how was it Lee could so easily dominate her thoughts and make her forget that most important fact? How was it seeing Lee in his red underwear could make her forget everything except what it was like to be held in his arms before she peeled that same underwear off?

It had to be stress. She understood the strain of being stalked and nearly killed could push her over the edge. But she almost found herself not caring about getting those answers. More and more, all she seemed to care about was Lee. She cared about the pain in his leg and wished she could make it all go away. She cared about the hurt in his eyes, knowing she was the one who'd put it there. And again, she wished she could make it all go away. He didn't want her here, and she cared about that. She wanted to be wanted by him.

Because more than ever, she wanted him. That want, that very need, hadn't lessened a bit in the past eight months. It was still there, perhaps even stronger than before because now he was here within her reach, within her sight. Every aspect of the man touched her senses and aroused her desire.

Yes, she wanted him. She wanted the past back again. Plain and simple.

And impossible.

She simply wanted to forget there was someone out there who wanted her dead and stay here with Lee. She wanted to be in his arms again, in his bed, in his life. She wanted what she'd had in the past with him, and more. But it was a wistful wish. She'd been the one to throw it all away. And even if she knew she was wrong, Lee didn't want her. He'd made that pretty clear.

Still, it was a new day, she thought, tearing herself away from the doorjamb and moving back down to the cold, impersonal room he'd given her—impersonal except for the quilt on the bed.

Erin slowly ran her hand across it, loving its softness, its familiarity. Just feeling it was enough to make her remember more, make her wish for more. She wondered what Lee would do if he came out of the shower to find it back on his bed in the master bedroom.

Grabbing some clean clothes, she headed for the other shower. At least she'd slept well, which was more than she could say about the past few nights. And no matter how hard she tried, she couldn't deny the fact that it was the safe feeling she got from being with Lee, the feeling of security she got being once again under this roof, that contributed to the way she'd slept.

The shower invigorated her, leaving her clean and feeling like new, renewing her strength with hope that she could face whatever the day brought. Looking in the mirror above the sink as she absently toweled her hair dry, she heard Lee's faint steps going down the hall and down the stairs. She couldn't stop her pulse from quickening, knowing he was so close.

It was Lee, she realized, who gave her the feeling of beginning again. She wanted to be in this house with him, this place that had always felt more like home than any other place, even her father's house. She knew she could trust him, that she wasn't alone.

More frightening than anything was knowing that it wouldn't last long. He'd help her get out of trouble, the way he did everything so efficiently, and then he'd tell her to leave so that he could get on with his life. This was, after all, only a job to him.

Getting dressed, Erin tried to put out of her mind the idea that once her life was safe again, she would have to live without Lee. She had to remind herself to think only of the present. To enjoy each moment with him while she could.

The smell of coffee and frying sausage hit her long before she reached the kitchen. In the doorway, she stopped and watched him, remembering all too well how they both enjoyed cooking.

Seeing him standing at the stove in his bare feet, wearing no shirt and a clean, faded pair of jeans that hugged him like a second skin, brought back a rush of memories that hit her like a fast-moving car. For a long moment, she couldn't even catch her breath, it was so hard to believe that almost a year had passed between them. Wasn't it just yesterday that she'd come down to find him cooking her breakfast just as he was now? And he was cooking sausages no less, her favorite breakfast food.

The radio was on, the announcer giving the morning news.

God, nothing at all had changed. Nothing. Not the room. Not the house. Not the rich, inviting smell of breakfast.

Not the man at the stove. The muscles of his broad shoulders rippled smoothly as he flipped the sausages frying in the skillet. His skin was tantalizingly smooth, tanned like soft leather. Erin knew how it would feel if she slid her palms across it. His dark hair was still rather long, covering his neck, appearing perhaps more wavy than before, and it still glistened wetly from his shower.

His legs were long and lean and muscular. Though she could see that he didn't stand on them equally—he tended to lean more toward his right, keeping the weight off his left.

She also knew that simply living each moment with him, waiting for him to make her life safe again, would never be enough. Never.

Unable to look away, she wasn't even aware that she moved closer. Closer. Close enough now that he was right before her. Close enough to catch the soft scent of the soap he'd used a short time before mixed with the masculine scent she recognized as only his. Close enough that she could feel the heat of him.

And even this didn't seem close enough for her. Erin was drawn to him like a moth to flame. She wanted to touch him. Just touch him. To reach out and put her hand on the smooth warmth of his back, follow it with her cheek and then her lips to make sure that the tanned flesh was the same as she remembered.

And she would have done just that if Lee hadn't turned around. His action was quick and smooth, but she was too close and the large spatula in his hand slapped right into her shoulder. His sudden move and her attempt to avoid the spatula sent her reeling off balance.

Just that quickly, Lee dropped the spatula and grabbed her, his strong hands grasping her shoulders in an effort to steady her.

Lee had known she was in the room. He had felt her watching him the moment she'd come down the stairs. He had felt the warmth of her, and the cold shower he'd taken had been just a waste of his time when it came to damping down the fires she stirred within him. He hadn't realized she'd been so close. And to find her that close, the softness of her body beneath his fingers now, made him feel as though a giant fireball was coursing through him like a comet.

She was dressed in jeans and a soft pink T-shirt that stretched tautly across her breasts. The entire outfit outlined her curves, showing them off instead of hiding them as her suit of the day before had. She suddenly looked just like the girl he'd made love to in the guest house, no longer the career woman who had shown up at his door yesterday.

How long they stood like that—his hands on her shoulders, her hands grasping his arms in reaction, their heated gazes locked—he had no idea. All he knew was that if he moved mere inches, the rest of his body would be touching hers. Just inches, and their lips would touch, and he'd become a part of her. Just inches, and he'd taste that familiar, yet excitingly exotic taste of her that he'd missed for so long.

He suddenly wasn't hungry for breakfast, for the sausages he told himself he was cooking because he liked them, not because she did. He was, however, starving. Starving for her.

Those few inches between them were crossed easily, without his even knowing whether he had crossed them or she had crossed them or they had met somewhere in the middle.

His lips touched hers lightly. A gentle brushing. Hardly a touch at all, like the touch of a feather. But the fire surged through him, leaving Lee hot and weak, wanting to pull her down to the floor with him. Leaving him wanting to crush her against him and explore every aspect of her, to make sure nothing about her had changed. Both of his legs threatened to give way under him.

She tasted so good. And he could feel his strength, his very will to survive, slipping away into the kiss, a kiss that very quickly reached into his soul....

Lee never knew where he got the strength. Perhaps it came from thinking her kiss would find his soul empty since she'd already ripped that part of him out. All he knew was that he gripped her arms tightly enough to leave bruises and tore himself away from her. It left him feeling as weak as the kiss itself had. His chest constricted; it hurt to breathe. Wanting her as he did caused the lower part of his belly to ache with unbearable need.

She stared up at him with uncertainty in her eyes. "What?" she asked.

As if she didn't know, he thought. As if she thought she could just waltz back in here after all those painful months and take up where she'd left off. Trying to keep a semblance of composure, of self-control, and careful of his leg, he leaned down and picked up the spatula from the floor. "Breakfast is burning," he snapped, turning away. He couldn't look at that uncertain, even hurt expression in her eyes any longer.

Damn, he couldn't believe he'd kissed her like that. How could he let his emotions drive him to do something so stupid? He'd almost let her all the way back into his innermost self again, a place he could never let her reach, never let her touch. He couldn't let his passion get in the way of his job. He had to protect her at all costs. But he had to protect himself, too.

Lee could still feel Erin close behind him, as he absently flipped the burnt sausages. If he turned again, he'd bump into her again. He stared at the sausages, unable to look anywhere else, refusing to move. He was afraid if he looked at her, he wouldn't have the willpower to fight off his wanting her.

He cleared his throat, trying to work past the lump that had lodged there. "They'll be ready soon," he muttered. "Do you want some eggs?" He felt his strength slowly returning. Concentrate on the cooking, he told himself. Then concentrate on the case, on protecting her. Forget about the past. It's gone and it can't be retrieved. Forget about the future, too. Any wishes regarding it were impossible.

"Sure," she replied from just behind him.

She was so close he could feel the warmth of her breath touch his back. He fought down a shiver against it. He tried to ignore the heat of it. Think of the present, nothing else. Forget the past. He could do it, he determined. He really could, if he tried hard enough. He thought it was getting easier.

At least he thought it was until she said, "You were always the one who liked to cook breakfast for us."

Lee had to close his eyes for a long moment as that single reminder ripped through him and wiped away any of his ability to concentrate on the present. "Thanks a lot for that reminder," he murmured.

He took the sausages from the skillet and moved away from her to get the eggs from the refrigerator. *Ignore her*, he told himself again. *Ignore the heat of her that seems to be hitting you from all angles. Just pretend she isn't even here. Remember all the plans you made, all the things you thought about doing when the sun came up. Well, now it's up. Put the plans into action and forget her.* The only problem was, he suddenly couldn't remember any of them.

So concentrate on the radio, he told himself, forcing his thoughts into something as trivial as beating the eggs. It wasn't easy, but he tried, keeping his mind on the rest of the breakfast and listening to the news on the radio. The big stories of the morning were a major train derailment and the capture of a suspect in a recent homicide. But Lee's ears perked up at the mention of the theft of a large painting in New York.

Erin left him to fix the breakfast and didn't say any more. Lee knew he should feel grateful that she was keeping quiet, but he didn't. Somehow, having her acting as a guest didn't seem to fit their situation any better than his treating her as though they were back together again and she was somehow part of his household.

He set two plates of food on the table and Erin sat down. He tried not to notice that of the four chairs surrounding the table, she was sitting in the chair that had been hers when they'd lived together.

"You never did answer my question about Kaffel," Erin said, falling easily into the role of the stubborn reporter. "Do you hate him?"

"No, I don't hate him," Lee replied. "Neither do I trust him. It was his fault my witness was shot before he could testify."

"That was a long time ago, Lee," she reminded him.

Lee said nothing. He just took a big bite of his breakfast.

"So how do we go after Burke?" Erin asked when Lee refused to talk any further about Kaffel. She poured herself a glass of juice from the pitcher in front of her and pointedly kept her eyes averted from him.

Noticing how she was obviously avoiding him, he did his best not to glance her way. He took a bite of eggs, but breakfast suddenly seemed less appealing than a plate of sawdust.

"*We* don't go after Burke," he replied shortly after swallowing, then choosing his words.

Erin took a bite of sausage, ignoring the fact that it was blackened on one side. "You don't expect me just to sit around here and wait for him to come after me, do you?" she asked.

"I expect you to sit around here, yes. But I don't expect to let him come after you," Lee returned.

She thought for a long moment. Lee could just imagine all the gears turning inside her head. "I can't just twiddle my thumbs and wait. I'll go crazy."

"The idea is to keep you safe, remember? If that means staying here, slowly going crazy and pulling your hair out strand by strand, then that's what you have to do, Erin. It's my job to protect you, and you're going to help me by doing whatever I say. Understand?"

"More than you know," she replied.

More than he knew? he mentally questioned. Not hardly came his just-as-silent reply. He met her defiant sparkling gaze and tried to ignore the heat that rushed through him. How was he going to share this house with her and keep from giving in to his want for her?

Chapter 5

Lee carried a stack of clean towels into the upstairs bathroom—Erin's bathroom. And the first thing that hit him was the scent of the soap she used. The second thing that stopped him was the sight of her things on the counter next to the sink. A few items of makeup, a hairbrush, deodorant and a toothbrush.

It wasn't much, but it was enough to tell him she'd staked her claim. Lee supposed that if she had continued wearing sleek little professional suits, he'd be seeing panty hose hung about the place, too. He all but dropped the towels onto the counter before walking out.

They had spent the past day and a half living with one another in the same house and avoiding each other at the same time. They shared the quick meals he fixed. Their conversation was forced and remained on the topic of Burke or Doreli. Erin questioned him every time the phone rang. Was it news? No, there was no news. The FBI was still investigating, waiting for Burke to make a move, to give them a reason to grab him. He didn't. So they couldn't. And Doreli hadn't been seen at all.

So Lee and Erin were forced to wait in a living arrangement that was slowly driving him out of his mind.

It seemed the only thing they had in common was wanting to find out more about Burke and watching the news, which they did together the night before. It was almost cozy, Lee thought, as they sat in his living room in front of the television, with Erin curled up on the sofa and Lee in the recliner with his legs propped up.

Just something more to remind him of those good old days they used to share.

Lee couldn't avoid the pain in his leg, but he did what he could to avoid Erin. If she was in his office working at his computer, he stayed in the kitchen. If she was in the kitchen, he was upstairs exercising or reading or, as he was now, doing laundry. He had never in his life thought laundry was this important.

A few moments later, the rising aroma of frying hamburger drew him downstairs. There in the kitchen, he found her standing over the stove. His stove, he reminded himself.

"What are you doing?"

Erin turned at the sound of his voice and smiled.

Lee ignored the smile, the easy, comfortable look in the deep green of her eyes. At least, he tried to ignore it. As with everything about her for the past day and a half, he told himself he was ignoring it, even if the rest of his body was responding with a rush of heat that pulsed through him, ending in the pit of his stomach.

"Cooking supper. Cheeseburgers," she said. "Remember how we used to have cheeseburgers at least once a week—"

"This is still my house," he cut her off shortly. "I'll cook. And I don't want a cheeseburger."

She tried to offer him another smile, but this one didn't come so easily. "I don't mind, really. You know I like to cook as much as you, Lee. And it's not like I'm making a seven-course meal. Besides, this waiting and doing nothing is driving me bananas."

Too bad, he thought. They were in this together, so they might as well be feeling the same thing. He stood his ground. If she wanted to put her personal things on the bathroom counter or work at his computer or read the morning's newspaper before he could get his hands on it, then fine, but she wasn't going to invade his kitchen, too. She was already invading too many other things. And he had to keep just one aspect of his life totally his and his alone. He had to. If he was going to keep his sanity and his heart intact, he would.

"I said I'll cook," he repeated, stepping closer.

That was his mistake—stepping closer. The warmth of her, the scent of her, touched him and mixed with the mouth-watering smell of supper cooking. It didn't help that his stomach grumbled with hunger.

"But I can see your leg is bothering you," she said, trying to keep her voice light.

"How nice of you to notice," he muttered, trying to push his way past her.

"Why don't you just sit down and rest?" she suggested, not budging from her spot at the stove.

"Erin, get out of my kitchen," he snapped.

"Lee, you're acting like a child," she chided, not giving in an inch.

Yes, he knew he was acting like a child, and he didn't care. He couldn't stand it any longer. All he had done since he'd opened his door to her was fight his own emotions over Erin Flemming, and he was tired of the struggle. He was tired of the fact that she thought she could sweep back into his life as though she'd never left.

How many times had he thought about leaving her to the men he knew were sitting outside watching over them? He wondered why he hadn't done it yet.

Tom's men and the FBI in unmarked cars were both out there. Lee could see one out the living-room window and the other out his bedroom window. Hell, he felt like a prisoner caught in the middle. Caught with Erin, too. And the hardest thing was, it could take years to come up with something substantial on Burke. Doreli could disappear, and probably already had, since he hadn't been seen anywhere by anybody. Worse yet, he could be doing this to Erin for reasons that had absolutely nothing to do with the well-known Forest Burke. And that would send them right back to square one.

But at this point in time, Lee had Erin still to contend with. She looked him straight in the eye and refused to move away from the stove. Their supper began to burn behind her. Another few moments, and the smoke alarm would probably go off.

"Get out of the way, Erin," he said, his throat tight.

"Go sit down, Lee." Her eyes sparkled like emeralds, her coppery waves shimmered as she shook her head to emphasize her refusal. "Prop your leg up and take it easy."

"Get out of my damned kitchen!"

"No," she replied, her voice never rising. She lifted her chin, though.

He wanted to shake her, but he didn't dare touch her. He was suddenly terrified at the heat he would feel coming from her. He might as well stick his hands in the skillet with the cheeseburgers if he wanted to burn himself.

"At least turn the heat off so they don't catch on fire," he snapped, using every ounce of willpower he possessed to bring himself under some sort of control.

Erin reached behind her back and turned off the stove

without even looking. Lee wished he could turn off the heat he felt in himself just as easily. He wished just as much that he could walk away from this job, from her, and let her have the kitchen, too. But he wouldn't. Now that he was this close to her, he refused to back down.

"Lee, what's the matter with you?" she asked evenly, never taking her eyes from him. "You're like a simmering pot just waiting to boil over. I came here for your help, and you've given it. I thank you for it."

He chuckled at her words. "Oh, well, you're so welcome, Erin," he said bitterly.

"Why don't you just stop it?" she cried, her emotions finally seeping out. "If anyone deserves to act like a caged animal, it's me. It's my life sliding down the sewer. Now, I'm doing everything I know to help this along," she continued. "Do you think this is easy for me? Do you? My life has been turned upside down and torn out of my hands."

"Well, gee, welcome to the club."

She glared at him, her green eyes dark and smoldering. "What more can I do? What more do you want?"

As though she had to ask, he thought. As though she couldn't look at him and know, when she seemed to know everything else. Well, if he had to show her point-blank, then so be it. He'd show it all to her.

"Just this!"

He grabbed her so quickly, he wasn't even aware he'd commanded his hands to move. Suddenly, she was in his arms, pressed close to him, her whole body touching his. In all the right places, too. And he'd been wrong. She was hotter than the skillet behind her. She seemed to singe right into him, becoming one with him. There was no way he could ever let her go.

He took possession of her mouth in an instant, just as he'd dreamed of doing for the past nine months. Hot, fast, complete. She was his now, he thought, feeling her response, feeling the way her lips came to his and parted with just as much need. She opened herself up to him, letting him take whatever he needed.

And Lee drank her in, feeling his blood, like flowing fire, race through his veins at the mere taste of her.

Passion. Need. Both came crashing together into the two of them at the same time, like a bolt of lightning, stunning them both, stopping them both, causing them to cling to one another as though their very lives depended on it. Fire consumed him. It was hotter than anything he'd ever felt before. Hot enough to melt the remaining chunks of ice that had encased his heart since she'd left him.

He had to have her. Right there. Right then. It would be easy, he realized. She felt so pliable against him, melting as he thought he must be. She was hot putty in his arms, hot putty pressed against his entire body.

Her breasts pushed against his chest with her sharp intake of breath. He'd never make it to a bed upstairs. He'd never make it to the sofa in the living room, either. He could take her to the kitchen table. But somehow he knew he couldn't even make it across the room.

That left the floor.

Erin pulled his T-shirt free of his jeans, working around his shoulder holster, and ran her warm palms over his back. He had to stop himself from ripping off her blouse. And suddenly, even the floor seemed too far away.

He managed to free a few of the buttons on her blouse, just enough so that he could get his hands under the soft cotton and feel the silky warmth of her skin. He couldn't touch her enough. Drawing himself down toward the floor, he held her and took her with him.

The hunger of his belly was now forgotten, replaced by a stronger, more urgent hunger that filled him somewhere closer to his soul. Lee could think only of having her. She would be his completely and his dreams would be coming true. She would quench his burning need and he would have her forever....

The glass backboard of the stove that housed the digital clock exploded just above their heads. Across the room, glass shattered at the same moment. Gunfire from an automatic weapon of some sort tore through the kitchen.

Lee didn't care what sort it was as bullets whizzed past them, slamming into the oven and the overhead cabinets. He pushed Erin flat on the floor and threw himself on top of her.

Which, of course, was just where he'd wanted to be moments before. But not like this.

She cried out and held on to him. All lingering desire was wiped away in an instant as Lee's instincts took over. Dragging himself away, he kept as low to the floor as possible while keeping himself between Erin and the one or more gunmen who had to be somewhere outside the sliding-glass back door, judging from the direction of the bullets. Lee didn't want to take the time or the chance in raising his head to find out for sure. He dragged Erin with him—not that she would have given him much choice to do anything else.

She clutched his arm so tightly he thought she must be drawing blood with her nails. More cabinets splintered around them, more glass shattered, but Lee didn't care about the damage. Only their survival counted now.

In a split second, they'd gone from heaven to hell as bullets continued to spray the room. Lee couldn't even begin to guess why they weren't being hit.

Thank God for the island counter that stood in the kitchen between them and the back door, giving them a shield to huddle behind. They'd both be dead if it wasn't for that. "Come on," he muttered, pulling out his gun. He fired two rounds, covering them as he pulled her out from behind the island and slid her across the floor toward the door that led into the dining room.

"They'll be able to see us if we go through there," she argued, fighting against him just enough that he could feel it.

"We can't stay here and wait for them."

Lee pushed his way through the doorway and rolled beyond to the opposite wall, taking her with him. Bullets sliced through the air around them and splintered the wall and woodwork around the door. Something burned his left arm but any thought of it was wiped away when Erin cried out again.

"Are you hurt? Are you shot?" he screamed at her, the very thought almost enough to cause his heart to stop.

"No, I just hit my head on the frame," she said.

Lee glanced at her, taking in the way she was crouching, pressing one hand against her forehead.

The phones were in the kitchen, his office and upstairs. He couldn't reach any of them. He wondered momentarily where Tom's men and the FBI were. He had to assume they couldn't help or they would have already. So he had to consider that he and Erin were on their own.

There wasn't time to analyze Erin's injury or the pain in his own arm or think about help that probably wasn't coming. More glass shattered from within the kitchen. That sound was followed a moment later by the sound of a footstep in the kitchen, crunching the pieces of glass on the floor.

Crunch...crunch...

More footsteps in the kitchen, coming closer.

He could make a stand, Lee thought. He had his gun, and he could make a stand. But he still didn't know how many there were or if there were others waiting outside. If something happened to him in the process, Erin would be left unprotected.

They could worry about Erin's head and his arm, as well as the missing men, later. Now, they had no choice. They had to get out. Or chances were they'd be getting out later—in body bags. Wasn't that Tom's rule? Don't go up against these guys alone.

Lee grabbed Erin by the arm, more roughly than he meant to, and hauled her to her feet. There was only one other door out of the dining room. It led to the basement. From there they could reach the garage.

Crunch…crunch…

The only problem was, they'd never make it around the large table and to the door. The gunmen were too close. And Lee didn't even know how many there were.

"Where are they?"

How Lee could hear the gunmen over the pounding of his own heart and the continuous crunching of glass under their feet, he would never know. But he heard the whispered words loud and clear.

"They're in here somewhere, now shut your mouth," the closer of the gunmen replied.

"But Burke said to make it clean. This isn't clean," the other argued.

"I said shut your mouth!" the first hissed just as he stepped into the darkened dining room.

Lee and Erin were standing just inside the doorway, pressed flat against the wall. Lee didn't think. He merely reacted, his years of training coming back to him as though he hadn't been away at all. Silently, he holstered his gun. Grabbing the barrel of the assault weapon in the doorway, he easily swiped the gun from the man's hands, then used the butt to smash in the man's face. Quickly and smoothly, he turned the weapon around and fired it at the second man who stood in the kitchen. The man dropped to the floor on the other side of the island.

Lee didn't know if he'd hit the guy or not. And he didn't

care. Nor did he waste valuable seconds finding out. He merely grabbed Erin, who stood stiffly beside him, and pulled her out of the room and down into the basement.

The basement was dark, and Lee didn't bother turning on the lights. The single-car garage took up half of the basement. Lee pulled Erin toward it. In the dark silence, he could hear her breathing, quick and shallow. God, she was probably going into shock. Just what he needed.

They reached her car, which was still parked in the garage, and he shoved her into the passenger seat. "Keep your head down," he instructed, slamming the door. Making his way around the car to the driver's side, he jumped in beside her.

"You left your keys in the ignition. Good girl," he muttered without looking over at Erin. The little sports car revved to life with a turn of the key. He set the gun he still held between the door and his seat where he could grab it easily and quickly if he needed it, but it was pointed at the floor where it couldn't hurt anyone if it accidentally went off.

"The door..." Erin said beside him, sounding as though she had to force the words out.

"Hell," Lee muttered, jumping out in a flash to hit the automatic switch. The door slowly moved up, seeming to Lee to take forever and making too much noise. All the while, he expected the dark figure from his dreams to come dashing in from the rain now falling or from the basement behind them. But no one came at them. The door rose high enough for the car to clear and Lee put it in drive and stepped hard on the gas. Lee was only grateful that yesterday he had parked his own car several yards from the garage door. Otherwise they might have crashed head-on into it or been blocked in. As it was, he had just enough room to maneuver around it, driving into his own front yard to do so.

Rain hit the windshield in an instant, and Lee flipped on the wipers and the lights. The lights, however, didn't seem to brighten anything in the cloudy darkness of the evening. At the end of the block, Lee stopped beside the parked police car. It took only a glance to see the blood and know the policemen weren't going to be of any help to them even if they were still alive. He didn't take the time to wonder where the FBI might be.

"Oh, my God," Erin moaned beside him. "I think I'm going to be sick."

"Not yet you can't," Lee replied, speeding off down the street. "Put your head between your knees and take several deep breaths."

She did as he said.

"Where are we going?" she asked, her voice sounding muffled.

For the first time, Lee glanced down at her. Then he gave in to the urge and gently placed his hand on her shoulder, massaging her gently. "I don't know," he replied. She sat up. Another glance and he could see how pale she was still. "Better?" he asked.

"I think so. Maybe."

He didn't take his hand off her shoulder. Even when she leaned slightly toward him as though his hand wasn't enough.

"Shouldn't we go to Tom?" she asked.

"Not yet," he said, looking straight ahead and still not really seeing the streets before him. He was automatically heading toward the Dan Ryan Expressway. He could feel the blood trickling down his arm. He felt the hot pain but he could still flex his fingers, he could still grip the wheel, so he said nothing. He couldn't think about it yet. Not until he found them a safe haven.

"Not yet?" she echoed in question.

"Only Kaffel and a few of his men knew we were there.

So did Tom and a few of his men. Someone told Burke. Until we know who, I can't trust any of them." He was finally forced to take his right hand off her shoulder and use it to grip the steering wheel. The fiery pain was beginning to spread down his left arm and into his fingers. He'd have to stop soon.

He felt Erin shift in the seat and knew without looking she was leaning against the headrest. They drove around the city as darkness engulfed them. Lee wished he could think where to go. But he couldn't. He needed help, and Erin's breathing was still quick and shallow.

Without thinking, he pulled into the drive-through at a fast-food restaurant. Probably neither of them would keep down any food, so he ordered them both extra-large sodas, thinking the sugar would help them. The young girl working the window looked at him strangely as she passed him two large cups, and he knew she must be able to see the blood he could feel on the back of his arm.

But he took the sodas and tried to smile.

"Are you all right, mister?" she asked.

"Just dandy, thanks," he lied.

Lee handed the drinks to Erin, who took them automatically and put them in the cup holders fixed to the dashboard in front of her. He drove off before the girl could say more.

"I don't think I can drink any of this without getting sick, Lee," Erin said, her voice sounding weak, drained.

"Drink it anyway. I don't want you going into shock." She was already there, he decided as he looked at her in the dim glow of the streetlights. Her eyes were large and shining, her face chalky, her lips pale. "Do it," he ordered.

Erin took a sip through the straw and he could see the way she had to force it down.

"Those men almost shot us," she said shakily.

Was she trying to convince herself that it was all real?

"Yes, Erin," he replied, trying to watch his driving through the rain coming down in buckets.

"They would have killed us if you hadn't kissed me like that. We'd both be dead...." Her voice faded away into the drumming of the rain as it hit the car.

"But we're not," he countered, wishing he didn't have to drive. Wishing he could take her in his arms and keep her warm and help her through this ordeal with more than just his words. But they couldn't stop. Not until he was certain there was no one following them.

Lee flipped the heater of the car on high when he heard her teeth begin to chatter. The horror of their situation was hitting her hard and fast. He had to find a safe place for them to stop. And he had to do it soon.

Lee had to admit that the shock of what had happened was hitting him, too, but it was a different kind of shock. It was almost as though he could feel his protector mode kicking into high gear as the circumstances became more desperate. He hadn't frozen; he hadn't been terrified. He had reacted with all his training and he had gotten them both out—alive. Knowing she couldn't see him in the darkness, he grinned against the pain in his arm. Boy, did it feel good to be back.

He drove on, letting the rich, wonderful feeling rush through him for a short time before he brought it under control. He didn't want it to overwhelm him and interfere with the job that lay ahead.

His next stop was an automatic teller machine. He was thankful he hadn't left his wallet up on his dresser as he'd done a few times in the past several days. After withdrawing as much money as his card allowed, he reached for his own soda. Needing the drink to keep himself going, he swallowed half of it before setting the cup back into the holder. "Drink some more," he ordered without looking at her.

"I'm too cold," she said, her voice sounding small and far away.

"Listen, Erin," he said. Forcing himself to drive with the arm that felt as though it was on fire, he reached over with his other and grasped her hand—tightly. "I need you with me, okay? Stay with me. I need you to help me." Lee never in his wildest dreams would have thought he'd be saying those words to Erin Flemming. But he was, and they were true.

"I'd rather just go to sleep."

"No, you can't," he said, his voice rough. "We won't drive much longer, I promise. I'll find us a place to spend the night. And I'm going to need your help when we get there. Do you understand?" He didn't give her a chance to answer. "Now drink up and stay awake. Talk to me. Sing with the radio. Do whatever it takes, but stay with me."

"All right," she replied softly. She took a drink. "I've never been able to refuse anything you've ever wanted."

Those words made him think. Just how true were they? Would she have stayed if he had asked differently or been more persistent?

He forced the questions from his mind. He couldn't handle them at this point. There were too many other things to worry about. Such as where would they be safe? Who was the traitor who told Burke where to find Erin? At least now they knew it was Burke who was after her. Not that there was much consolation in the knowledge.

He had switched on the radio before and told her to sing with it. He was half listening to it when the news came on and he took note on hearing about a painting recently stolen from a private collector in Chicago.

"Do you think Burke has something to do with these robberies? Do you think that's why he wants to stop me before I can connect him to them?" Erin asked, sounding no stronger than before. But at least she was staying awake.

"All I know is that he's after you. Let the FBI and the police worry about the thefts." Lee knew he didn't have the strength to worry about it himself.

He took another long drink of his soda and wondered at the most important question swirling around in his head. Would they even make it to safety anywhere before he blacked out? Heaven help them, he didn't want to pass out at the wheel and crash and kill them both. Nor did he want to leave Erin alone and unprotected. And Erin looked worse than he felt. He didn't think she could drive. More than that, he didn't know if she could face the reason he would need her to drive. At least not yet.

Minutes passed like hours, the windshield wipers counting the seconds.

"Where are we going?" she asked, breaking the silence again a short time later.

"South. I'm almost certain no one has followed us. So I'm going to find a motel."

"A motel?" she echoed.

Lee looked over at her and tried to grin lightly. "Yes, a motel. One of those out-of-the-way motels where you pay in advance, by the hour if you want, and never get disturbed unless the place is on fire."

"A dump, in other words," she added. She finished her soda, slurping momentarily through the straw.

"You got it," Lee said over the noise.

"What if they find us or see the car parked in the lot?" she asked.

"That's why I'm picking a so-called dump. There are enough of those to keep anyone looking for us for days," Lee explained.

Erin sounded stronger, more in control now, for which he was eternally grateful. And she turned down the heat, too. But he didn't look at her. He looked straight ahead, trying to keep his mind on his driving, trying to keep his concentration clear. It would be so easy to give in to the pain in his body and lose control of the situation.

Finally, he spotted just the kind of motel he was looking for, one with the rooms in the back. He pulled in, parking the car behind the main building where it couldn't be seen by anyone driving by.

"I'll be right back," he said, reaching for the door handle. He would have liked to send Erin in to get a room, but he wanted to request a specific room, hoping to get one of the back rooms hidden by the office building so he could keep the car parked out of sight. Besides, she didn't yet look strong enough to ward off whatever scum might be lingering in the office. Most of all, he didn't want her seen by anyone.

"Don't leave me," she said, reaching out and grabbing him by the arm.

"I'm just going to get us a room for the night, Erin. I'll be right back. I'll leave the car running in case anything happens," he explained, trying to gently pull loose from her grip. The heat of her surged through him at her touch, and Lee did his best to ignore it. Yet he had the feeling he was never going to be able to ignore Erin Flemming, not without lying to himself.

Still, that didn't mean he wouldn't keep trying.

"What's going to happen?" She refused to let him go.

"Nothing. Just wait here for me."

"What if something does happen?" she insisted.

"Drive out of here and leave me."

"I could never do that, Lee," she said slowly, looking at him, her eyes sparkling in the darkness.

Lee fought the urge to remind her that she'd left him before and she'd made it look easy. That thought did give him the strength to pull out of her grasp. "Yes, you can, and you will. But nothing's going to happen. Just sit tight and lock the doors, okay? I'll be right back."

He climbed out into the rain. Feeling wonderful, the cool rain woke him up and cooled him off. He let it soak him, not even bothering to cover himself at all, hoping that whoever registered him in the office would see only how wet he was and never be able to recognize him or identify him should he ever be asked to do so.

Lee didn't have to go into the office. He was able to rent the room by talking to the attendant through a sliding window near the door. Lee was glad. In the darkness and with the rain soaking his clothes, the attendant would be unable to see his arm.

"You sure you want a room for the night, not just an hour or two?" the attendant questioned.

"Yes," Lee replied, giving him nothing but short answers and cash through the small opening.

"Do you want sheets for the beds?"

"Aren't they already there?" Lee asked.

"Nope. Too many people steal them. And those who don't, never need them anyway. They're an extra ten bucks."

Lee passed through another bill and signed his name as John Tompson before grabbing the sheets the guy stuffed through the window.

Erin jumped when Lee startled her with his knock on the window. She unlocked the door, and he pulled it open, quickly climbing in. Absently, he handed her the rain-spattered sheets. She took them without a word. Then he started the car and moved ahead a few yards to park in front of room number eight. It was just what he wanted—out of sight from the highway.

Ushering Erin quickly inside, he paused just inside the door. Closing it and locking it, he switched on the light, illuminating the bland, lifeless room, exposing two naked beds, a chair that had definitely seen better days and a dresser that badly needed refinishing.

"It smells in here," Erin muttered.

"It certainly isn't the executive suite, is it?" Lee had to agree, "but right now, I think it's the safest place."

Erin let out a heavy sigh. "I suppose it doesn't matter. I'm so tired I'm going to put the sheets on a bed, fall into it and sleep."

"I need your help first," Lee said. "And I need one of the sheets."

"What for?" Erin turned to really look at him for the first time since their narrow escape.

At the same time, Lee held up his arm to look down at it, knowing just what to expect.

"Oh, my God! You've been shot!" she cried. "Why didn't you say something? What the hell's the matter with you anyway? Are you crazy? You could have bled to death. Your shirt is soaked with blood!"

"Calm down," he said, trying to force himself to do the same. He sank onto the nearest bare bed and slowly undid the buttons of his shirt. His arm hurt when he moved his fingers that way.

"Here." Erin stepped closer, seeming to come out of her shock just as quickly as it had set in. "Let me help you."

She helped him peel away his bloody shirt.

"Oh, Lee, we should get you to a hospital," she said, peering at his wound.

"It's just a flesh wound. The bullet just grazed the skin, that's all. It's already stopped bleeding."

"I can see that." She grabbed one of the sheets and wiped away the dried blood as gently as she could. Her touch still caused him to flinch. "But you still need stitches and something for infection, not to mention a tetanus shot. A dirty motel room with dirty sheets isn't what you need."

He was glad to see the sight of his injury snap her out of her shock. It was worth it, even if it did feel as though his arm was on fire. His tone of voice, low, gentle and yet firm and commanding at the same time, was enough to cause her to look up and meet his gaze.

"Erin," he said, "we can't go to a hospital. Every doctor has to report any gunshot wound to the police."

"Oh," she said, her total attention now on his wounded arm.

"I had a tetanus shot eight months ago. Besides, it just looks bad because of the blood." Lee let her touch him, telling himself again and again that the warmth of her fingers was just exaggerated because of the pain in his arm, because he'd lost a bit of blood. He wasn't his best because of his injury. That was why her copper curls, which were laced with raindrops, looked so enticing he wanted to reach up with his other arm and lose his fingers in all that hair. That was why her lips looked so red and soft and inviting. That was why that small V of skin at the top of her buttoned blouse looked so desirable—because he'd lost the blood that should be nurturing his brain.

Lee tried to close his eyes and block her out, but her touch was so real, so warm. Her closeness and the soft, familiar woman scent of her invaded him, reminding him of those heated moments when his hands had been on her as they stood in front of the stove, reminding him of the way she felt so soft pressed against him. He wanted her. Again, only stronger this time, if that was even possible.

Forget about the pain, forget about the danger. He wanted her. He wanted every aspect of her—her body, her heart, even her love. The fire that was suddenly burning deep inside him seemed much more urgent than any bullet wound. Something inside told him that having her in his arms would erase all the pain.

"Let me wet this," she said, her voice sounding tight.

Or was it just his imagination? Or his own hopeful thinking that her touching him might be affecting her as much
as it was him? She took one of the sheets and left, heading
into the small bathroom.

"Why don't I just come in there with you?" Lee asked,
starting to get up and follow her. A wave of dizziness
washed over him, and for a moment, he wasn't at all sure
he could stand.

"Sit down. I'll be right back," she called out to him.

He did as she said, suddenly terrified that he was going
to do something ridiculous like fall flat on his face onto
the dirty carpet. While he listened to the water run in the
bathroom, he took his own advice and leaned over, putting
his head between his knees. Once the water was off, he
sat up and breathed deeply, feeling a little better. But even
the dizzy feeling hadn't been strong enough to erase the
feeling of desire that only strengthened when Erin came
close to him and touched him with her soft hands a moment later.

She held a warm, damp sheet, and Lee let her clean his
arm. The warmth felt good, her gentle touch even better,
despite the fact that he didn't really want to admit it. She
was quiet, intent on her job. Lee was just as quiet, trying
not to be so intent on *her*. Her warm breath touched him
as she let out a tired sigh.

"Are you all right?" he asked softly.

"I should be asking you that," she replied, just before
ripping one of the sheets to bind his arm. "Are you?" she
asked.

"It hardly even hurts. But then I probably have my
nurse to thank for that," he weakly joked, trying to lighten
the mood and not to think just exactly how she was really
making him forget his pain. His words turned out to be a
lie when she tightened her makeshift bandage around his
arm and pain shot all the way to his fingertips. Lee gritted

his teeth against the pain, telling himself over and over it could be so much worse. He knew from experience just how much worse a gunshot wound could be. He was reminded of it every time he took a step.

"I think that'll do, unless of course, you change your mind and decide to find a doctor. We could probably bribe one into not reporting it," Erin said, making a final adjustment to the bandage.

"Honest Erin offering bribes?" Lee quipped with a grin and a raised brow.

She didn't reply, only smiled at him.

"No need to bribe anyone. You did a great job. Thanks. I couldn't have done it one-handed," Lee returned, slowly flexing his fingers, and finding the action not that hard to do.

"I'll be right back, then," she said. "I'll see what I can do with your shirt." She left, this time taking his shirt into the bathroom. Again, Lee could hear water running.

On the bed, Lee fought the urge to lie back and rest. He was afraid he'd fall asleep where he landed. Instead, he leaned forward, resting his head in his palms. He looked up at Erin when she returned a few moments later, only to find her looking exhausted. Absently, she rubbed the back of her neck and stifled a yawn. It was another experience he knew well—the way an adrenaline rush could leave you feeling absolutely drained once the danger was over and you came crashing back down to earth.

"I hung your shirt over the shower-curtain rod. I think I got most of the blood out," she said.

"Thanks, that's great. Listen, why don't you put one of those sheets on a bed and get some rest," he suggested.

"What will you do?" she asked, looking rather pleased at the idea.

"Keep watch for a while, make sure no one comes looking for us," he said, still enjoying the feeling of his protector mode.

But Erin wasn't satisfied with his reply. "But you need your rest, too."

"I'll get it later. I'm fine for now."

"All right," she agreed after a moment. "I'll rest for a while, but only if you promise to wake me in a couple of hours so I can stay up and watch while you get some sleep."

"Fine, I'll wake you in a couple of hours," he agreed, just to make her happy, thinking he wouldn't wake her unless he absolutely had to. On the job, he had been used to working on very little sleep and grabbing what he could when he could. He had the feeling that, like his protector mode, it wouldn't take much to get used to that again.

He got up and moved to the window, moving the curtain a fraction of an inch to peer out into the darkness while Erin covered the bed with a sheet. Outside, it was quiet except for the muffled sound of the falling rain. Lee let the curtain fall back into place. Then he moved the worn chair in front of the door. If anyone did find them, he was going to make it as hard as possible for them to get in here. He turned back to find Erin had kicked off her shoes and was already on the bed, not too far from where he'd been sitting.

She covered herself with another sheet, and Lee moved to help her. "Thanks," she muttered, already sounding half asleep.

"Get some rest."

"Don't forget to wake me," she insisted.

"I won't," he assured her. "Does the light bother you?"

She murmured a negative response and drifted into sleep before his eyes. She looked so small, so fragile, so lovely sleeping so close to him. Her breathing became even and slow. And Lee watched her, wondering just how anyone could ever try to hurt her.

Well, no one would if he had any say in it. And he planned to stay at her side and do whatever it took to insure that. But he had to face facts. The fight with the gunmen, the race to safety, the gunshot wound and his loss of blood had left him tired, too. He needed to sit down, even if it was for a moment or two.

Unable to move even a few feet away from her, he sat down beside her on the bed. Sitting close enough that his thigh brushed against her, he propped himself up against the fake wooden headboard of the bed. He'd just rest a few minutes like this, then he'd get up and stay near the window where he could check outside every so often.

They had a long night ahead of them, and as soon as he was sure no one had followed them, he would grab a few hours of sleep. Then in the morning, he'd find them an out-of-the-way greasy spoon to get something to eat, and together they would decide what to do.

But for now, he was too tired to think beyond that. He closed his eyes, trying to come up with some sort of plan. He should call Tom, too, and he would—just as soon as he got some rest. All he could think about now was Erin, so near he could feel each breath she took. He thought he could even feel her heart beating in unison with his. And that was all he felt, he soon realized. The pain in his arm was slowly fading, and for the first time in a very long time, there was absolutely no pain in his leg. None....

Chapter 6

Erin opened her eyes to darkness. For a moment, she couldn't remember where she was. Then she was aware of the warmth of Lee pressing up against her back, and she didn't need to remember where she was. Out of everything that was going wrong in her life, having Lee close to her was not one of them. This was perfect. His warmth touched her everywhere. His closeness told her she was safe.

He was touching her hair. Tenderly, softly, with nothing more than the warmth of his fingertips, he touched her. Erin didn't move. She didn't want to break the spell he was weaving. She didn't want to lose the comfort of his touch.

Gently, Lee pushed her hair away from her face. His fingers lightly brushed her face and Erin closed her eyes, resisting the urge to lean into his hand. She knew if she did, he would know she was awake and he'd move away.

This is where you belong, Lee, she thought to herself,

relaxing against him. *This is where we both belong, in each other's arms.*

Lying in the bed, close to him, it was so easy for Erin to forget the loneliness and the stress of his job. It was easy to forget that Burke wanted them dead. Next to Lee, Erin could shut out everything except the warmth and security of his closeness. Erin wanted just to stay awake and feel the tenderness of his touch. The rest of the world and its dangers were now far away. Life was as it should be and Erin didn't want to sleep through a minute of it.

That was why she was surprised to wake up later to find the room still dim, the cloudy light of morning trying to force its way through the heavy curtains covering the windows. And Lee was gone. With him went his warmth. A chill passed through her, one so cold no amount of blankets could ever erase it.

"Lee?" she called out hesitantly. Sitting up, she recognized the sound of the shower. She relaxed back onto the bed, knowing he was close, and they were both safe.

Lee stood under the hot spray, letting it wash over him. He stood slightly sideways to keep it from wetting the bandage on his arm. His arm still ached but it felt more stiff than anything else. And he would probably need Erin to rebandage it when he was finished.

A tingle went through him at the thought of her touching him with her gentle, soft hands, and he tried not to think about it.

But putting her out of his mind was impossible. The truth was, he couldn't stop thinking about Erin. He remembered how he had awakened to find himself still next to her on the bed, his hand in her hair. He had meant to get a few hours of sleep, but he'd planned to do it sitting in the chair where he'd wake up at the slightest sound should any of Burke's men find them.

But no one had bothered them. The chair was under the

doorknob just where he'd put it last night. When he'd pulled himself away from Erin to get up and look out the curtained windows, he hadn't seen any sign of Burke's goons. There was no movement around the motel at all.

It had seemed like a good time to grab a shower. Lee told himself he needed one to ease his stiffness and wake him up.

At the same time, he couldn't help but feel the shower was more of an escape. More than to ease his aches and pains and to freshen up, he'd had to get away from Erin, put some distance between them, to be gone when she woke. He couldn't be there to see her wake up. He hadn't been able to get through the night without touching her. There was simply no way he could feel her sleepy warmth, see it in her eyes and keep his hands off her.

There was one more thing that caused him to distance himself from her. His leg. For the first time in eight months, he wasn't waking up with pain. Nor had there been any discomfort to deny him sleep. For the first time in all these past lonely months, he woke up to find the woman of his dreams pressed up against him and his leg free of pain.

And there was a madman who wanted nothing more than to kill him and Erin.

How in heaven could things feel so right when he and Erin were running for their lives?

It was impossible. Yet, it was happening. And Lee didn't want it to happen. He didn't want it to feel right. Because he knew as soon as he saw Erin through this— and he vowed he would see them both through—it wouldn't be right. She'd leave, and his life would never be right again. Just as it hadn't been right the whole time she'd been gone.

Lee knew he couldn't survive having her leave him a second time. He couldn't. So he had to be the one to do it. Now. Before he got so close to her that he wouldn't have the strength to do it. Neat, clean and quick—that was the easiest way to stop what was happening between them.

He just wasn't sure how to go about doing this. Nothing had actually happened between Erin and him. Right?

He continued to tell himself that as he ignored the want he felt flaring up within him every time he looked at her.

Yes, he'd kissed her, and last night he'd slept up against her. But that was all. It was nothing. Really. It meant nothing. Really. So Lee didn't have to say anything. All he had to do was keep his distance. Starting now.

Turning the water off, surprised that it had stayed hot as long as it had, he stepped out of the shower and dried himself with a clean towel. The hot water had worked out his stiffness and he felt fresh and invigorated, ready to face the day. But first he had to face Erin.

Erin was awake and flipping channels on the ancient portable television in the corner of the room. But all she was getting was snow. Not that Lee cared, as long as he didn't have to see her with that dreamy, I-just-woke-up-and-I-need-love look. "What are you doing?" he asked anyway.

"Trying to get some news," she said without looking at him.

Lee wondered if she even knew he'd spent the night next to her. He wondered even more if he should care. He couldn't help it. He did care, enough that he couldn't push the thought of it out of his mind.

She finally turned around. He wore only his jeans, and the hungry stare she gave his chest made him feel naked. How could she get to him so easily? And why her, of all people? Why couldn't he have met someone nice and beautiful and kind in all the months she'd been gone? He must have been touched by a thousand different nurses. Why couldn't one of them have turned him on like the woman before him? This woman who had the power to tear his soul to shreds?

The top buttons of her blouse had somehow come undone, revealing just a hint of the lace she wore underneath. He mentally swore as he pulled on his shirt and started doing up the buttons, ignoring the pain the movement brought his arm. Erin had done a good job washing most of the blood out, but there was still a faint stain on the sleeve. Nor had the cuffs dried completely. Lee couldn't take his gaze from Erin, not caring about the shirt just then.

Clearing his throat, he asked, "Are you hungry?" He wanted out of this dump. He wanted to go someplace where there would be other people around, where he could look at something other than Erin's beauty, where he could feel he was once again part of a normal world. True, he still had to keep the two of them safe from any more of Burke's men, but he was tired of feeling so isolated with only Erin to hold on to. He looked away, fighting a battle within himself, for she really was all he wanted to hold on to. He just didn't want to admit it.

"Starving," she answered.

"Then let's get out of here and find some place to grab a bite."

"What do we do after that?" she asked.

"Call Tom, but I want to do it from a public phone booth."

"What then?" she probed.

"We'll worry about it over full stomachs."

There wasn't much to get together and they'd paid in advance, so a short time later, after Erin had had a chance to freshen herself up and wrap strips of a clean sheet around Lee's arm, they found themselves at a nice little out-of-the-way greasy spoon.

"I always liked these kinds of places," Lee muttered as they slid into a booth with smooth red seats. He took a long whiff. "You can raise your cholesterol a few notches just by breathing the air."

Erin only offered a smile, watching him closely. He wondered what she was thinking, even though he wished he didn't. So he continued talking.

"I mean, just look at that old woman behind the counter. I'll bet she was here when the place opened. I'll bet she insists on serving people real food, nothing fast and easy and full of things most of us can't even pronounce."

They ordered a moment later, and it was just as he said—all real food made from fresh ingredients. Golden brown home fried potatoes, creamy scrambled eggs, long strips of crisp bacon. The coffee was fresh and strong and hot, its warmth settling into his bones.

"What are we going to do, Lee?" Erin asked over a final cup of coffee.

Lee had known the question was coming and he still had no easy answers. "I know what I'd like to do," he said. He couldn't seem to forget the feel of her when he awoke. Nor could he forget the kiss of the day before. The passion of it seemed to overshadow the terror he should be feeling that they could have been shot—that he *had* been shot. That it could have been so much worse than it was. Yet, he found it comforting, sitting in a greasy spoon where the air was thick with conversation coming from the construction workers at the counter and the sound and aromas of the food frying on the other side of the counter. It was comforting sharing it all with Erin. He knew it made no sense, but he couldn't help the feeling.

Lee looked at her across the small table and found that he didn't want to be out in the world after all. He wanted to take her back to the motel, dump that it was, and make love to her. He wanted the two of them to be all alone in the world. A world where they'd feel safe, where they could lose themselves in each other, free from cares and worries and doubts. Just the two of them.

"What?" she asked.

He nearly told her exactly what, but managed to stop himself at the last moment.

"I'd like to kill Burke, that's what," he said instead.

"Well, you have to get in line," she replied, taking a sip of coffee.

A thought hit him so suddenly, he nearly flinched. "That's what we'll do," he said.

"Kill him?" She almost choked on her coffee.

"No, but we'll go to him," he declared, feeling more in control than he had since this all started.

"What are you talking about?" she said, setting her cup down with a thud. "When I wanted to go find him, you said no, and Tom said not to—"

"That was before his men shot up my kitchen and my arm. Listen, do you remember the name of his hometown?" Lee asked, ignoring her objection.

"Jamesbrook. Why?"

"Because we're going there, that's why. We're going to flush Burke out."

"What about the FBI? What if it messes up their investigation?" she asked.

"I don't give a damn about the FBI," he said. "I'm tired of playing cat and mouse with this man and his thugs. And who knows. If things work out, maybe we'll be able to find some evidence so that the FBI can nab him."

"What if he's not in Jamesbrook anymore?"

"Questions, questions, questions," he muttered. "Don't you ever get tired of asking questions, Erin?" he teased, unable to keep the amusement out of his voice.

"It's my job, remember?" She smiled, apparently liking the way he had lightened up. "Besides, what about Tom?"

"Oh, yes, I remember your job," he returned, not telling

her that there was little about her he was able to forget. "I also remember that with the way you probe into things, you'll be able to find Burke even if he isn't in Jamesbrook. And if it will ease your mind, I'll call Tom before we leave here."

Her smile grew. "Good. But do you think we could get some clean duds before we head to Jamesbrook?"

"Duds?" He chuckled. "Sure. Why not? We'll need a few other things, as well, if we're going to catch Burke at his own game."

The smile he flashed her was brilliant, casting sunshine on the gloomy day.

Erin realized then that Liam McGrey had safely, securely and easily slipped into the realm of his life where he belonged most. He was back to being more like the man she'd known and lived with, no longer the dark, brooding man who'd opened his door to her a short while ago. But knowing this raised so many questions. Why now? Did his easiness have anything to do with her? Or did it have more to do with doing the job? The sense of needing to protect, that Liam had so strongly, was coming from the need to protect *her*. It was what he called his protector mode.

Just looking at him, she could see that mode in full swing. With its coming, the torment that she'd sensed in him seemed to have vanished.

All Erin could do was return his smile. True, she had no desire at all to die, but if she had to die now, if Burke somehow succeeded in his plans, she felt she would at least die a happy woman. And all it took was knowing that Liam was closer to being the complete man she'd known before he was shot. No, before that—when she'd left him. He was no longer that haunted man who wanted to throw her out of his kitchen.

Seeing Liam like this, with that gleam in his eyes that

she hadn't seen in the past few days—a gleam she had the feeling hadn't been there for the past eight months—Erin felt sorry for Forest Burke. He might try to kill them both. He might even succeed, heaven forbid. But she knew Liam McGrey would give him one hell of a fight.

"Call Tom," she said. She was still finishing her coffee when Lee came back from the phone at the rear of the restaurant. "What's wrong?" she asked, taking in his look of frustration.

"Tom just confirmed that Burke's still in Jamesbrook, but he ordered me to take you to the safe house and not go after him. He said the two policemen outside my house were shot but not killed and he raked me up one side and down the other for not calling sooner. I think I'd rather quit my job for good than take orders from that man," he muttered.

Erin fought the urge to laugh. "He's your best friend. He's worried about us."

"I know. I shouldn't have doubted him. I should have called him sooner. Are you finished?" he asked.

"Yes," she replied after taking a final drink.

"Well," he said, tossing down several bills to pay for their breakfast, "I guess it's on to the safe house we go."

"If I didn't know better," Erin teased, "I'd think you're disappointed that you don't get to chase after Burke."

"I'm just disappointed that we're having to be the prisoners while he's out there running free," Lee replied.

The safe house was just as Lee imagined it would be when he found it a short time later. It was a nice, quiet house at the edge of a modest subdivision. Lee pulled into the drive and stopped, letting out a heavy breath. Yes, it looked like a nice house to come home to. It was just that he was coming to it with Erin, and Lee didn't want to play house with Erin again, not after that earth-shattering kiss in his kitchen.

Lee didn't have long to think about it, though, as a dark car pulled up to the curb near the drive and stopped. His first thought was that the two men inside had been sent by Tom.

"Are they friends of yours?" Erin asked.

Lee shook his head. "I don't recognize them, but then I've been away from the office for a long time. Stay in the car," he instructed, reaching for the door handle. His gaze caught movement in the side mirror and he stopped just in time to see the man in the passenger seat shift a gun from one hand to the other. "Get down, Erin," Lee ordered, starting the car again.

She did as he said, sliding down in the seat, but she questioned him at the same time. "What is it?"

"Just stay down!" He put the car in reverse and backed out of the driveway. His foot slammed down hard on the gas and they went speeding down the street once again, moving past the unknown men who were now out of their own car and starting toward Lee and Erin. One of them yelled and was forced to jump out of the way in order to keep from being hit. The other drew his gun and fired at them. But Lee was already careening around the first corner, avoiding any direct hits.

Lee made several more turns in an effort to keep the men from following them. Neither spoke, and Erin didn't even move, staying low in the seat and not looking anywhere but at the dash in front of her and at Lee.

"Hell," Lee muttered after a long, frightening silence.

"How did these men find us, Lee?" Erin asked.

"Tom," Lee replied, saying the name slowly. "Tom was the only one who knew where I was taking you."

There was nothing Erin could say that would ease the pain she could hear in Lee's voice. Wordlessly, she sat up, reached over and took his hand. Not only did he let her, but he seemed to grab hold of hers, like a man clinging to a life preserver.

"What now?" Erin asked.

"We go back to plan A," Lee replied tersely.

A short time later, Lee took Erin to a shop that, like the rest of the places he found, seemed nothing more than a hole in the wall. For the first time, he let go of her hand to get out of the car.

"Why this place, Liam?" she asked quietly once they were inside, walking past the racks of clothes.

"You said you wanted some new duds, remember?"

She could still feel his pain at discovering that Tom had betrayed him. "Yes, but we could get them anywhere," she countered.

"It hasn't been modernized **ye**t," he replied.

"Modernized?"

"No computer system to run a credit card through. So if anyone's tracking us, they won't know we've been here until the credit card slip actually gets sent in," he explained. "Pick out whatever you want," he added without looking at her. He was checking out a rack of men's shirts.

"How did you find out about this place?" she asked, pulling off a deep red shirt that she thought would look great on him with his dark hair.

"One day, after a painful therapy session, I couldn't stand the thought of going home to an empty house, so I drove around the city for a while. I saw these two boys fighting on the sidewalk and a man from this store came out and broke it up. I don't really know what possessed me to go in and check the place out, but I found myself liking it. It had an old-fashioned, hometown atmosphere about it, making me feel comfortable, I guess. Or maybe like I've stepped back in time. Do you think this would fit me?" he asked, holding up a shirt.

"Yes," she replied, looking at the tag.

"Fine." He moved on to some jeans. "Find something for yourself so we can get moving."

"Moving where?" she asked quietly, already knowing, but having to hear it from Lee.

"To get Burke," Lee replied.

Erin chose a few things and Lee paid for all of it. Then they went down the block to another store, where pieces of electronic equipment and photographic equipment were sold. It's probably all hot, Erin thought, but didn't voice her opinion. Instead, she just watched Lee pick out a pair of binoculars and pay for them with cash. He handed Erin one of three large bags. "Ready."

"Yes."

It was raining again as they exited the store. But with Erin's slim, but perfectly curved body moving gracefully ahead of him, Lee didn't feel it.

"Is there anything else we need?" she asked.

Lee was glad she didn't look back at him or she'd catch him watching the subtle movement of her hips. "Just some gas," he said absently. "And I'm sure I can get a map at the gas station, too."

After hours of driving and several cups of coffee from drive-through fast-food places, they reached Jamesbrook in the early afternoon.

"What a quaint little town," Erin noted.

"Doesn't look much like a place that would harbor a killer or a thief, does it?" Lee returned.

"No. But then they never do."

"I wonder what the locals think of the FBI watching Burke," Lee mused.

"Maybe they've been so good at their jobs that the locals haven't noticed," Erin replied. "Besides, you know there are a lot of different ways to run an investigation. And I doubt Burke's estate is located anywhere near a populated area."

"You're probably right," Lee had to agree.

Even the gloom of the cloudy day couldn't take away the inviting charm of the rustic houses. Set on the banks of the Illinois River, the place looked like a colonial town set smack-dab in the twentieth century.

"I wonder where Burke's estate is," Erin said, never taking her eyes off the scenery out her window.

She could feel Lee looking at her, and she turned to meet his glance. "I'm going to leave that up to the roving reporter in you," he said.

Erin could only smile. "Thanks, I'll be glad to find out. Why don't we stop for a late lunch at the first place we come to. And I'll bet I have the answer to that question before we even finish our meal."

Lee grinned at her. "You're on," he said taking the bet. "And if you don't, you have to buy lunch."

"With what, my good looks?" she quipped, her voice filled with humor at the way they were suddenly talking just like they used to. It felt so good to let down their guard and be the people they were before she'd left him, before a spray of bullets had found their mark in his leg.

"I guess we'll have to settle for doing dishes to earn our lunch," he teased.

"Ha-ha," she said, trying not to laugh. "Besides, I don't have to worry. I'm not going to lose. I'll know exactly where Burke's estate is before you're halfway done eating your lunch."

"Well, you'd better prepare yourself and put your roving-reporter hat on, lady, because we're here," he said, his voice still filled with lighthearted amusement. He pulled into a parking place in front of a large brick house that was now converted into the Jamesbrook Inn.

They had both changed clothes at the gas station earlier, so they were as presentable as they could manage. The rain had stopped hours before, even though the sun didn't seem to stand a chance of making an appearance today. The air was damp and chilled, touching Erin with something close to cold fingers as she climbed out of the car. A plan to find out the location of Burke's estate hit her in the same instant, and she smiled.

It was warm and cozy inside, the atmosphere as inviting as the rest of the town. A plump, older woman with silver hair greeted them just inside the door. "Welcome to the Jamesbrook Inn. This is your first time, isn't it?"

"Yes." Erin smiled easily. "But we've heard how good the food is here, and we thought we'd try it out since we're taking a small vacation to celebrate."

"I'm Jennifer Renolds," the woman introduced herself. "My husband Frank and I operate the Jamesbrook Inn. What's the celebration?"

"Liam—" Erin nodded her head in his direction "—and I just got married."

Lee had to bite his lip to keep his mouth from dropping open. He narrowed his eyes at her. Just what the hell was she trying to pull anyway?

Jennifer Renolds didn't notice his look, she was too busy shaking Erin's hand. "Well, congratulations, dear! This does, indeed, call for a celebration. You've come to the right place."

"Yes, well, we had initially planned on a big church wedding, but our families have done nothing but fight over the details, so we just decided to up and visit the justice of the peace all by ourselves." Erin smiled and ignored Lee's glare. "I just hope we haven't given Liam's poor mama a coronary. She was so hoping to have the Landfair Family Singers at the wedding reception. But I suppose we'll have to end up planning a party of some sort. That should keep just about everybody happy."

"Oh, that would be nice, since you should really have your family and friends present to wish you well," Mrs.

Renolds agreed warmly. "But then, you young people are so different than we were when Frank and I married. I'll give you the table near the fireplace. It's the coziest. Unless, of course, you'd like a private room," Mrs. Renolds added.

"The table near the fireplace sounds great," Lee choked out.

They followed Mrs. Renolds into the main dining room. It was as quaint as the rest of the place, with homey touches here and there. Three other tables were taken, but the patrons didn't spare Lee and Erin more than a passing glance. Lee gave himself credit for keeping his frustration under control enough to hold Erin's chair and pretend to be the happy groom. He gritted his teeth and smiled, not saying a word until after Mrs. Renolds had placed menus before them and left.

"What the hell are you doing, Erin?" he asked, still seething.

"What do you mean?" she asked innocently, smiling at him sweetly. "Did you want the private room after all? I'm sure we can change. We'd just have to signal Mrs. Renolds."

"No, I don't want the private room," he snapped. "I'm afraid if I got you alone, I'd strangle you. Don't you think this is drawing a bit too much attention to us?" Actually, Lee realized it didn't draw any more attention to them than if they'd just sat down, saying nothing. But the idea of being married to her hit him somewhere just below the belt, making the act of breathing nearly impossible.

"Exactly. If anyone comes looking for us and asks Mrs. Renolds, what's she going to say? Yes, there was a man and a woman in here today, but they were just celebrating their marriage."

Lee had to agree with the logic of it, even if he didn't like the idea. It definitely didn't make the game any easier for him to handle. Pretending to be married to Erin was too close to what he really wanted, so the idea was doubly upsetting.

Mrs. Renolds returned to take their order, carrying a bottle of what she called their best house wine. "On the house," she said, beaming her congratulations.

They ordered. Erin paid particularly close attention to the menu. Lee suddenly couldn't have cared less. He was still trying to come to terms with the idea of Erin as his wife. He wasn't even hungry anymore. At least not for food.

He poured the wine and tasted it. Its heady warmth spread down his throat. "It's delicious," he said, looking up at Mrs. Renolds. Not that he really noticed. He had the feeling it could have been iced tea just then and he wouldn't have cared, not with the idea of Erin as his wife warming his insides.

At the same time, Erin said, "We thought we'd stay here for the night, too, to make the honeymoon official before the rest of the family finds out. Is there a place where we could stay? We heard something about an estate close by. Brook or something like that. Do you know anything about the place?"

Lee tried not to choke on his wine and at the same time ignore the warmth that continued to spread through the rest of him. The very idea of a wedding night, an official honeymoon, with Erin, started a fire deep within him.

"The Burke estate, just a few miles out of town on Highway 24," Mrs. Renolds said knowingly. "But it's not open to the public for anything. There's a bed and breakfast at the south side of town called O'Malley's Place. The O'Malleys are nice people and very accommodating."

"Thank you so much," Erin responded, giving that perfect smile of hers.

For the first time, Lee could genuinely smile, too. "Yes,

thank you, Mrs. Renolds.'' It was the information they needed, but it didn't extinguish any of the fire in him.

Mrs. Renolds went off with their order.

"Gosh, I got the info even before we got our meal. Do I get anything extra for winning the bet so quickly?" Erin asked pertly, giving him the prettiest smile Lee had ever seen.

His heart was suddenly pounding, and heat pulsed through him to the point where he thought he might have to step outside into the cool air of the afternoon. To really be married to her, to really be able to go on a honeymoon with her. He tried to push the idea out of his mind, but soon found it impossible. He must be crazy to even think such things.

Erin, however, seemed quite pleased with her ability to find the answers. After finishing their late lunch, they set off in search of Highway 24. It took even less effort for the two of them to see that Burke was still at his estate. Using the binoculars they'd purchased along with their new clothes, Lee watched the house from out on the street, looking through the iron fence that surrounded the grounds.

"He's there, isn't he?" Erin asked beside him.

"Sure is. I just saw him on the veranda outside one of the upstairs rooms." With all the pictures Lee had seen of Burke, he felt he would have known him anywhere. "From the looks of things, he's getting ready for something, like a reception or a very major auction," Lee muttered, the binoculars still pressed to his eyes.

"Oh? Let me see."

She sounded like a child eager to look through a telescope at the moon for the first time. Lee handed her the binoculars. Their fingers brushed at the exchange, and he did his best to ignore the heat of her touch. He still hadn't been able to put out the fire she'd set in him at the inn.

"Look over on the left side of the house, through that giant front window," he instructed, hoping his voice didn't sound as rough as he thought it did.

She followed his gaze. "They're setting up tables."

"Lots of them," Lee added.

"From everything I read, big parties are his specialty," Erin said.

"Maybe we could use the big party to get in there and take a look around," Lee suggested.

"What if he already had the party and what we're looking at is the cleanup?" Erin asked.

Lee shook his head slowly, even though she was still looking at Burke's estate with the binoculars and wouldn't have seen him. "I don't think so. From the public relations stuff you had, Burke seems to like to start his parties after lunch and have them go until late at night, serving an unforgettable supper at six o'clock. Then he has everything cleaned up immediately after. If he had this party yesterday, it would have all been cleaned up and we wouldn't see any trace of it, not even those tables. And if it was happening today, it would be in progress already. No, I'm betting that this is for tomorrow."

"So what are we going to do?" Erin finally met his gaze in a hot flash of green. "Rent tuxedos and try to get past the doorman with the excuse that we lost our invitations?"

Lee took the binoculars from her and looked through them again. "I guess using your press credentials is out, right?" he asked, not really expecting an answer.

"Since I was forced to leave them in my purse at your house, yes, that's out. Maybe we could make our way around the back, climb a tree with limbs that hang over the iron fence and jump into the party," she ventured.

"I think before I tried that," Lee countered, "I'd hijack a car before it could arrive and then steal an invitation."

"Oh, that should work," Erin said in mock agreement. "We should probably buy a couple of ski masks first. Or maybe we could just put bandannas over our noses like the old Western bank robbers. Are you going to use that little automatic piece that you took from Burke's man? If you think it's too intimidating, we could buy a toy gun when we stop at the discount store to buy the ski masks. Go for broke and buy one that squirts water."

"I find ski masks too hot for this time of year, despite the cold rain. What would you think of a couple of rubber masks of politicians?" he suggested. Through the binoculars, he swept his gaze past the house, but he couldn't see any other activity going on through the heavily draped large windows. There was a woman in a black uniform sweeping off the covered front entrance. But that was all.

"I'd rather have cartoon characters," Erin said, amusement filling her voice. "Hermie the Hippo is my favorite."

She was enjoying this, he realized. "You're having a good time, aren't you?" he asked, still scrutinizing Burke's house.

"Well, yes, sort of. I mean, when I can forget that Burke wants to kill me, I am. I'm finding this to be a lot like the old days when I was just a simple reporter looking for a simple story."

"Do you miss that?" Lee asked before he could stop himself.

"Yes. I do miss those days when life wasn't so extreme. I miss the days when stories about children writing winning essays were as important as political campaigns." There was no longer any amusement in her voice.

And Lee knew better than to look at her. He could almost feel the fire in her gaze, fire hot enough to melt him.

"Maybe we won't need invitations," he said, growing serious again.

"Why would you think that?" Erin asked.

''Not all of Burke's auctions are by invitation only. A few of those PR photos you had of him showed him smiling at public showings. Do you think you could put on your reporter's hat and find out about tomorrow?''

''Sure.''

Lee still didn't look at her. Feeling her beside him was enough to send heat surging through him. Feeling her watching him was almost too much to handle. Still using the binoculars, he looked elsewhere, moving past the house, the grounds, then down the street in front of them.

''Damn!'' he swore, nearly dropping the binoculars.

''What is it?'' She was suddenly alert next to him.

''I'd say it's the FBI continuing their investigation. They've parked down the street. We should probably get out of here.'' He handed her the binoculars without looking at her and started the car.

''Are you sure?'' she asked.

''No. But I don't want to find out firsthand. No doubt your license plate number has been sent across every computer between Chicago and New Orleans. Even if the FBI didn't stop us to ask questions, they'd still report seeing us to either their friends or Tom. I doubt Alex Kaffel is going to be very happy with us being in the midst of his investigation. And until I get closer to Burke, close enough where a leak isn't going to hurt us either way, I can't trust any of them. Not to mention that being stopped by Tom or the FBI would keep us from getting to Burke.''

Erin's car was small enough for Lee to make a U-turn and drive off without having to pass the dark car parked farther ahead.

''So where are we going now? To a discount store to buy rubber masks?'' Erin asked.

''How about O'Malley's Place?''

''Are you serious? Do you mean to tell me you don't

plan to put me up in another motel as glamorous as the one last night?'' Erin teased.

"I have enough cash to pay for our stay at the bed and breakfast, so don't worry," he reassured her.

"Maybe by tomorrow, we'll figure out some way to get Burke to make a move and all this will be over and we can go home," Erin said, her voice full of optimism.

For a long moment, Lee couldn't even reply. Because for a split second, when he'd suggested their spending a night at O'Malley's, he'd been thinking about the idea that it could be like a wedding night for the two of them.

But Erin had shattered the notion by mentioning home. Going home. And her home was not his. Could Lee even go home to the cold, lonely rooms of his house after this was over?

He was still pondering the question when he pulled into the parking lot of O'Malley's Place. It was a beautiful Victorian house and held added appeal by having the parking situated in the back where the cars couldn't be seen by anyone passing by on the highway. Lee thought the place couldn't have looked more inviting if it had a sign in the window that read Come And Spend Your Wedding Night Here.

Killing the engine, he closed his eyes for a brief moment, trying to push the idea out of his mind. Maybe he'd be better off giving her the cash and then spending the night in the car. He wasn't sure he could spend another night with Erin, especially a night in a place as warm and cozy as this one.

But you've got to protect her, he reminded himself.

Taking a deep breath, he questioned his own sanity. Hell, he might as well forget about protecting her, not with all the things he wanted to do to her himself.

"What's the matter, Liam?" she asked beside him.

She placed a gentle hand on his arm. The warmth of her

touch seemed to burn its way right into his soul. He really should stay in the car.

"Is your leg hurting?" she asked.

"No," he choked out. No, this was so much worse than any pain in his leg.

"Then why don't we go in?" she suggested. "I don't know about you, but I'd love a shower."

She climbed out of the car, and he had no choice but to follow. The cloudy sky echoed with a distant sound of thunder, and Lee stopped a moment to listen to it. Maybe he should just stand outside a while for his shower. Heaven knew he needed a cold one, and it looked as though that same heaven soon was about to provide it.

Chapter 7

Lee signed the register that James O'Malley placed before him. "You're not going to tell anyone we're here, are you?" he asked, forcing his voice to sound light. "Because I'm sure by now Ellen's mama has probably gotten some idea that we've run away and gotten married and messed up all her plans. She's probably sent her dogs out to find us, and we'd really like to spend our wedding night undisturbed."

This idea of pretending to be married seemed to be working for everyone except him. In fact, he had the feeling that Mr. O'Malley's major question would be, "Why don't you act like an eager groom?" Not that it wasn't easy to pretend. That was his whole problem; it was too easy to pretend. It was too easy to want it all to be real. The smile Lee kept on his face was beginning to make his jaw ache.

Thank goodness Mr. O'Malley was polite enough not to ask the question.

Erin hit him on the arm even though she was amused. "My brothers are not dogs, honey," she chided.

"Of course, Mr. Robertson," Mr. O'Malley said, taking the register, still eyeing them both with a bit of wonder and a small smile. "We remodeled the Sunshine Room specifically with honeymooners in mind. We even put in a bath big enough for two with those jets that make lots of bubbles," Mr. O'Malley went on, his smile growing. "Will you need any help with your luggage?"

"No," Lee replied with a grin. "We never planned this. Would you believe this morning at work, Ellen called me to tell me her mama's plans for a cake, and I just said, 'I'm picking you up in five minutes and we're going to the ol' J.P. If your mama wants cake, she can eat it herself.' I figure if we let her plan it all now, she'll most likely think she can plan out the rest of our lives, too." Lee had to look away, despite the way the lies seemed to come more and more easily. In fact, the very idea of being married to Erin, of spending a wedding night in a place like this, was getting easier and easier to imagine.

"That's been known to happen," Mr. O'Malley said, his heavy Irish accent coming out more than ever. "Let me show you to your room."

He led them up the stairs to a lovely yellow room. Lee barely took in the old-fashioned wallpaper in a yellow flower print or the antique furniture or the matching yellow curtains draped on the windows. What held his attention was the huge, canopied bed. Of course it was a big bed, with enough room for himself and Erin.

Was it his imagination, or was Erin staring at that beautiful, inviting bed, too?

Hell, he'd spent last night pressed up against her on a bed. Why did this one hit him so much harder?

Because this one was a wedding-night bed, that's why, came the answer. It was warm and comfortable, meant for a long night of loving, not a quick roll in the hay as the other was. That answer hit him like a swift jab to his solar plexus, making it suddenly hard for him to draw in a breath.

"Well, here you are. You should have everything you need, but if you don't, just pick up the phone. Mrs. O'Malley's usually on the switchboard. The door locks from the inside, but if you, ah, have any need to leave, you can get a key from me."

"Thank you," Erin muttered.

Lee couldn't say a word, his throat so tight he felt as though he must be choking on something.

"And," Mr. O'Malley went on, "we serve supper in the dining room if you'd be wanting anything, but it's extra."

Suddenly, he was gone, leaving the two of them alone in the beautiful room. Lee could just imagine this room with its large windows and cheerful decor on a brilliant summer morning with the sun pouring in. Dropping the bags, that held everything they had, he sank into a nearby overstuffed, high-back chair, propped his feet up on the ottoman and closed his eyes.

He didn't have to open them to know that Erin sank onto the bed. He heard her movement as the mattress shifted. More than that, he imagined her there.

"What do we do, Lee?" she asked quietly.

Make love, he thought. Start the wedding night. Forget about Burke and Doreli, and most of all, forget about my best friend, Tom. "Rest," he choked out, still not opening his eyes. "Just rest."

"Does your arm or your leg hurt?" she asked.

"No." Surprisingly, it was the truth.

"Good. I'm going to call Burke's secretary, pretend to be some rich socialite and see what I can find out about Burke's party tomorrow."

Lee heard the mattress shift again with her movements. "What if Mrs. O'Malley is listening in when you go through the switchboard?"

"Do you think we need to worry about it considering Mrs. O'Malley doesn't have our real names?" Erin asked.

"Probably not," Lee replied, never opening his eyes.

He heard Erin speak softly into the phone, but he didn't concentrate on her words, only the soft sound of her voice. Several moments later, he heard her gently replace the receiver.

"Well, you were right," she said.

Lee opened his eyes to find she had turned to face him. The smile she wore was the most beautiful sight he'd ever seen.

"What?" he forced out.

"Burke is planning an art showing and an auction tomorrow starting at two-thirty, followed by a big dinner at six. The showing is open to the public and the auction is open to anyone who can show proof that he's able to pay for whatever he bids on. So do we go to an art showing?" she asked.

"Yes. And we'll go shopping again in the morning. We want to be dressed for the occasion," Lee replied.

For a long moment, neither of them spoke. Their gazes touched and held, almost like a tender caress. Then the spell was broken when Lee made himself close his eyes once again. He had to shut her out before he got out of the chair and swept her into his arms.

Erin cleared her throat. "Do you mind if I go take a shower and a dip in the whirlpool?"

"No, go ahead," he muttered. "I'll probably do the same after you're done."

A moment later, she was gone. Even though Lee never saw her go, he was aware of every move she made. He should just be glad with the news they had regarding

Burke. He should just be happy there was a possibility that things could all be cleared up as early as tomorrow, providing they could find something out about Burke at the showing. But all he could think about was Erin.

He heard her move past him to go into the bathroom. Her soft scent touched him like a gentle breeze as she went by. A moment later, he heard the water running in the shower. He thought he even heard her sigh softly.

It would be so easy, he realized, to get up and join her. He could wash her back; she could wash his. His breath caught at that thought and he gripped the arms of the chair to keep from moving. He resisted the urge to laugh. For the past eight months, he'd done whatever necessary to keep his leg propped up to ward off the pain. Now, suddenly, it seemed as though that same leg was crying to take him right into the bathroom. And without any pain at all.

"You're just overtired, that's all," he whispered out loud.

But his words, even spoken out loud, didn't convince him in the least. He wanted her more than ever. His arm was beginning to ache, but not from the minor flesh wound that was healing rather nicely. No, it was from the way he was gripping the chair. Taking a deep breath, he tried to relax. And finally, after using every technique he'd ever taught himself when he'd played the waiting game as a cop, he was able to do it. Not completely, but enough to rest.

For the first time, he felt free of so many things. There was no pain in his leg to remind him of the one day in his career he wanted to forget. There wasn't some criminal witness he had to protect for his testimony. If it wasn't for Burke, he could almost convince himself that here in this cozy room with Erin so close and still safe, life was as he wished. He couldn't help but smile at the thought. He could even smile through the hurt of Tom's betrayal. He could do it because he knew there would be a time and a place to deal with Tom.

"What are you smiling about?"

Erin's voice brought him back to earth in a snap. He was suddenly wide awake, looking at her. He grew warm instantly seeing she was wrapped in nothing but a giant yellow towel.

"Nothing," he answered just as quickly.

"Oh," she said, sounding disappointed. "I thought maybe you knew something I didn't. The bathroom's all yours."

"Thanks," he muttered, despite the fact that he no longer felt like getting up. He wanted to stay right where he was and look at her. Her skin was pink, her wet hair glistened with a coppery sheen and her eyes were shining.

"I can rebandage your arm with the gauze we bought, too, after you're through," she offered.

"Okay." Lee still couldn't stop looking at her. Seeing her this way was almost enough to make him forget the way she'd hurt him before, or the fact that she was probably going to hurt him again when this was over.

"So how did you get shot—the first time?" she asked.

Her question hit him like a bucket of ice water being thrown in his face. For a moment, he couldn't reply. He could hardly breathe. He stared at her, and she stared right back at him.

Lee knew that look. Knew it all too well. It was the look she got in her eyes when she was searching for answers and determined to get them. He would have liked to have seen that look in her eyes before now. Witnessing Jenkins's murder must have scared her enough to erase that look. Well, now it was back. And as much as Lee was glad to see it, he wished to hell it wasn't directed at him.

"Why do you ask?" he asked, trying to put her off.

"Because I can't imagine it happening to you. You're so good at your job, the best."

"It happens to the best sometimes," he said, forcing his voice to remain free of any emotion.

"I know. So how did it happen to you?"

He should have known he couldn't deter her.

"I was protecting a witness whose testimony would put away some major underworld criminal. We were holed up in one of the best hotels in Chicago. It was almost time for a shift change and I was waiting for my relief. When the elevator arrived, I thought it was that very relief stepping out. It wasn't. After that, things happened pretty fast. One minute, I was reaching for my gun, the next minute, I was on the floor, thinking my leg was gone." It was the shortest explanation he could give, and he hoped it would be enough. He should have known it wouldn't be.

"What happened to the witness?" she asked.

"He was fine. He managed to hide in the bathtub and the thugs didn't get much time to search since my back-up got there pretty quick."

"Did anyone else get shot?"

"The cops who'd been in the lobby were killed. It was a very professional hit. And we never found out who leaked the information about where we were hiding the witness," he said. He'd told himself over and over that there was nothing else he could have done, but it didn't make the idea that it happened easier to swallow.

"You've protected witnesses and dealt with various emergency situations before. What made this one so different?" she asked.

In one smooth move, Lee stood up, needing to move away from her. Not wanting to face her probing questions. "I don't know. Someone leaked the information. Those guys with guns knew the setup. They knew when to come up. They knew everything." He paused. Then without thinking, he added, "It was the most terrifying moment of my life."

There, he'd said it. He'd actually admitted his fear.

That search-for-answers look left her eyes in a flash. Those same eyes widened. "You make it sound as though that's a terrible fault," she returned, her voice now hardly more than a whisper.

"It is a fault. I froze up. I was so afraid, I couldn't even move. And all I could think about for a split second was you, telling you that I still loved you and telling you that I was sorry because your worst nightmare was coming true. It turned out to be my worst nightmare, too, and I just didn't know it until I was lying there in my own blood, thinking that the guy was going to finish me off any moment."

"But you wouldn't let me stay at the hospital with you. It's like you blame me for something," she probed. "You do, don't you?"

"You left," he said, keeping his voice flat. "Yes, I blamed you for that. Maybe I still do, no matter how much I try, I can't stop loving you." He forced himself to walk to the bathroom, leaving her there, ignoring the stunned look on her face.

Closing the bathroom door, he locked it and leaned against it, not believing what he'd just admitted. Hell, he might as well just put a sign on his back telling the whole damned world that Erin Flemming had broken his heart and left him to bleed to death. Looking up, he caught sight of his reflection in the large mirror over the sink. "Why can't you get over her?" he whispered to his reflection. "Why can't you get beyond this?"

He knew the answer just as he knew the sea was salty. He still loved her, even more than before, that's why. He loved her more than his own life, more than he'd ever loved anyone else.

Lee didn't want to love her, not anymore. Love meant nothing but pain and emptiness. He knew that firsthand.

She knocked on the door and it vibrated against his back. "Liam?"

"Go away, Erin." He couldn't let her in. Not now, not after his admission.

"Let me in."

Lee moved away from the door and turned on the water in the whirlpool, hoping to drown the sound of her voice, hoping she'd take the hint and leave him alone.

She only knocked harder. "Liam, let me in so we can talk about this. You can't throw this in my face and then walk away."

Watch me, he thought. True, he couldn't walk as well as he once did, but he could still walk. He ignored her, unbuttoning his shirt.

"If you don't let me in, I'll call Mrs. O'Malley and ask her to get a locksmith!"

"You would, too, wouldn't you?"

"Damn right!" she yelled through the door.

Lee reached over and unlocked the door, but didn't open it. And he only did it because he knew she'd be on the phone to Mrs. O'Malley. He was determined to draw as little attention to the two of them as possible. She opened the door herself.

She was still wrapped in nothing but a towel. Lee looked at the water filling the tub.

"You shouldn't have kicked me out of the hospital. You should have let me stay with you," she said.

"Why? So you could rub my nose in the idea that you didn't want to live with me anymore because you were worried I might get shot?"

His bare chest must have bothered her, he realized, for she seemed to be at a loss for words as she stared at it for a long moment.

"I wouldn't have rubbed your nose in anything. I thought you needed me," she said, her voice softening.

"I did need you. But I didn't need the pain that came along with needing you," he admitted.

"I stayed at the hospital," Erin said. "Even though you wouldn't let me in your room. I stayed and questioned the nurses and the doctor, making sure you were going to be all right."

That was enough to get him to look at her. His dark gaze met the clear green of hers. "When?"

"I was there every day until they sent you home."

"You were so worried that you never tried to call after that?" Lee asked.

"I did call, not that it made any difference. I'm sure you were too busy," she snapped.

Her eyes were flashing green fire, her arms crossed tightly against the top of the towel. She was suddenly angry, no furious, and Lee didn't have the vaguest idea why. He stared at her, wondering what had set her off. "Talk about going from zero to bitch in less than five seconds," he muttered.

"What?" she nearly screamed at him.

"Erin, listen." He tried his best to speak calmly. "I know this business with Burke is getting to you—"

"This has absolutely nothing to do with Burke!"

"Then what does it have to do with?"

"You, Liam! It has to do with you! And me! I called you. I had to tell you—" She stopped suddenly, and Lee knew she meant to say something but caught herself at the last moment.

"Tell me what?" he probed.

"Just things, just daily life things."

That wasn't all. He could see much more in her flashing eyes. "It doesn't matter," she went on. "You were obviously busy."

"What are you talking about?" he asked. "I was too busy? I never even knew you called. Why didn't you call back?"

"Jennifer answered the phone." Erin said the name Jennifer as though it left a bad taste in her mouth.

"Jennifer?"

"Yes, Jennifer. Some woman with a French accent. I was gone hardly more than a month, and already there's another woman in our house—your house. Are you telling me there's been so many women that you don't even remember that one?"

Lee nearly laughed, but he held himself back, knowing that she wouldn't take his laughter very well just then. "Well, actually, there've been four or five, and it did take me a moment to remember that one."

Erin let out an angry huff and rolled her eyes. "Did you forget me just as easily?" she demanded.

Lee could only wish. "She was my cleaning woman. I called this cleaning service about a week after I was released from the hospital because a few of the guys came over to—to…" To cheer him up, to give him something else to think about besides Erin Flemming and the fact that he might never walk again. To get him drunk so he could forget her, even if it was just for a little while, that's what, because he'd been such a bear since Erin had left him. "To have a party of sorts, you know, play cards, drink beer, that kind of thing. The house was a mess, and I couldn't have cleaned it if I'd wanted to. So I called the first service I found in the phone book, and this woman came the next day. I've been calling them ever since. Sure, I cook and I put the dirty dishes in the dishwasher and I can run the washing machine. But I don't do windows or scrub floors or toilets. They do that. They helped a lot and I should have called them right after I got out of the hospital instead of waiting. Even though I had a nurse who came, her only job was to check on my health and prepare me for therapy. And yes, there's been a lot of them over the past eight months. There's Jennifer, the one you spoke to. She was the first and will probably always be special.'' His voice was suddenly filled with amusement. ''Of course, she wouldn't go out with me. She was afraid her friends would think she was robbing the cradle. Then there was Abigail. She was cute, but she was young and not really interested in cleaning, so she didn't last. Then there was Ed.''

''Ed?''

''Yes, Edwina. She had this thing for corners. Seeing dust and dirt gathered in them nearly sent her into a frenzy.''

Erin smiled and sank onto the edge of the tub, her anger obviously gone, her eyes seeming to drink in every word he was saying.

''And how could I ever forget Cindy,'' he declared, his eyes lighting up. ''She's my favorite, and still comes every two weeks or so. She's a woman after my own heart.''

''Oh, yeah? How?''

''She bakes me chocolate chip cookies.''

Erin laughed. ''I should have guessed.''

''So you never called again after Jennifer answered the phone?'' he asked, growing serious.

''She said you were washing, and I thought...'' She let the sentence fade away. ''I guess after that I was scared to know what I thought was the truth.''

''You really thought I had another woman there,'' he finished for her.

''Yes, I did,'' she said slowly, meeting his gaze over the now-bubbly whirlpool. Lee had touched a switch that caused it to pulse to life.

''I have a confession to make,'' Lee said, his gaze holding hers with the strength of a vise.

"Oh?"

"I thought about calling you all the time."

"You did?"

"Yes."

"So why didn't you?"

"Because I couldn't make up my mind if I wanted to cuss you or tell you how much I wanted you and plead with you to come back."

Erin smiled. "I suppose it's rather funny how we never connected. It's almost as though something was keeping us apart," Erin said slowly.

Lee nodded, his expression rueful. "I remember thinking that it must have been fate or some higher power keeping us apart, too."

"But now it's brought us back together," she said softly.

"So it has," he said just as softly, his gaze now seemingly lost within hers.

For a long moment, only the sound of churning water broke the silence. Suddenly, Erin looked down at the tub, breaking the spell that had held them.

"So are you going to get in or just watch the bubbles?" she asked.

Lee had never taken his eyes off her. God, all the wasted months, all the time lost, he thought. But there were still those original reasons for her leaving him.

Right now, though, those reasons were so unimportant, almost nonexistent.

Not taking his gaze from her, he asked, "Are you getting in with me?"

The question startled her and she didn't reply for a long moment. "I just... Do you want me to?" she whispered.

"Yes."

Slowly, she stood up, and Lee watched her every move. With determination, he released the snap of his jeans. Her gaze moved down to follow his fingers. Lee heard a pounding and couldn't determine if it was his heart or just the rumbling of the water. Not that it mattered.

Suddenly, nothing mattered. Nothing but the two of them. Now. In this place. In the water.

Lee slid out of his jeans, hardly even aware what he was doing. He was only aware of Erin, the way she watched him, the way her heated gaze touched him as she unwrapped her towel and let it drop to the floor, where it formed a yellow pool at her feet.

As the seconds passed, all he could do was look at her, drinking in the sight of her as a man dying of thirst would gulp down water. "You're more beautiful than ever," he breathed. At least he tried to breathe. It seemed like so long ago since he'd seen her, really seen her. At the same time, it could have been only yesterday.

"You're not so bad yourself," she said. The smile she gave him was small and inviting at the same time. Slowly, she reached out to him.

Lee took her hand.

"And soft, too," he added.

"All you've felt is my hand. How can you be so sure?"

"I'm sure."

They climbed into the large tub together. Lee felt the warm water caress his skin like silky satin. And Erin's touch had the sensual feel of velvet. It was her touch that sent a surge of heat coursing through him.

"I want to kiss you," he murmured.

"Then why don't you?"

"I'm afraid to get close to you."

Erin looked away for a moment and didn't reply as though she had to weigh her words carefully before speaking. "The last thing I'd ever want is for you to be afraid of me. I won't break."

But I might, he thought. "What's the first thing you want?" he asked instead of voicing his thoughts.

"For you to kiss me. Like you did before all the shooting started. For you to kiss me and touch me. Like you used to. I need you. I've needed you for so long...."

With tentative fingers, he reached up to caress her cheek. "I have a question first," he said, his throat feeling tight, almost painful.

"What?"

"Is there anyone else, anyone like Jack, perhaps?" Lee knew it was an awkward, probably even a stupid time to ask, but he had to know. He had to be certain that there wasn't anyone for her to leave him for. She might have enough reasons of her own; he wanted no more. He wasn't even sure how he would react if she said yes. Here they both were, naked, warm water bubbling over them, feeling like heaven. He was feeling her warmth, and he had the feeling, too, that if she said that yes, she had someone waiting for her, he wouldn't be able to step away from that warmth and leave her. Still, he had to know.

"No, there's no one," she said.

His lips were on hers almost before she was finished with the words.

She tasted so good. She was fire, passion, goodness, sweetness. All rolled into one. His senses reeled as she took him back into the past, when life had been less complicated.

At the same time, she kept him firmly grounded in the present. Right there. Right then. With her.

In Erin Flemming, Liam McGrey had found eternity.

Lee wanted to touch her everywhere, to feel what he'd missed for so long. She was familiar and excitingly new at the same time. She was soft but firm in all the right places. He thought perhaps her breasts might be a bit larger and fuller than before, more womanly, inviting. He placed his hand on one, relishing the soft groan his touch brought from her.

Pulling her close, he moved her until she straddled him, settling her against him. Her bottom might have been somewhat rounder, but it was still so firm, fitting to him perfectly. For the first time, he didn't regret the months that had separated them. If they had stayed together, he probably wouldn't have noticed these pleasing, subtle changes in her.

He wanted to stay like this with her against him forever. They fitted together like two puzzle pieces.

One kiss melted into another and another, until his body was doing all but crying out in agony for her. Her hands were on him as much, if not more, than his were on her. She was driving him nearly wild.

She pulled away from his heated kiss, only to look into his eyes with a heat that was just as intense. "Show me how to love again, Liam," she said softly. "Show me what it's like to feel that again."

"Yes."

As he moved to make her a part of him, Erin gasped at his touch, her head falling back slightly as her breathing quickened.

Lee nearly came undone. He never thought he'd feel this way again. Never.

It was so good, so real, so complete. Having her become a part of him again like this was what he needed to fill that empty place deep inside him.

He gently clasped her face, a hand on either cheek. "Look at me," he grated, his throat dry, his voice tight. "Look at me while I love you."

He wanted to see her eyes. He wanted to see her feelings. He wanted to see inside her soul. He wanted to know that this was as real for her as it was for him.

She looked at him, her gaze capturing his and igniting

inside him like a torch thrown into a dry stack of hay. And he saw everything he wanted to see. He saw her want, her need.

And he gave her what she needed, while at the same time taking from her all that she gave him. Together, they made love, making up for all the lost time.

"Stay with me," he groaned, knowing she was as close to him as he could have her and yet wanting her even closer.

"I'm right here," she replied.

Yes, he knew that. But she misunderstood. He meant for her to stay forever, not just for the moment. He would have liked to tell her that, but the passion within him erupted then, and there was no chance for words. As he lost himself in her completely, he could only hope that whatever she felt would be enough to last.

Whether it was the heat from the whirlpool or the heat from Erin, Lee had no idea. He just knew they couldn't stay in the water any longer or they were going to burn up. Slowly, he stood up, pulling Erin out of the tub with him.

"We should check your arm and put on a clean bandage," she said.

"Later."

"But this one got wet," Erin insisted, touching it lightly.

In one smooth move, he pulled the tape and removed the wet bandage Erin had put on hours before. "See, it's fine. It would probably do it some good to leave it open, for a while anyway."

"Are you sure? It would only take a minute to put on a clean bandage."

"I'm sure." And to prove it to her, he swept her up into his arms. He carried her to the bed.

"Put me down," she said, laughing.

"Why?" Lee asked, stealing a quick kiss before letting her answer.

"Your leg," she reminded him.

"What about it?"

"Doesn't it hurt? I got the impression it hurt you all the time," she said, holding on to him.

"It used to. In fact the only time it usually didn't was when I was knocked out with pain medication. But funny, it doesn't hurt now."

And Lee didn't want to think about it hurting, afraid that thinking about it would bring on the pain. Nor did he want to think about the fact that it wasn't hurting and hadn't hurt much since he'd slept close to Erin. Could the pain be in his head just as his therapist had suggested? Could the pain in his leg come from the one he never wanted to deal with in his own heart, caused by Erin's leaving him? The very thought terrified him. So he forced it to the back of his mind, refusing even to dwell on it. Instead, he set her down on the bed and lowered himself beside her.

"What did you mean when you told me to show you how to love again?" he asked.

Erin couldn't meet his eyes for a long moment. And when she finally replied, her words came slowly. "You asked if there was someone else...."

Lee felt something tug at his heart, but he tried to ignore it and just listen to her. Still, if she had lied to him, Lee had the strange feeling he'd walk out of the room without looking back. He couldn't face another betrayal.

"I went out with someone. It was months ago. He was nice. He had a good job, a nice house, great car, everything. He was every woman's dream."

Lee swallowed the questions that threatened to spill out.

"I thought—" For the second time since they'd come

to the bed and breakfast, she stopped herself from saying what she was thinking. "I thought Dex would be good for me, too. But there was nothing. Just nothing. No fire, no passion, nothing. I thought it was just me. You were my first and only..." She paused and looked at him. "I thought that I was letting you..."

"Stand in the way somehow," he finished for her.

"Something like that. I was determined to feel something. Anything. I invited him over for this candlelight dinner and wine and music. But when it came to after dinner, I still didn't feel anything but cold. And rather silly. I mean, I could have been kissing one of the pillows on my bed for all the enjoyment I got out of kissing him."

"What happened?" he asked, holding her close, thinking there was no way now he could ever let her go.

"It only got worse. The more I tried, the less I felt. By the time I finally shoved him out the door, I felt nothing but empty and foolish and humiliated."

Lee held her tighter, turning her slightly so that her back was pressed against the front of him. Pushing her hair away slightly, he placed a soft kiss on her neck.

"What did you do after that?" he asked quietly.

"I spent the next three months pouring myself into the job," she said flatly. "It's probably what's gotten me into all this trouble—thinking only about the job."

"I suppose I can't picture your being anything other than hot, Erin," he said softly. He wanted to tell her he was sorry she ever felt that way, but he wasn't. The fact that she wasn't passionate with anyone other than him told him a lot. And he liked it. Too bad he couldn't get rid of the nagging little question of how long this passion-only-for-him would last. Or if it would be enough to see her through any of the loneliness or worry that drove her away before.

He couldn't begin to answer either question. He could

say, however, that the passion was far from ending right now.

Erin was soft and hot and wanting him again as much as he wanted her. She placed her hand behind her, gently stroking his thigh. She might as well be tossing jet fuel on the fire inside him.

"I want you. Now." And forever, he nearly added. But he was unable to take the chance and utter the words. He leaned forward and kissed her neck again, feeling her tremble beneath his touch.

"Then please take me," she murmured, pressing herself against him to the point where he didn't think he could possess her fast enough.

Lee did take her. Then again, later, deep in the darkness of the night after they'd slept a short time in one another's arms. And again, just before dawn. Each time he made love to her, he felt as though he took her farther than the time before. By the last time, with both of them facing the windows, as they moved with the rhythm of the slow-rising sun, Lee felt as though he'd taken her to the ends of the earth.

But it wasn't far enough to keep her safe from Burke or Doreli. Still, Lee couldn't help but wonder. Was it far enough to make her want to stay with him forever? Because now, he had to trust her again since he knew there was no way he could let her walk away a second time.

No way.

Chapter 8

"You be sure to come back and visit us again," said a very plump, redheaded Mrs. O'Malley the next morning, once Erin and Lee were through with the hearty breakfast she had set on the table before them. They were just about to leave.

"We will," Erin promised. "Maybe we'll even spend every anniversary here," she added.

Lee felt his heart constrict with her words. After a night of passion unlike any he'd ever known, he didn't want to face the day. And Erin's statement was just another lie on the icing of the cake he was trying to force down. Anniversary? They weren't even married. And after facing Burke today, they might not even live to worry about being married. He reached out past the awkwardness that had fallen over them some time between waking up in one another's arms and getting dressed, and he grasped Erin's hand, needing to touch her.

"Thank you for everything," he choked out. "It was

wonderful." It was also the biggest understatement in the world. The past night spent with Erin had been almost like a second chance at life, a chance at perfection that Lee was afraid might never pass his way again.

The sun was shining this morning, but Lee thought it wouldn't last long. There was still a dampness in the air and the threat of storm clouds moving in. Or was it the threat of what lay ahead with Burke? Or was it the idea that all of this was coming to a head and would soon be over? Then, if they got through it, which Lee planned to see that they did, he would have to figure out just where he stood with Erin. And he might even have to stand back and watch her leave a second time. Lee didn't know. Still, he shivered against the dampness as the two of them stepped outside.

In the newness of the day in the bright morning sunshine, Jamesbrook looked like a make-believe small town in a Norman Rockwell illustration. Welcoming. Inviting. Warm.

And there really wasn't a cloud in the sky to threaten them, at least not yet. So why did Lee feel so cold?

"What's wrong?" Erin asked, climbing into the car with him.

Lee tossed their bags into the back seat and climbed behind the wheel. "What makes you think anything's wrong?" he asked.

"It's just a look about you, that's all," she replied, never taking her eyes off him.

He wished she couldn't see through him so easily. He wished it almost as much as he wished he could see through her, so that he would know by just looking at her if he should back away now. And start to rebuild the wall around his heart to protect himself the next time she left him.

"What is it?" she asked again.

Oh, nothing, he wanted to say. Except they were heading out to meet a coldhearted killer before he could come after them, and he wasn't liking the idea at all. There was something deep in his gut that told him something was going to happen, something bad. Call it gut instinct, call it a premonition. Call it whatever you wanted, but it didn't sit well, and it was strong enough to leave a bad taste in his mouth.

Maybe it was just that he'd spent the best night of his life making love with Erin, the only woman in the world who would ever hold his heart, and now he had to face the day. He had to look at the two of them in the light and face just where they were in this relationship.

Lee swallowed hard at the nagging thought of what exactly it was that they had. Yes, there was undeniable passion. But it was the uncertainty of their relationship, the doubts about their future together, that made him unable to look directly into her eyes. True, he wished he could read her feelings as well as she could read his. But the truth was, he didn't want to see what her feelings were this morning. Not really. He didn't want to see if there was any regret over their night together. So he didn't look.

And he didn't let her look into his eyes either.

There was more to this sick feeling inside him than that.

Lee finally forced himself to speak to her. "Erin, no matter what happens today, I want you to know..." he began. *That last night was the best night I've ever had.* He didn't say the words. They sounded too much like a cop-out. *That he loved her.* No, he wouldn't admit that, either. She'd probably think he was just saying the words because he had to after making love to her.

Maybe she was thinking the same thing. He didn't know. The only thing he knew was that she saved him from having to say anything. "Everything's going to be fine, Lee. We're going to get through this. And we can talk about us after it's all over, okay?''

"Okay," he agreed, starting the car.

They drove through town, taking in the early morning activity. A truck was delivering milk to the small grocery store, and a mailman on foot was delivering mail. Lee said nothing, but he wondered how everything could all look so normal, so everyday, when the two of them were well on their way to facing the man who wanted them dead.

"What are we going to do? We never did decide," Erin reminded him. "We can't just drive up to Burke's front door. I doubt he's going to have the welcome mat out for us."

"Remember, we were going to get dressed for the occasion." He looked over at her. "Let's go get some fancy new duds, as you call them. Whatever it takes for us to look appropriate for Burke's showing this afternoon. What do you think?"

She smiled at him.

It was enough to cause his breath to catch in his lungs. He wished more than anything that she hadn't done that. It reminded him too much of last night when she smiled at him and climbed into the whirlpool. And when she smiled at him as he carried her to the bed. And when she smiled at him as she woke up beside him.

You might as well face it, McGrey, he told himself. Her smile can make your heart race and drive you insane, and it doesn't matter how or why or when she sent it your way. Your reaction is always going to be the same. The only change in that reaction might be that it would get hotter with each smile. Lee tried not to think about any of that now. He had to think about Burke and be ready when they faced him. If he wasn't, they didn't have a chance.

"I think something black for the both of us would be good, don't you?" Erin replied. "Black is sophisticated, chic, fitting—for Burke's funeral.'' Her words were slow and hinted of seduction, matching the smile she'd just given him.

They ended up having to drive all the way to Peoria in order to find a mall with a store where they could get the clothes that Erin wanted for what she continued to call this special occasion. They changed in the rest rooms.

Erin stepped out of the ladies' room looking like nothing less than a dream dressed in black. The dress could have been made for her, Lee thought, watching her walk to the car. Low cut and short sleeved, it revealed just enough cleavage to cause a man to want to see more. Even when she slipped on the sleek, fitted jacket that went with the dress, Lee couldn't stop staring as they made their way across the parking lot.

Once they reached Erin's car, Lee tried to occupy his hands by knotting his tie. But seeing Erin in her dress had only succeeded in making his fingers clumsy.

Erin waited quietly beside him. He tried not to look at her but it didn't help. He could still feel the warmth of her closeness. He could still smell the soft, sweet, woman scent of her. Out of the corner of his eye, he saw her brush her fingers through her curls, trying to calm them. He didn't tell her that it did no good.

"There's nothing like trying to get dolled up in a mall rest room," Erin said, sounding slightly out of breath. "Maybe we shouldn't have checked out of O'Malleys."

"If we didn't, we might have had to tell more lies, lies that would only be hard to remember. Besides, you look great," Lee said, still doing his best to fix his tie and avoid looking at her. "But I think I should have left this dress-up part to Tom." It was hard to concentrate on Burke, getting into Burke's showing and playing the part of an art lover. Because when he looked at Erin in the black dress, all he could think about was what was underneath the dress and how much he wanted it.

"Thanks. You look pretty dashing yourself. That black double-breasted suit fits you. You should wear one more often."

He finished with the tie and gave her a sideways look. "I don't think so."

Lee took out the gun he had under his jacket and checked it.

"Please be careful with that," Erin said. "I'd hate for you to shoot yourself somewhere important."

"Don't worry," he assured her. "I don't plan on ever getting shot again. Twice was definitely enough." He holstered the gun again and then helped Erin into the car.

They drove back to Jamesbrook in plenty of time for the showing which was starting at two-thirty.

"Are you ready?" Lee asked as they pulled up to Burke's estate.

"I guess."

Erin's little sports car didn't look too out of place. The young valet who took the keys from Lee even commented that he couldn't wait to drive it. Lee made sure they didn't arrive first or last so they could walk right in with the crowd.

"I don't know, Lee. This suddenly seems too easy," Erin whispered once they were ushered into a wide hall. "I feel like we've just entered the lions' den, only the lions haven't been let in yet."

"Don't worry. We're going to beard this lion in his den, Erin," he whispered back. "Look at this one, darling," he said more loudly. "Do you like it?" He gently pulled her to the nearest painting and pretended to be interested. A woman in a maid's uniform came by carrying a tray and offered them champagne. Lee declined for both of them. He needed to keep his head clear.

Another couple approached and admired the painting. Once they were gone, Lee asked, "Where do you guess Burke would be?"

"Probably in the torture chamber in the dungeon, if I had to guess."

"He's probably even got a hunchback as a sidekick." Lee took Erin's hand again and maneuvered them to another painting, heading toward a doorway. At the door, he made sure there was no one about and ventured into the next room, Erin at his side. They moved in the direction the maid had disappeared once her tray was empty. They found themselves in a large, formal dining room. It was empty.

"Come on," Lee said softly. He pulled her with him. Erin didn't protest.

She did, however, grasp his fingers tightly enough to nearly cut off his circulation. It was the only indication that she was afraid.

Across the room, a door led to the kitchen where the maid and another woman were intent on artistically placing hors d'oeuvres on silver trays. Without a sound, Lee pulled Erin back and led her to the other door in the room.

This one led to the hall off the foyer. They were now on the tiled floor and it was virtually impossible not to make a sound. Just ahead was a wide, curving staircase. Its railing was wrought iron, the stairs carpeted. The two of them climbed up it silently.

At the top of the stairs, they paused to listen and glance down a long, carpeted hallway lined with doors. Only silence greeted them. Erin still clung to his hand. At that moment, Lee needed her as much as she seemed to need him. He wouldn't have let go of her hand to save his own life. The first two rooms they checked were bedrooms. Void of any personality, both rooms held nothing more than a bed and dresser.

"That motel we stayed in the night before last was more inviting than this," Erin whispered. "If I didn't know better, I'd think Burke lived in a display home."

However, the third room held enough personality to make up for the other two.

"Burke's room," Erin whispered again.

Lee pulled her in and closed the door without a sound.

Yes, there was no mistaking Burke's room. Decorated in Southwestern taste, Lee was reminded of the way the man dressed. True, he wore the best suits a tailor could make, but he had the habit of topping them off with bolo ties instead of neckties. In more than one picture, Lee had seen him wearing snakeskin boots.

Snakeskin for a true snake, he thought, remembering.

The man's room was decorated lavishly, with plush carpeting and expensive wall hangings. The coverlet on the bed was in earthy Southwestern colors, but it was folded back neatly to reveal the satin sheets underneath.

Erin looked out the French doors that led onto a balcony overlooking the backyard of the estate. A lake was in the distance, surrounded by trees. A bit of garden could be seen below. The flower beds had been readied for planting, but this early in spring nothing was yet blooming.

She stared out for a long moment, until Lee came up behind her. "What is it?" he whispered in her ear. He was close enough that her softness touched him. He breathed in the scent of her.

"To think Burke lives in a place like this and is nothing more than a criminal," she replied quietly. "I don't understand so much greed or unfairness."

"Yeah," he agreed. "I'm sure he'll grow to appreciate all this when his only view is through the bars of his cell."

Lee thought the doorway across the room led to a bath, until he heard voices beyond it. Both he and Erin pressed an ear to the door and listened.

"Has there been any word on where they might be, Mr. Doreli?"

The question was formal, the words very crisp and precise.

Burke. Lee mouthed the single word to Erin. She nodded.

"No, sir," came the reply from someone who had to be the infamous Jimmy Doreli. "Nothing. We searched all night again, but we found no trace of Erin Flemming or her protective friend. Perhaps they've left the state."

"Perhaps," Burke muttered. "In the meantime, I shall call my contact to see if he knows anything regarding his colleague. I want this business with that pesky reporter stopped for good before the end of the day. Guests have filled the gallery downstairs. Why don't you go down and make sure things are falling into place for the auction this afternoon. I don't want anything going wrong. If we're going to get *The Cornucopia* and the other works safely out of the country, there can be no mistakes. Our federal friends are watching everything very closely these days. When these deals are complete, I think we should take an extended vacation in Europe."

"That would be nice, sir."

"You've checked for recording devices and microphones today?"

"Of course," Doreli assured his boss. "Everything's clean and clear."

"Good. This is becoming so tiresome," Burke muttered.

"Yes, sir. Can I send Mrs. Dobbs up with anything for you?" Jimmy Doreli asked.

"No, thank you. When I'm finished with my call, I'll come down myself. I want to see how everything is progressing. I'm sure you understand the importance of my mingling with the guests at the showing," Burke replied.

"Of course."

Erin and Lee heard another door open and close with Doreli's departure. Faintly, they heard Forest Burke pick up the receiver, drop it on the desk and follow it with a muttered oath at his clumsiness. A moment later, they heard his voice.

"Hello," he greeted the person on the other end of the line.

A pause.

"Don't get so irate. I'm well aware that I'm calling you at your office, but no one's watching you. They are all too busy watching me, and I assure you, my telephone is clean. They will never connect me to you."

Another pause.

"Now, have your people found Erin Flemming?"

Another pause.

"What do you mean, you don't have a clue? That man she's with is one of you. He's even been to your office and has been reinstated. Doesn't he call in?"

Your office. The words buzzed through Lee's mind. The only office he'd been to was Tom's. Oh, God, why did it have to be Tom? he cried out silently. Thinking it and knowing it for certain were two different things. Knowing it for certain caused an anguish worse than being shot. Why did it have to be Tom who had betrayed him and hung him out to dry? Please, not Tom, the only man Lee felt had been a true friend.

Lee closed his eyes and tried to swallow down the sick feeling mixed with the unstoppable frustration that swept over him. Oh, Tom, how could you, you bastard? He wanted to strangle Tom with his bare hands.

He still held Erin's hand, and she squeezed his tightly. Looking into the green pool of her eyes grounded him and brought him back to reality.

He'd deal with Tom later. After he finished with Burke.

He didn't know which one he would enjoy tearing apart the most.

"Well, you'd damn well better keep me informed," Burke went on. "I want this problem taken care of—for good—by the end of today. I plan to leave the country first thing in the morning to get away from all these federal agents who seem to enjoy watching me so much. And I don't need this complication following me."

His words "for good" sent a tingle up Lee's spine and left the hair on the back of his neck standing up. He knew what that meant, even though Burke didn't say the word. Final. Complete. *Dead.* By the end of today.

Lee looked at Erin. She knew the meaning of his words, too. It was written in the paleness of her face and her wide, shock-filled eyes.

Well, it would be taken care of—for good—by the end of today, but it wasn't going to go the way Burke had planned it. Lee would make certain of that. He just wasn't sure how. The thought nearly brought on a grin, but he fought against letting it out, knowing full well that Erin would think he'd lost his mind if he starting grinning now.

In the next room, Burke slammed down the receiver. A moment later, they heard the door close with his leaving.

Erin let out a heavy sigh.

"When I get my hands on Tom, I'm going to kill him slowly," Lee whispered, fighting the rage and frustration that still swept through him at knowing who the leak was. "I can't believe I ever trusted him."

"You don't know for certain it was Tom," she said.

"Who else could it be?"

"Anyone who saw us come to the office. We didn't meet Tom secretly by any means. And until you know for certain…"

"Tom knew we were going to the safe house," Lee persisted.

"How many other officers in your department know that safe house exists?" Erin asked. "The leak could have told Burke about a number of safe houses and Burke could have had men watching all of them."

She was right, of course. But it didn't ease the pain he was feeling, and Lee didn't want to deal with it. So before she could continue, Lee gripped the doorknob and turned it.

"What are you doing?"

Lee had the door open and was quietly making his way in before she got out the question. Since he still held her hand, refusing to let her go for even a second, he took her with him.

"He could return any minute." She tried to pull him back, but she was no match and could do little but follow him to the desk.

"He's probably downstairs stuffing his ugly beak with Mrs. Dobbs's hors d'oeuvres." Lee's voice was filled with anger.

"He does sort of look like a bird, doesn't he?" Erin returned.

"Like some bird of prey," Lee muttered. His anger at Tom was flowing through his body. He gritted his teeth against it.

"You're breaking my fingers," Erin complained mildly.

Lee let out a heavy breath and loosened his grip on her, but only enough so he was no longer hurting her.

"What are you going to do now?" she asked.

"Find out for certain if it was Tom," he snapped.

"How?"

His only reply was to pick up the phone and punch the redial button.

The phone rang on the other end, and Lee waited. He had every intention of telling Tom that he was coming to get him as soon as he took care of Burke. Then someone answered the phone.

But it wasn't Tom's voice on the other end. Lee smiled at the voice. This man would be even easier to take down. "You filthy traitor," Lee whispered harshly. "There isn't anywhere you can hide that I won't find you!"

"He's coming back!" Erin's urgent plea hit Lee like a brick.

Lee set down the phone, mentally picturing the terror that must be on the face of the man he'd just hung up on.

Yes, Burke was coming back. His muffled voice could be heard in the hall. He was almost to the door.

"Come on!" Erin pulled him around to the other side of the desk and through the nearest door.

Into a closet.

Lee swore silently. This was all he needed. To be stuck the rest of the afternoon in a tight space with Erin—with death waiting just on the other side of the door. Erin pulled the door closed just as the other door opened.

Had Burke seen them? Had he heard the closet door close?

Lee waited, holding both of Erin's hands, holding his breath, trying to ignore the loud pounding of his heart. A touch of light filtered in from beneath the door. Through the dark of the small space, he could barely make out the sparkle in her eyes. Just enough to see she was trying to look up at him. He knew what she was thinking. It was the same thing he was thinking.

This was it. If Burke had heard them, he'd be opening the closet door any second. And that would be the end.

Burke's voice grew louder as he came into the office. It took Lee a moment to realize exactly what he was saying.

"Thank God my security cameras are working, especially when my men all seem to be sleeping. Search the entire grounds," he said, sounding suddenly like a growling bear. "Everywhere! Those two walked right in with everyone else and no one even noticed! I want them found—now! Drag them out from whatever rock they're hiding under!"

Doreli answered. "Yes, sir, right away."

"And bring them to me when you find them!" Burke finished.

Lee couldn't help but smile at the frustration in Burke's voice. Burke obviously thought going after Erin was little more than fun and games. Well, Lee could show Burke fun and games. Lee could show Burke the real meaning of vulnerability. Maybe he still would, if he got the chance.

Together, Lee and Erin waited. Seconds ticked by. Lee could hear his pulse throbbing in his ears. He finally forced himself to take a slow, deep, calming breath. And realized he shouldn't have when all he succeeded in doing was breathing in a healthy dose of Erin's sweet, woman scent.

Oh, she was so close. How could he even think about her at a time like this, when Burke was just on the other side of the door? It was the fear, he realized. The fear tingling through him heightened every other emotion, too, and desire was at the top of the list.

There was a single suit jacket hanging in the closet, and the wool of it pressed against him. He fought against letting go of Erin to push it away. He fought against the urge to scratch his head where the fabric touched it. He fought against the urge to swallow. He fought against the urge to pull Erin closer to him, to hold her against him and feel the length of her, to shelter her when Burke pulled the door open to find them....

But Burke never came to the closet door. He barked some orders over the phone, then called the man managing the gate and yelled obscenities at him. "Just how in the hell did anyone get past you? What were you doing anyway, sleeping? How would you like to take a nice long rest—at the bottom of Lake Michigan?'' Burke went on to yell at someone else who was in charge of the parking attendants.

A few moments later, he slammed the phone down and then the door on his way out of the office once again. Lee sucked in a long breath and shakily let it out. Erin relaxed within his grasp. He chuckled softly, wanting to really let out a long hoot of laughter.

''What?'' Erin whispered.

''I wanted to give him a bad day, and it looks as though I have,'' he whispered back. Finally releasing Erin's hands, Lee reached up to push the suit jacket away. At the same time, Erin shifted, but reached for the wall to keep her balance in the small space.

She let out a gasp as that same wall gave way beneath her touch. Instinctively, Lee grabbed her to keep her from falling.

''What is that?'' she asked after regaining her balance, even though she never let go of Lee.

''It looks like a hidden staircase.''

Lee looked at Erin.

Erin looked at Lee.

''I think the FBI might be interested in this, don't you?'' he said, grinning.

Erin smiled up at him. ''I do. But I think we should make sure first.''

Taking her hand, Lee led her into the darkness, feeling his way down the narrow wooden stairs with his other hand. The secret panel slid back into place, as though on a spring, once they were through. Beneath his touch, the brick wall was smooth and cool. Once they left the closet and the wall closed again behind them, they were virtually in the dark.

''Lee?'' she whispered. ''I don't like this.''

Lee didn't like it either, this feeling their way around.

He took each step carefully, terrified that the stairs would suddenly end and they would step off and fall into some deep, dark, bottomless pit. Discovering this hidden place had seemed a golden opportunity until they'd been swallowed up in the darkness. Now, the hair on the back of his neck was standing up.

He reached the bottom first. Sensing the difference between the wood of the step and the earth floor beneath his feet, Lee stopped, his hand still on the brick wall. His hand hit the light switch with a suddenness that nearly startled him.

They were momentarily blinded by the bright light that hit them when he flipped the switch and had to blink against it for a few seconds. What they saw in the room once they were able to focus startled them even more.

"Oh, my," Erin breathed, still one step up behind him.

The room was filled with art. All sorts of art. Paintings, sculptures... There were also quite a few boxes.

Lee's hands were sweating, and for the first time, he let go of Erin and moved farther into the room. In size, it was hardly bigger than his kitchen at home. And yet it held so much.

"Do you know much about art, Erin?" he asked quietly.

"Like what?"

"Like enough to know how valuable any of this is. I'd hate to send in the FBI only to find it's all worthless."

Erin stepped down into the room as Lee walked around. "I couldn't begin to guess. But some of it looks like junk."

The air was so still, so quiet, so dead, Lee was almost afraid to move, but he stepped up close to a sculpture of an angel and tentatively touched it.

"You don't recognize any of this as being stolen?" he asked.

"No, but then my reporting usually dealt with issues, not news happenings," she replied.

"Burke talked about moving the painting *The Cornucopia*. I don't see it here. I wonder where it's stashed. I mean, this would be the perfect place."

"It certainly is neat and tidy down here," Erin noted. "See how the paintings are stacked just so."

"All except for this ugly one here near the stairs," Lee said, picking up the framed work and peering at it. "Who in his right mind would find enough beauty in this donkey to paint it. I wonder if this is the donkey's good side," he joked. "If it is, I'd hate to see the other side." He looked at it more closely, then held it away again. "I think I did a paint by numbers when I was a kid that was better than this."

"And I don't know about you," Erin added, "but except for the angel over there, I think most of this sculpture is pretty ugly, too. Why do you suppose Burke's got it hidden down here?"

"Maybe he's too ashamed to have it upstairs where someone might see it," Lee replied, his attention still on the ugly painting of the donkey he was holding. A donkey? He still couldn't believe it. And yet there was something about it that continued to catch his eye.

"I mean, look at this," Erin went on, rubbing her palm against the sculpture of a fat little girl holding an umbrella. "I suppose you could hide this in a bunch of greenery in a garden and it would look okay." She stopped suddenly. "It's rough."

"What?" he asked, turning his gaze to Erin.

"It's rough, feels like clay, almost like the mud pies I made when I was a kid."

"Mud pies?" Lee came closer.

"Yes. While you were doing your paint by numbers, I was making mud pies in the backyard."

"And your father approved of that?" he asked.

"My father helped me," she replied absently, looking more carefully at the sculpture.

Lee had a hard time picturing Erin mixing mud pies in the backyard of the Wilmette home, with the guest house and the shores of Lake Michigan not too far away. But he didn't have much time to dwell on it. What caught his attention was the dust that came off when Erin roughly scratched at the sculpture with her nails.

A moment later, the umbrella the child was holding fell away completely, revealing the point of a spear. Then, from under the child's face appeared the face of a man.

Erin gasped, starting and stepping away.

"What's the matter?" he asked, concerned.

"This I recognize. It's called *The Warrior*. It was stolen last fall from a museum in New York. The reason I remember is because I had worked for days on an article about a new landfill, and at the last moment, it got scratched, and the article about this piece being stolen took my space. There was a picture and I threw darts at it for a week."

Her words faded away as she stared at the sculpture beneath the sculpture.

Lee looked at the painting he still held. Pulling out a small pocketknife he always carried, he set to work gently cutting the canvas along the edge of the frame.

"I see now how Burke is planning to smuggle all the stolen art out of the country," he said a moment later after he'd cut away the top layer of canvas. Underneath was the original artwork. And even though he'd never seen this painting, Lee knew its name. *The Cornucopia*. "The real art's underneath. But it all looks like a bunch of worthless junk."

"So why is he having an auction? He could just pack this stuff up, looking like it does, and take it with him if he wanted to get it out of the country. The customs agents would probably laugh when they saw him with it.'' Erin absently kept scratching away at the sculpture to reveal more of the handsome face of the warrior.

"Maybe he didn't steal it for himself," Lee said, staring hard at the famous painting in his hands. "Maybe he stole it for somebody else, somebody who would pay him a great deal of money when they come to the auction tonight and bid on what others think is nothing more than junk. They'd be taking home priceless art for their own private collections or maybe even to sell to someone else, and no one would ever know. Besides, seeing someone as prestigious as Burke with junk that looks like this might be enough to raise suspicion."

"How perceptive of you, Mr. McGrey." The voice that echoed through the small room was crisp and now very familiar. It was the same voice that contacted the traitor who'd leaked their whereabouts.

Erin gasped.

Lee turned his head to take in Jimmy Doreli standing at the bottom of the stairs with a gun pointed at them. With his pockmarked face and pointed nose, Lee thought he would know the man anywhere. He was even uglier than his mug shot. Behind him stood Forest Burke. He looked exactly like all his photographs—well-groomed, arrogant, untouchable. Even now, standing on the cramped stairs, he stood straight and tall and haughty. Lee thought he could live to be one hundred and never forget a single detail about the man—his tailored suit, bolo tie and pointed snakeskin boots.

And Lee especially wouldn't forget the way he was smiling.

Chapter 9

"Gosh, you don't look anything like a hunchback."

Lee looked up briefly, silently praying that Jimmy Doreli wouldn't shoot them for what Erin had just said. He himself was finding it hard to believe she'd even uttered the words, considering Jimmy Doreli was pointing a gun at them. Besides, she knew Dorell wasn't a hunchback. She'd seen his mug shot. She'd seen him kill her informant.

A puzzled look passed over Jimmy Doreli's expression, but he said nothing about Erin's comment. He just held the gun steady on them. And Lee supposed Doreli wouldn't shoot them unless Burke ordered him to.

"Of course Mr. Doreli isn't a hunchback," Forest Burke said, sounding as though he might be talking to a small child. "But then you knew that, didn't you, Ms. Flemming? You have seen Mr. Doreli before, haven't you? On a pier, perhaps?"

Erin didn't answer, which was most likely all the answer Forest Burke needed.

Lee thought about the weapon he had hidden in the holster under his jacket. Could he reach it in time? Looking at Doreli, he saw that Doreli had his own gun pointed more at Erin. Maybe Doreli thought her more of a threat, considering the information she might have. Lee didn't know if he could beat Doreli in a draw, but with Erin in the line of fire, he couldn't take the chance. So he slowly raised his hands hoping that he'd get to use his gun before Doreli used his own.

"Well, Mr. McGrey," Forest Burke said, shifting his attention to Lee, his voice thick with formality, "how nice it is to finally meet you in person. Mr. Doreli?" Burke turned his attention back to his right-hand man. "I'm certain Mr. McGrey has a gun. Please take it."

Doreli moved without hesitation to do his bidding.

Lee felt the cold touch of a steel gun barrel against the back of his neck before Doreli roughly searched for his gun. Standing there and letting Doreli take his gun, his only weapon, was one of the hardest things Lee ever had to do. But he didn't dare fight for it. Erin was too close, and he wouldn't be any good to her if he got himself killed.

"You're a very interesting man, Mr. McGrey," Burke went on once Doreli stepped back with Lee's gun in hand and went back to pointing his gun at Erin.

The man was immaculate. From his perfect double-breasted black suit to his wavy dark hair, there was nothing out of place. He could have stepped right off the front cover of a man's fashion magazine. Lee wondered what would happen if Burke's hair ever got ruffled or if dirt got smeared on his clothes or if—heaven forbid—he ever stepped in anything smelly wearing those snakeskin boots.

"That's nice," Lee muttered.

"Yes, your being a Special Division Officer, your flawless record. Too bad you had to get shot."

Lee said nothing.

"Anyway," Burke went on, "I read your file, and I thought you were almost as interesting as Ms. Flemming. Speaking of whom, I can't tell you how much of an aggravation she has been to me." Burke spoke as though Erin wasn't standing directly in front of him. "I was beginning to wonder if she was part cat, considering how many lives she seems to have." Burke continued to smile a cold, heartless smile. "But now, it seems as though she's been caught with her paw in the canary cage, wouldn't you say?"

And it seemed that the only life in Burke's eyes was a calculated sparkle of glee at having caught her, Lee thought.

Lee still didn't say anything. He wanted more than ever to tell Burke to go to hell, but had the terrible feeling that those words would be enough provocation for Doreli to send him there instead. So he clamped his jaw shut. Tight enough that after a few seconds, his face began to ache. He wanted even more to leap on Jimmy Doreli and rip his heart out for threatening Erin with the gun. It was taking all the willpower he possessed to stay perfectly still and hold his hands in the air.

Erin didn't even appear to be breathing as she stared from Burke to Doreli and the nasty, deadly gun he held pointed at her.

"So," Burke continued, "I suppose the question is, just what exactly do I do with the two of you."

"You could let us go," Erin suggested.

Lee threw her a glance, but otherwise never moved. He recognized her false bravado in the way her voice shook slightly. She continued to hold her chin up, despite the way the color had drained from her beautiful face.

"At least let her go," Lee said, looking at Burke and trying to ignore Doreli and the way Doreli was looking at Erin.

Burke laughed. But it was a hollow sound, a sound as cold and deadly as his smile had been. "Surely you don't expect me to do that. This woman has been a thorn in my side for far too long." His face grew suddenly hard, the smile gone in an instant as though it had never been there at all. "I don't like anyone pushing his—or her—way into my life. I don't like anyone searching for answers they have no business knowing. And that's what you did, Ms. Flemming. You stuck your little reporter's nose into my life and my business. I guess you didn't understand that I grant interviews and give out information about myself at my choosing. No one else's."

"But I never really found out anything," Erin insisted.

"Yet you were trying, Ms. Flemming," Burke countered. "And talking to the wrong people, such as Jenkins, didn't help put you in my good graces."

"If you had nothing to hide, you wouldn't have had to worry about it, now would you?" Erin snapped.

Hell, Lee thought, this isn't the time to get angry, Erin.

Forest Burke drew close to her, close enough that Erin took an involuntary step backward, only to bump into one of the sculptures. Lee half expected Burke to slap her or, worse, order Doreli to shoot her.

"You deal with so-called issues at that rag you call a newspaper, don't you, Ms. Flemming? Issues like child neglect and spousal abuse and environmental protection?" he asked. The question was casual, but his voice was cold, slicing icy daggers through the air, directed right at Erin.

Just hearing it gave Lee goose bumps, and he couldn't begin to think how much fear Erin must be feeling. And he still had no idea what to do, how to get them out of this. Doreli pointed his gun steadily at Erin. Lee was afraid to even breathe, much less move. Or reach for Erin and pull her away from Burke.

"Yes," Erin finally replied to his question, knowing full well Burke already knew the answer.

"Well, let me tell you, you've never dealt with an issue that compares to dealing with me," Burke grated, his gaze chilling enough to match his words.

Erin swallowed so hard that Lee could see her do it. He had to take a chance if he was going to get them out alive. He looked again at Doreli. And he remembered Erin's words about entering the lions' den. Doreli was looking at Erin like a lion getting ready to pounce and devour her. He was all but licking his chops. The man was definitely enjoying every moment of this, and even more, he was anticipating what might come in the future. He stared at Erin with an open, uncontrolled hunger.

Oh, great, that was just what they needed.

"Get some rope from those crates over there, Mr. Doreli," Burke instructed. "Tie them up so we don't have any more trouble out of them while we figure out the best way to take care of them once and for all."

"Yes, sir," Doreli replied, handing his gun, as well as Lee's, to Burke and hastening to do his bidding.

Doreli tied Erin up first, fastening her wrists together with a rough length of sturdy rope. All the while he kept glancing at her with a gloating I've-got-you-now smile on his face. Of course, Erin didn't miss the look in his eye or the evident lust. Not missing a beat, Erin spit at him, catching him smack on the cheek.

God, this is it, Lee thought with certainty. We're dead. Burke would shoot them both now. If nothing else, Doreli would give her a good hit, maybe enough of a blow to break her neck before she even reached the floor.

To Lee's amazement, Doreli's smirk only broadened, leading him to believe that their predicament was even worse than he thought. Yes, there were things worse than death. Lee could see them in Jimmy. Doreli's cold, feral eyes. The words he uttered next were enough to send chills up Lee's spine.

"I'm going to enjoy taming you, you little spitfire," Doreli said with a deadly, terrifying calm. Absently, he wiped away the spittle with the back of his hand. "I'm going to enjoy every minute of it. A lot…" Holding Erin's tied hands in one of his, he reached up with the other to touch her cheek, his thumb brushing against her lips.

Lee couldn't wait any longer. He couldn't stand here and watch Doreli put his hands on Erin. He couldn't let himself think about what Doreli wanted to do to her.

Lee could see Erin was trying to maintain a brave front, despite the way she visibly paled even more. She cringed at Doreli's touch and tried to back away, but there was no place for her to go. She was up against a sculpture already. Lee could see her wanting to scream or cry. Her glistening emerald eyes were threatening to spill over with tears at any moment. Yet she refused to look away from Doreli. She refused to back down, just as Lee had known she would.

Lee wanted to hug her for her courage. If he ever got the chance…

Lee lunged at Burke, who was still holding both guns. He seemed to be entertained by Doreli's actions. Lee's only hope was to knock one of the guns far enough away to give him enough time to get his hands on the other one.

He collided with Burke, knocking the tall, self-possessed man off his feet with the unexpected move. His hope became reality as one weapon flew out of Burke's hand. Where it landed, Lee had no idea, nor did he care.

It was the chance he needed. Lee grabbed the other gun and swiped it out of Burke's grip. That was all that mattered. He had managed to get his own gun. Feeling elated at the idea of giving Burke a taste of his own medicine, Lee felt a crazy urge to laugh.

He held his gun on Burke. And smiled.

All they had to do now was march Burke out of here, down the street to the FBI guys who sat watching their cars. Piece of cake. Pure and simple.

Then Erin screamed his name. The loud, shrill sound echoed through the small room.

Blinding pain hit his leg in the next instant. He groaned at the blow, thinking it was happening all over again. The shooting, the instant flash of white-hot pain. Except this time, he never heard the shots fired.

Still, it swept his feet right out from under him, and the floor came up to meet his face before he ever realized what exactly was happening.

Oh, God, not again, he prayed. Please, not again. He didn't think his body could survive another bullet. Not in the leg, not anywhere.

The pain began to lessen, and Lee groaned again. Trying to focus, he blinked against the light that seemed too bright. He thought he could see Erin kneeling beside him, but for a moment, he saw two of her. Even when the two blended together into one, she was still rather fuzzy.

When she cleared, he could see she really was crying now. The tears had finally spilled over and were now coursing down her cheeks in glistening streams. And Lee had never felt so helpless in his life. Even when he'd lain waiting after getting shot in the leg, knowing some unknown assailant was coming and it was only a matter of time... Even then, he hadn't felt this helpless. Even then, he'd had his gun in his hand and felt he'd had a small chance.

It was then that he noticed he no longer had his gun. It was also then that he noticed Jimmy Doreli standing over him, and he knew in an instant he hadn't been shot. Lee had been so intent on watching Burke, the man with both guns, that he had missed Doreli's quick action. Doreli had kicked his bad leg right out from under him. And he hadn't even seen it coming.

All this time, they had joked of Burke resembling a bird of prey, when it had been Jimmy Doreli who was able to swoop down without a sound like a hawk capturing a rabbit.

Panic rushed through Lee like molten metal, and it quickly mixed with the pain pulsing through him.

Forest Burke chuckled, an empty, hollow sound echoing through the room. "It certainly pays to know an enemy's greatest weakness, doesn't it?" he remarked coolly.

Lee didn't reply. He merely tried to force himself to his feet. He tried even more to keep what little control he had left from slipping away. But it was hard to do when the realization hit him so strongly that he and Erin were about to die and there was nothing in the world he could do to stop it. They were going to die and no one would ever know about the leak or about Burke's secret little room that held countless treasures or about how Burke planned to get those stolen treasures out of the country. The FBI was going to watch Forest Burke leave the country in the morning and there was no way they would ever be able to stop him. Despite the millions of dollars of evidence surrounding Lee right now.

But worse than anything, no one would ever know the fact that Liam McGrey loved Erin Flemming more than life itself.

"Thank you for being so quick, Mr. Doreli. Please tie his hands behind his back now, before he tries anything else," Burke instructed.

"Yes, sir," Doreli replied, grabbing another piece of rope.

"If you try any more tricks, Mr. McGrey," Burke said, turning his attention to Lee, "I will shoot Ms. Flemming."

Lee was still in too much pain to try any tricks. Burke must have obtained his medical records in order for Doreli to know the exact spot on his leg where one of the bullets had shattered the bone. Any unexpected kick would have probably knocked him on his backside, but Doreli had known precisely where to kick to cause the most pain.

Still, Lee tried one more trick. One that neither Doreli nor Burke, nor even Erin, seemed to notice.

He held his breath while Doreli tied his hands behind his back. For all the good it would do, he had no idea, since Doreli was tying the rope tightly enough to cut into his wrists. He had to try. He had to hope that it wasn't over for him or Erin just yet.

Not after sharing last night with her. Not now that he had the chance to have her back once again.

No, he couldn't give up. He couldn't give in. He wouldn't. It was as simple as that.

Yet things didn't look good for either of them. Erin, with her hands tied in front of her, and Lee, with his hands tied behind him.

And things seemed to be going from bad to worse as Burke reached down slowly and picked up the gun Lee had dropped. "I think, when the time comes, that it would be ironic for you and Ms. Flemming to die by your own gun, don't you?" Burke asked.

"Yes, I do," Lee agreed, trying to overcome the palpable tension in the small room, trying even more not to show Burke the fear and pain burning through him enough to cause his head to ache.

"It probably won't make a great deal of difference to you, though," Burke added.

With a sudden clatter of footsteps, another one of Burke's hired men came down the stairs in a rush.

"What is it now?" For the first time, Burke sounded irritated.

"The FBI's arrived. Apparently, they were checking every car that arrived here today and they've identified Ms. Flemming's car. They've come to investigate and want to speak with her."

Burke's eyes blazed with anger, but it was the only sign Lee could see that revealed any of the man's emotions.

Lee enjoyed it, despite his own desperate situation. "The FBI," he taunted. "Why don't you show them in? We'd love to speak with them. Wouldn't we, Erin?"

He shifted his gaze to her, taking in her shocked expression. She nodded. "And after we've explained why my car is here, Mr. Burke could explain why these art treasures are in this room," she added.

"Shut up," Burke snapped, his angry gaze burning into Lee. Burke, however, was the first to look away. To the second man, he said, "I'll be up to deal with the FBI in a moment."

"Yes, sir," the man said, leaving as quickly as he arrived.

Burke turned his attention to Lee and Erin once more. "The FBI," he said, his voice cold and harsh and as tight as a garrote.

Lee would have rather the man yelled and ranted and raved. At least that behavior would be more predictable than this.

"You've brought the FBI down on me in my own home. I assure you, you will both pay for that mistake," Burke threatened in that same frightening voice. "Mr. Doreli, keep them down here until the FBI have gone. I suppose I shall even allow them a search to get them off my back. There are quite a few guests upstairs. When you take this pair out, make sure it's done so that no one sees them. I won't be able to supervise, and I want it done right." He glanced at Doreli. "If there is any trouble, I'll have your head on a platter. Do you understand?"

"Yes, sir."

"Take them back to Chicago and finish this once and for all. Then take them to the middle of the lake and put them with Ms. Flemming's friend, Mr. Jenkins. She seemed so eager to see him on the pier. Why I ever thought Jenkins trustworthy enough to be in my employ, I'll never know," Burke muttered under his breath before turning away.

Erin gasped at Burke's words. Lee didn't make a sound, trying to keep his heart from racing in his chest. They were getting close to the end, and there was still nothing he could do. His hands were tied. He felt like kicking himself. He should have called Tom. He should have trusted his friend. But now it was too late. The only thing he could hope for was that Tom would get the report of Erin's car being identified or that the FBI could help them.

A moment later, Burke was gone, leaving Jimmy Doreli standing there, holding his gun on them.

"I could always scream," Erin ventured. "That would get the attention of the FBI."

Jimmy Doreli only moved the barrel of the gun and pointed it at Lee. "Go ahead," he said with a cold smile. "I'll shoot your lover in his good leg. And I suppose it's true that someone would probably hear the shot. But you know, guns go off all the time while they're being cleaned or simply by accident. True, I'd have to act like an idiot when I confess that my gun accidentally went off. Then I'd have to show my permit to carry it, and it could become a big hassle.

"Of course," he continued bitingly, "there is always the chance that even though they may hear the shot, they won't be able to find this room. In either case, they wouldn't be of any help to you or to Mr. McGrey."

Erin clamped her mouth shut.

Doreli leaned up against the wall casually, still smiling, still holding his gun steady. "You may as well get comfortable. It's hard telling how long we'll have to wait before we can leave."

Lee found himself suddenly caught in the heat of Erin's gaze across the small room. Slowly, she moved, stepping around the sculpture she stood against to get to him.

"No," said Doreli, straightening slightly.

Lee wondered if Doreli was taken off guard more by the look that passed between him and Erin, or if it had merely been Erin's movement.

Doreli motioned to Erin with his gun. "You stay over there." He turned to Lee. "And you stay over there. You're not getting close, where you can scheme together."

Erin flashed Lee another heated look before giving in and staying where she was. Slowly, she sank to sit on the cool, earth floor.

Lee looked at Doreli, holding the gun, standing so sure of himself. With his hands tied behind his back, Lee doubted he could reach the man before Doreli could shoot both him and Erin.

Doreli saw Lee looking at him, and his smile only grew. He knew exactly what Lee was contemplating. "Come on," he beckoned. "Try it. Let's see how fast you can run with your leg in the shape it's in."

Lee could hardly stand on it now, even though the pain Doreli had caused was slowly fading. "Go to hell," Lee finally got the chance to say. Then, he, too, sat down to wait.

He looked at Erin, her knees drawn up, her head resting against them. Lee wished he could hold her, sit close to her and offer her some assurance that they would get out of this alive. But he couldn't. Besides, it would be a promise he wasn't sure he could keep.

Minutes later, Lee found this to be the hardest wait of his life. Sitting on the cold floor with an even colder gun pointed at him and the man with his finger on the trigger just itching to pull it, Lee thought he might just lose his mind. No waiting game in all his years of being a cop, not even the past long months of healing and therapy after the shooting, had been this bad.

And Lee knew it must be just as bad, if not worse, for Erin. At least Lee had had years of training and experience to prepare him for the bad situations. Erin had only reported them, seeing them secondhand, hearing about them from witnesses. He doubted she had ever lived through anything as shattering as this.

"Are you all right over there, Erin?" Lee finally gave into the urge and asked quietly.

"Yes," she said. "You?"

"Be quiet," Doreli ordered.

"I'm fine," Lee replied, ignoring Doreli, not even so much as looking at him. Instead, he looked only at Erin and gave her a small smile, the only assurance he could from across the room.

"I said be quiet," Doreli said, this time a bit more forcefully.

The room grew quiet again, except for Lee's loud, frustrated sigh. Seconds grew into minutes, and Lee had no idea how many slow, agonizing minutes ticked by.

He did, however, notice that Doreli was watching Erin again. The very thought that that thug wanted to put his hands on Erin burned in Lee's gut. He tried to push the rage aside and use it to his advantage. While Doreli was otherwise occupied, he slowly, silently, struggled against the rope that bound his wrists together behind his back.

And all the while, he mentally called out to Erin. *Erin, do you know that I love you? Do you know that I have since the first moment I met you? Do you know that I always will?*

He could only hope that somehow she would be able to read his mind.

He should have told her last night. He should have told her this morning during Mrs. O'Malley's hearty breakfast, or later in the car. Hell, he should have told her the moment he opened his front door to find her standing there. Now look at the two of them, he thought, his hope fleeing him. He might never get the chance to tell her.

It could have been hours, or merely long, exaggerated minutes, until Burke returned. He came down the narrow, hidden stairway, still wearing his perfect dark suit, his boots heavy on the wooden stairs. Only this time, he wore a flushed, frustrated, annoyed expression to go along with it. Lee would have liked to laugh, but he didn't think that would go over well, so he kept his silence.

"The FBI have finally gone," Burke muttered through gritted teeth. "And now it's time for you to leave, as well. I will not bid you goodbye, for I'm grateful to be rid of you. Get them out of here, Mr. Doreli. Mr. Raimmey is waiting out back in the van and will drive for you. Call me as soon as everything is taken care of so that I may celebrate with a glass of champagne."

Burke left without another word.

Silence hung in the air in his aftermath.

Doreli broke it. "You heard him. Let's go. On your feet." Grabbing Erin by the arm, he roughly hauled her to her feet.

Lee cringed at the sight of Doreli's hands on Erin's soft skin. Lee vowed that somehow Doreli would pay slowly and painfully for putting his hands on her. But all in good time. This wasn't over yet.

With his gun constantly at their backs, Doreli maneuvered them up the narrow stairs and once again into Burke's deserted office.

"One peep out of either of you," he warned, "and I shoot McGrey in his other leg."

"You seem to like that threat," Erin observed quietly.

Standing in the empty office next to Lee, with Doreli holding them at gunpoint, Erin leaned against Lee. It felt good just to have her brush her arm against his. She was so warm, so real. So alive. And Lee was going to do whatever it took to keep her that way. He only wished he could tell her somehow. He promised himself that if they ever got out of this alive, he would never again put off telling anyone anything. But now, all he could do was give Erin's arm a slight rub with his own.

"I do like that threat," Doreli responded. "Very much. You might keep that in mind before you open your mouth again. And as for you—" he glared at Lee "—if you try anything stupid, I'll hurt your girlfriend. Understand?"

Better than you know, Lee thought. Yet he merely nodded, not trusting his voice should he choose to open his mouth. If and when Lee got the chance, Doreli was going to pay for all of this. For all the threats. For knowing just what threats to use to keep them both in line. Yes, he was going to pay. Big time. A moment later, before they left the plush office, Lee asked, "Doesn't it bother you that you're nothing more than Burke's gofer?"

"Shut up."

"But think about it. All you do is take orders. You stay loyal, you do whatever the head honcho tells you. But the FBI is watching him. And sooner or later, they're going to find something to pin on him. Do you think he's just going to 'fess up and go to jail to do his time like a naughty little boy going to bed without his supper? No, he's going to name names. Yours will probably be first on his list. Why, do you ask? Because you've been so loyal, that's why," Lee persisted. He had no idea if any of this was getting through to Doreli, but at this point he was willing to try almost anything.

Doreli stopped pushing them toward the door. "I said shut up."

Maybe Lee was getting to him. Lee pushed on. "I've seen it a million times. Hell, in my job, I protected men like Burke who ratted on their men. Burke will expect you to do all his time for him. And the state will actually protect him in order to get his testimony," Lee said. "He's so slimy, he'll probably even point his finger at you and make a deal with the district attorney so fast when the time comes that you won't even know what hit you. And while you're rotting away in a cell doing his sentence for him, he'll be free and clear, wasting no time moving some other dumb clod into your position—"

Doreli hit him with the butt of his gun. Lee saw it coming, but ducking was about all he could do with his hands tied. Erin tried to help, too, by throwing herself at Doreli. But neither action stopped Doreli from slamming the butt of that gun into the side of Lee's face.

God, that hurt.

Almost more than what Doreli had done to his leg.

The pain of it left him dazed. He was hardly aware of Erin clutching his arm with her bound hands. Her voice, however, rang through his head like a church bell.

"No! No! Don't hurt him! Let me help him." Erin helped him to his feet. "Just lean on me, Lee."

Lee leaned on her. He couldn't help it. He couldn't fight the pain of what must be thousands of tiny explosions going on in his head and still stay on his feet at the same time.

Doreli hurriedly ushered them down the rear stairs and into a waiting van. Lee moved along, leaning on Erin, blinking against the new wave of pain Doreli's blow had just given him, hardly aware of his surroundings. In the van, there were no back seats. Just when Lee had nearly regained his bearings, Doreli shoved them into the hard, empty place. Leaving them to land as they would, he slid the door closed and climbed into the front passenger seat. A man Lee assumed was Raimmey sat behind the wheel.

As they drove away from the house, Doreli shifted in his seat and turned toward them. "You might as well get comfortable for the ride. It will take a few hours to get back to Chicago."

Lee's head pounded with a headache that he thought could kill a horse, but at least he could focus again as he pulled himself into a sitting position against the wall of the van. Erin struggled up, moving to sit close to him.

"Why not just take us to the river? It's closer," Lee forced out, trying to hide the fear he could feel welling up inside him, threatening to spill over, as the pain in his body ebbed.

"Don't give him any ideas, Lee," Erin snapped.

"And take the chance your bodies will wash up on the shore so close to Mr. Burke's house? I don't think so," Doreli answered. Yet he was looking at Erin again as he spoke.

Lee mentally cursed him. The man might as well put a stamp across his forehead that read "I want that woman."

Well, Doreli wasn't going to have her. Not while Lee was still alive.

Lee slowly shifted, again working the rope binding his hands. Was it his imagination, or were they just a bit looser? Slowly, while trying to relax his muscles and give himself all the room possible, he continued his efforts.

Doreli was probably too intent on Erin and the upcoming excitement, and he didn't seem to notice.

Lee moved faster.

Doreli shifted again, saying something to the driver that

Lee couldn't hear. Lee concentrated on the rope. Freedom was close. He could feel it. Taste it.

Yes, the knot in the rope was loosening. Another few moments, and he would be free.

But then, with Erin's words, everything came to a sudden, complete halt. Everything.

"Lee," she said softly, leaning close enough to him to entice him with her soft scent, "I love you."

Chapter 10

Erin had to tell Lee. She had to tell him everything. If time was running out for the two of them—and it definitely seemed to be—she had to tell him while she still had the chance.

Telling him she loved him had thrown him off guard. She could tell by the look in his eyes, in the frozen expression on his face. He looked as though he didn't believe a word she'd said. He looked as though she'd just dropped a jug of ice water down the back of his shirt.

So Erin said it again. "I do love you. Really."

"Erin—" he began, his hoarse voice hardly more than a whisper.

"Liam, please," she cut in, "let me talk. Let me say everything I want to say before you stop me. I'm afraid that if you don't let me say it now, I may never get the chance."

"You still might, you know," Lee murmured. "This isn't over yet."

"I know it isn't," she said, totally ignoring the two men in the front of the van, concentrating completely on Lee. His handsome face was now marred with a huge, darkening bruise left by Jimmy Doreli. But his black eyes sparkled. Erin wished she could simply get lost in those mysterious depths. "I'm just afraid that if I do get the chance some time later to say everything that I feel needs to be said, I won't be able to find the courage."

She paused for a long moment, never taking her eyes off Lee. She fought the urge to take his face in her hands and kiss away the pain she knew he must be feeling still. Even more, she wished she could simply erase all the pain he had experienced in the past eight months.

"You?" Lee questioned, not looking at her, "without courage? I don't think I'd believe it even if I saw it."

Erin couldn't help but give him a little smile. "I'd like to cut out Doreli's heart for what he did to you," she said softly.

"You have to get in line, honey."

Lee shifted, rubbing the length of him up against her. Erin didn't move, feeling the strength in the muscular body that brushed up against her. More than ever, she needed those strong arms around her, just as much as she needed to put her arms around him. But she couldn't, and she knew he couldn't, either, so she didn't move.

"I wanted to tell you that it was stupid of me to leave without talking to you when you asked," Erin began.

"What?" he asked. "Erin, that's over and done with. Why bring it up now?"

"Because I'm sorry for all the wasted time, that's why," she said simply, still feeling as though she could get lost and be safe in those eyes. But then she'd always felt that way.

"But your reasons for leaving were justified," he reminded her. "So forget it." He brushed up against her again.

"Oh, don't I know it," Erin replied wryly. "What I didn't know was the fact that leaving didn't really change any of them. Leaving didn't ease the loneliness or take away the worry." She tossed a glance at Doreli in the front seat. When she saw he wasn't watching them, she pulled and twisted against the rope that held her hands tied. "It only made them worse.

"Oh, I'll be the first to admit," she went on after a slight pause, "that I thought I was doing the right thing, but all I was really showing was my own selfishness."

Doreli glanced over at them. Erin stopped struggling against the rope. Waiting a moment for him to turn and once again face the front, she then continued working at the binding on her wrists.

And she quietly continued with her confession. "After I left you, things didn't get easier, only harder. It was like a vicious cycle. I poured myself into my job to try to find some satisfaction like I had when I was with you, only it wasn't enough. So I would spend even longer hours at the job, but it still wasn't enough. I was so lonely, I couldn't stand it."

"Lonely?" Lee prompted. "How could you be lonely? You were meeting so many new people, weren't you?"

"Yes. But I was still the loneliest person on the face of the earth." She paused and looked at him. "Because you weren't there to share it with."

Lee tensed again. Erin could feel it. She could see it in his expression. He was so easy for her to read sometimes. It was one of the things she loved so much about him. Easy at times, a complete mystery at others, making him so complex to her she wanted to spend the rest of her life studying him.

Too bad the rest of her life was nearly reaching its end.

"I should never have been so quick to leave," she finished.

"You weren't that quick, remember?" he asked. "You were with me at the hospital."

"I should never have left to begin with," she returned.

"But your unhappiness with me might only have gotten worse," Lee offered quietly. "And sooner or later, you would have come to blame me for it. I've seen it happen to other guys I work with."

Would she have? Erin had no idea. She only knew that she shouldn't have left him, that she shouldn't have wasted all that time she could have spent with him. And now she had no one to blame but herself. "No, leaving you was a bad decision. I began to question more and more if doing my job was the way I wanted to spend the rest of my life. When this Jenkins business came up, I had already decided to take a leave. I needed to take another look at myself." The entire time Erin talked, she was working to loosen the rope that bound her.

"Quit that."

Erin lifted her head to find Doreli watching her closely, looking again as though he would like nothing more than to devour her whole. Drawing on every ounce of courage she possessed, she stared at him hard, but at the same time, she quit fighting against the rope.

Doreli finally turned away.

"Are we going to get out of this?" she asked quietly. The last thing she wanted to do was give up. But, boy, their chances didn't look good. And with every passing minute, she knew they were just that much closer to death. Granted, it was two against two, but her and Lee's hands were tied and the gun Doreli held on them made things as unfair as they could get.

"We are if I have any say in it," Lee said, causing her to wonder if he had something up his sleeve. Knowing

Lee, he probably did. She was certain when he said, "Keep talking, Erin."

"What?"

"Just keep talking."

"What are you doing, Liam?" she whispered.

"Never mind. Just talk some more."

"About what?" she asked, suddenly feeling at a loss for words. She had already emptied her heart to him.

"It doesn't matter," he muttered.

Doesn't matter? It was enough to cause her to wonder if anything she'd said so far mattered. "Have you even listened to anything I've said?" she asked, feeling just a bit perturbed. Here she was thinking the end was so near. What was he doing? And what was he doing every time he rubbed against her?

Hard telling, but he wasn't exactly listening to her, she suddenly realized. And he probably wasn't going to listen much to whatever more she kept talking about, either.

"Of course I have. Tell me more about how lonely for me you've been," he said.

"Why should I?" she whispered. "So you can feed your growing ego?" How could she have been so stupid to admit all those feelings, to put her heart on her sleeve, when he wasn't even paying attention?

Lee looked squarely at her, making her feel naked and vulnerable, even more vulnerable than when Doreli pointed his gun at her. "Erin," he said, "for nine months now, I felt as though I've done little more than try to keep from thinking about you."

His admission shook her to her very core, letting her know that while she'd been letting go of her heart, taking the chance that he could take it and crush it in his bare hands, he really had been listening. True, she thought she could read him so easily. But she would have never known what he just told her. It was one of those mysterious aspects about him, she supposed. "Really?" she asked without thinking.

"Yes, really," he confirmed. The tender expression that suddenly crossed his face reached right out and grabbed her heart.

"But what about when I came to the hospital?"

"It was too hard to talk to you. It's why I never called you, even though I must have thought about doing it a million times. I was feeling as helpless as a baby sometimes because I couldn't get up and get my own glass of water. I didn't want you to see me that way. But the truth is, there hasn't been one day go by that I didn't want you or think of you or see something to remind me of you."

"I feel the same way," she whispered. "Night after night, I would lie awake, remembering what it was like to sleep next to you. Sometimes, I would wander around the house and try to come up with a good reason for even being there. I mean, the place should have felt like home. But it didn't. Not like the home we shared. It was just a place to eat when I had to and sleep when I could."

"That's pretty much how our house became after you left."

Erin searched his eyes, seeing the truth of his words in them. "It's not our house," she returned. "It's your house."

"It's always been our house."

"And you stayed there," she added. Lee's words seemed to hang in the air, just waiting for her to reach up and take them into her soul. She remembered the few days before, when she'd knocked on his front door. It hadn't been at all as if she was coming to visit. It had been as though she was coming home and she had merely forgotten her key.

"I guess secretly I was just waiting for you to return. God knows I should have sold the place after the shooting.

I sure didn't need any extra stairs to climb. I can't tell you how many times I slept on the couch to avoid them,'' Lee explained. ''As well as to avoid our bed,'' he murmured, keeping her gaze caught in the warmth of his.

Lifting her bound wrists, Erin reached over and placed a gentle hand on his arm.

''Oh, Liam, why did it have to take this to bring us back together?'' she asked, feeling tears in her eyes again. Blinking against them, she was determined never to let Jimmy Doreli and that thug with him see her cry. It was bad enough that she had let tears fall when Doreli had hit Lee. And she hadn't even been aware of those tears until she had Lee once again on his feet and moving.

''Fate works that way sometimes,'' Lee simply replied.

''Well, we are not going to die. We're not going to let Doreli kill us,'' Erin vowed. ''We just can't. It's as simple as that. Not now that the same fate has brought us back together again.''

Lee merely offered her a sad smile.

''You're up to something, aren't you?'' she whispered.

''Just be ready for anything,'' he warned.

Erin wasn't sure whether it was the hard way he said the words or the way he continued to smile as he spoke them, but her heart picked up speed. ''For what?''

''What are the two of you sweethearts talking about back there?'' Doreli demanded, turning to them, cutting off any reply Lee might have been about to give her. ''You wouldn't be vowing endless love for all the eternity you'll soon be spending together, now would you?''

''We were just discussing which one of us wants to kill you most,'' Lee replied evenly. ''Since we can't decide, we're probably going to have to flip a coin when the time comes to ending your pitiful life. You wouldn't happen to have a quarter we could borrow, would you?''

"Oh, God, Liam..." Erin couldn't believe Lee had just said those words to a man with a gun.

Doreli undid his seat belt with a snap and spun out of the seat, bending low to stalk into the back of the van, coming toward them like a panther on the prowl.

"Oh, boy," Erin muttered under her breath. "Now you've done it." She had complete confidence in Lee, complete trust, but seeing Jimmy Doreli approaching him with murder in his eyes and a gun in his hand, didn't do much for one's confidence.

Doreli ignored her, his attention glued solely on Lee. "I've had about enough of your smart mouth. I think I'll just shoot you right here and now and toss you out into the nearest muddy ditch."

"But then you'd either have to tell your keeper you didn't do the job according to his specifications, or you'd have to lie. Which do you suppose would be worse when it comes to dealing with a man like Forest Burke?" Lee asked innocently.

Erin closed her eyes for a brief moment, thinking that to Lee it probably wasn't going to make much difference. He was going to be dead either way. She wished she could think of a prayer—any prayer—but her mind drew a blank. All she could come up with was a mental *please, God, oh, please.* The tiny hairs on the back of her neck were standing up, and a fear unlike any she'd ever felt in her life churned in the pit of her stomach.

Doreli drew closer, a look of pure hatred and uncontrolled anger in his dark, cold eyes. Erin thought it was a shame that his vicious expression was probably the last thing they'd ever see.

Her heart racing, her breath trapped in her throat, Erin began to work even harder at freeing her hands. Doreli had reached them, and whatever was going to happen was going to happen in the next second or two.

Erin didn't want to be tied up when it did.

And it came even sooner than she expected.

One moment, Lee was sitting beside her. The next moment, he was on his feet, struggling with Doreli, fighting for control of Doreli's gun.

The action took Doreli by surprise as much as it did Erin. Lee took advantage of the fact that Doreli was thrown off balance by his move. Smoothly, he swung Doreli around, trying to sweep him off his feet and get the gun out of his hand at the same time.

But Doreli nimbly avoided falling and made a graceful landing.

"He must have had dance lessons as a kid," Erin muttered.

Doreli would have been able to keep his balance easily if Erin hadn't stuck out her foot and tripped him. He fell to the floor near her, but the gun stayed in his hand.

Lee, still holding on, went down with him, and the struggled continued.

The driver gave the wheel a snappy jerk, causing the van to swerve. "Hey! What's going on!" he yelled.

The sudden swerving was enough to toss Erin sideways. But she hardly had time to dwell on it because the man's shout was lost in the loud crack that filled the van when Doreli's gun went off. Erin screamed against the rush of air she felt and realized the bullet had gone right past her cheek and into the wall of the van. Thank heavens it hadn't hit Lee or ricocheted, she thought briefly. She was too caught up in the fight between the two men to think much more about it.

The struggle was pretty well even. Doreli wasn't as big or stocky as Lee, but he had the agility of a dancer, giving him the ability to slither like a snake out of any hold Lee could get on him. At one point, the two fighting men rolled over near her. Realizing the gun they fought over was pointed directly at her, Erin reached out with her tied hands and grasped a handful of Jimmy Doreli's hair. In the same moment, Lee pulled him away, leaving Erin holding that handful.

Doreli cried out at the pain of being partially scalped. And the gun when off a second time in reaction. But since Lee had just pulled Doreli away, the gun was no longer pointed at her. The bullet went through the front passenger seat where Doreli had been sitting just moments before.

Lee ground out an oath when Doreli tried to kick him in his bad leg a second time. With that oath came an extra bit of strength needed to pop Doreli smack in the jaw with one fist while trying to get control of the gun with his other hand.

The blow left Doreli momentarily stunned. But the impact of it caused the gun to go off again. This time, the bullet found its mark in something other than the van, as it slammed into the back of the shoulder of the driver who had been yelling on and off over the two fighting men. The driver slumped over the wheel.

"Erin, try and grab the wheel!" Lee yelled as the van veered sharply again.

Erin managed to scramble to her feet, working her hands free of the last of the rope, ignoring the icy cold terror that had long ago settled in the pit of her stomach. But the fear was so strong, so paralyzing, she had to fight against the urge to simply lie down, curl into a ball and hide her face so that she didn't have to watch anything that was happening. Now there was more than the threat of Doreli with a gun. There was the chance they could crash and die.

Erin reached the driver, grasped his shirt and pulled his unconscious body away from the wheel just in time to keep them from colliding head-on into an oncoming car. The blaring horn of the vehicle died away seconds later after it passed them. Still, it was a sound that seemed to freeze somewhere deep in her heart.

Leaving her feeling numb.

Oh, God, that had been so close. And it was the straw that broke the camel's back. She had just had too much terror, too much life-threatening fear to face in the past few hours. It seemed as though her mind was beginning to simply shut down. She wanted to get her foot on the brake to stop the van, but the driver's leg was in the way, his foot still pressing on the gas. Almost automatically, she threw the gearshift into neutral, so at least the van wasn't rolling under engine power any longer.

And everything started happening in slow motion. Erin didn't understand it. Even her own body wasn't responding to the demands her brain sent it. When she'd been concentrating on the gearshift, they had once again swerved across the yellow line into oncoming traffic.

There was another vehicle—a pickup truck this time—coming right at them. Erin had time to notice that it was red, that there were two people in it. It amazed her how much time there seemed to be to see little details, like what make of truck it was and the fact that the man behind the wheel had a beard. At the same time, Erin's hands couldn't seem to move fast enough. It was hard to get them to move at all, to steer the van out of the path of the truck.

They were going to hit one another.

There was even time for Erin to imagine herself flying through the windshield and landing in the cab of that truck. Distantly, she thought she heard Lee yell her name. Again she wanted to close her eyes to it, to not watch. At the same time, she couldn't.

"Oh, Liam," she said out loud, "I don't want to die. I don't want to leave you. Not now. Please, not now."

That was all it took. Thinking of Lee was what she'd needed.

Suddenly, at the last moment, as though the two of them had been playing a game of chicken, Erin spun the wheel to the right, weaving the van away and out of the path of the pickup truck so sharply that it crossed the right lane and continued past the shoulder and off the highway. She felt the bumps, the roughness of the grassy terrain, more than she noticed it with her eyes. She found it was a lot like being on a roller coaster, and she simply rode along, not even bothering to try to steer, just following the track the van chose for itself.

She saw the trees directly ahead and merely watched in horror. Along with everything else, they were still going to crash. Gripping the wheel tightly enough to turn her knuckles white, she turned back toward the left.

For a moment, just a split second, feeling the van turn, seeing the trees sliding past out of their path, Erin felt a sense of relief. They weren't going to crash after all.

But then she realized she'd turned too sharply this time. Combined with the fact their vehicle was top-heavy and the ground was uneven beneath them, the van spilled over, finally coming to rest on its side.

The unconscious driver slammed into the door beside him with a thud, and Erin couldn't stop herself from falling onto him. The groan that escaped him was enough to tell her that Doreli's bullet hadn't killed him. Then the window on the door beneath him broke beneath the weight of the van, popping pieces of glass into the interior and filling the window with the high grass they'd just been driving on.

Erin found it all so strange how one moment, things had been happening in slow motion. Then in the next moment, when the van finally tipped, everything happened in the blink of an eye. It was enough to leave Erin feeling as though the world had suddenly tilted the wrong way and there had been nothing for her to hold on to to keep from falling.

Erin blinked again, trying to focus on just which way was up as she pulled herself away from the driver.

Someone grabbed her arm. It was a strong hand, holding her with the strength of a vise. Erin turned, thinking it might be Doreli, ready to fight with everything she had, with every last ounce of her strength.

It wasn't Doreli.

It was Lee, the fire of his gaze mixing instantly with the fire in her own.

Erin melted into his arms. "Oh, Liam," she breathed.

"It's all right," he assured her. "Doreli's out of commission for a while."

Erin barely glanced behind him, only enough to see Doreli unconscious, resting against the side of the van, which was now the floor. "So is the driver, but he's still alive."

"Are you all right?" he asked, his harsh, whispered words lost in her hair.

"I think so," she replied.

"Hey, are you all right in there?" an unknown voice called from above them.

Looking up, they took in the two men who had climbed onto the side of the van and were trying to slide open the side door.

"We're fine," Lee answered back. "Can you help us out?"

"What about those other two?" one of the men asked. "Look," he went on, noticing the driver, "that one's bleeding. Shouldn't we get him out first?"

Lee quickly grasped Erin's hands. With a gentleness she had only felt in him and no other man, he rubbed the circulation back into them. "No, take her out first. These other two are dangerous and wanted by the police, and I'm not taking them out until they're tied up."

"Dangerous?" one of the men asked cautiously. "Are you a cop or something?"

"Yes, I am," Lee replied, still rubbing Erin's hands. Again, he met her gaze, locking it into the heat of his. "Protecting a witness they wanted to get rid of."

"Does this mean you're back on the job for good?" Erin asked softly.

"Yeah, well…" he began, unable to find an appropriate reply. He turned toward Doreli. "Go on out now. Your head is bleeding."

"It is?" Erin had been so caught up in Lee, in the fact they were still alive, she hadn't even noticed. Slowly, hesitantly, she reached up and touched the tender place at her hairline just above her temple. She couldn't remember when or how or on what she had hit it. Bringing her fingers down once again, she stared blankly at the trace of blood she saw there.

"Erin," Lee said, giving her a small shake and pulling her out of the shock that was settling over her at the sight of her own blood.

"Yes?" She looked up at him once again, his dark, hot gaze grounding her as nothing else could. Yet it didn't last. It seemed to her that as soon as her gaze touched his and he knew she was all right, he looked away.

"Go out now. See if you can find someone with a mobile phone to call the police. Then try to get a hold of Tom and tell him where we are and what's going on. I'm afraid if these two don't call in soon enough, Burke will disappear. And keep pressure on that cut on your head," he instructed, all the while avoiding her gaze.

Erin wanted to force him to look at her. She wanted to confront him, make him see that he'd gotten them through this with nothing more than a cut or two, that he was still as good as he'd ever been. That he could be even better as a cop than he was before, limping or not. But he was already gently pushing her aside, toward those men who were reaching down to her. "Go on," he said.

She tried to stand, careful of the uneven wall of the van beneath her feet, while Lee moved to tie Doreli with the same rope that had been on Erin's wrists. The two men above her reached down and helped lift her out.

By the time Erin found a mobile phone and called the police, Lee, with the help of other Good Samaritans who had stopped after seeing the van crash, had Doreli and the driver out of the van. Lee had taken their guns and, despite the fact both men were out for the count, had tied them both up.

The police arrived a moment later. Erin thought there was even more chaos after that. The police didn't trust Lee, even after he turned the guns over to them. The questions never stopped, at least until Alex Kaffel showed up.

Alex was everything an FBI agent should be, Erin thought. Rough, tough, and so determined to do his job that he appeared to be a man carved in stone. He brought in with him a sudden air of tension.

"What are you doing here?" Lee asked, his voice harsh.

"I decided there would probably be more action where you're concerned, McGrey," Alex replied. "So as well as continuing to watch our mutual friend, Forest Burke, I was keeping an eye on you. Or trying to, at least. You're not an easy man to keep track of. I found it very interesting when Ms. Flemming's car showed up at Burke's today. Not that I was surprised. I knew you could never stay out of my investigation. What did surprise me was that neither of you were there when we searched. Then when I heard the call come over the radio for dispatch to check out a Liam McGrey in connection with this accident," he said, "I thought I'd better get here. Are you guys all right?" he asked, looking from Lee to Erin.

"None the worse for wear," Lee muttered, looking as though he could never trust Alex Kaffel.

"I figured you were both at the bottom of Lake Michigan after the mess we found at your house. And you're damned lucky you aren't. You should have stayed out of this," Alex said.

"And how long do you think we'd have had to stay in hiding, waiting for Burke to make a move if Erin, if I hadn't forced him into it?" Lee asked. His voice was calm, but Erin could feel the tension radiating from him. "Not to mention that Burke's men came after us first, remember?"

Alex gave him no reply.

"What about the cops who were watching my house?" Lee asked finally.

"They're alive," Alex replied. "Barely, but the doctors do expect them to recover. Do you think Burke's men just took a chance that you were there?"

"There's a rat in the Specialists Division office. I figure that rat did a little too much squeaking," Lee revealed.

"And do you plan on taking care of that rat?" Alex asked.

"Yes, I do."

"Well," Alex went on, his attention drawn to the men Lee had tied up on the ground, "it looks as though you've done my job and caught Doreli for me."

"Yeah," Lee muttered. An ambulance arrived then, and Lee led Erin to it. "Take a look at her head," he said to the first paramedic who approached.

"Sit down right here, miss." The paramedic guided her to a seat, looking at her head as he spoke.

Lee turned to go back to Alex. He was still avoiding Erin's direct gaze. And Erin had had enough of it. She reached up and grabbed his hand. "Don't leave me."

It was enough to force him to look at her. The tender

way his gaze met hers was warm enough to melt ice. "I won't." And he held on tightly to her hand as the paramedic expertly bandaged her head.

She refused to go to the hospital for stitches, but promised to see her own doctor as soon as she got the chance and go right to the hospital should she have any problems such as blurred vision.

Alex Kaffel came back to them just as the paramedic was finishing up. "We were finally able to get a hold of your partner, Tom Weatherby. We're moving in. He's on his way to Burke's house right now. And so am I."

Lee straightened. Erin could feel the way he tensed up by the way his hand tightened on hers. "I want to be there when Burke's taken down."

"I kind of thought you would. I'll take you. But I want you to stand clear. This is an FBI operation."

"I'm going, too," Erin said.

Both men looked at her.

"Well, it's me he wanted to kill to begin with. You don't expect me just to walk away now and watch from a distance, or, heaven forbid, read all about it in the newspaper, do you?" she asked. "I want to see him arrested. I deserve to see him arrested."

"Fine," Alex agreed. "And McGrey?"

Lee met his gaze. "What?"

"I know how you feel about me, and you have every right to feel that way. When I make a mistake, I admit it, and I made a mistake when it came to your witness getting shot. I never meant for any of it to happen."

Lee said nothing as he held Alex's gaze.

"Anyway," the agent went on, "I just wanted to say that we probably couldn't have flushed Burke out without your help. And I know you don't trust me—"

"I trust you enough to go with you now," Lee countered.

Alex offered him a slight smile. "Then let's finish this."

"That sounds good to me," Lee said.

Erin was trying to rest in the back seat of Alex's car, but Lee could see it wasn't easy for her. She looked as keyed up as he felt.

Yet his anxiety had nothing to do with catching Burke. True, he wanted the slime put behind bars. He could even admit to himself that he would have liked to see him tortured, see him experience pain, for all that he had put Erin through—for all he had put them both through.

That wasn't, however, why he was feeling as though his insides were tied in knots. It was because of what Erin had asked, that one little question that had said so much. "Does this mean you're back on the job for good?"

Yes, he was a cop. It was all he would ever be. He could face that.

What he couldn't seem to face just now was the fact that in dealing with Burke and Doreli—and protecting Erin—he'd had a big taste of what it meant to be "back on the job again." A big enough taste to know he wanted to eat the whole cake.

What he didn't know about was Erin. If he was back on the job for good, did that mean she was gone again? True, she'd said a lot of things in the back of that van, but did she still feel the same, now that she was safe? Because his being a cop in Special Division might very well mean he'd be gone for days or weeks at a time. Just like before.

He didn't know what he'd be going back to. The uncertainty scared the hell out of him. Even after he finished telling Alex everything he and Erin had been through—about Burke and his secret, hidden room and the art treasures—after facing the realization of just how close the two of them had come to losing their lives, the uncertain future still weighed heavily on his mind. Was his job worth his love for Erin? Would he be forced to choose?

Even Erin's hand, when she gently reached over the front seat and touched his shoulder, didn't come close to pulling the weight off him so he could breathe.

"Liam, are you sure you're all right?" she asked softly.

"I'm sure," he replied, hating himself for the brisk, quick way he put her off in front of Alex, as well as for the lie in those two short words. However, Lee doubted he could tell her how he felt, even if he'd been alone with her.

The future terrified him, and that terror was mixing with the dull ache that had returned to his leg. The pain had been there ever since Doreli had kicked him. It was an ache that couldn't be relieved by the aspirin he'd gotten from one of the paramedics. Lee closed his eyes for a brief moment, knowing there was little that would ever relieve it. At the same time, he fought to keep from remembering the past two nights with Erin and how the pain had vanished.

As the now-familiar town of Jamesbrook came into view, he did his best to push everything from his mind except the thought of meeting up with Forest Burke again.

Alex Kaffel drove through the open gate and into Burke's wide, circular drive. Cars, expensive and luxurious cars, were parked everywhere, and Alex stopped among them. He and Lee climbed out and Lee opened the back door for Erin.

The look he gave her said, "We don't have to do this, you know."

The look she gave him back said, "Yes, we do. So let's go. Let's see this finished."

As though to confirm that look, Erin reached out and took his hand.

Her gentle touch was nearly his undoing. He felt torn

between the desire to pull her into the heat of his embrace and hold her so that neither of them would have to face Forest Burke again. He wanted just to keep holding her, holding her tightly enough so that she wouldn't even begin to speak about being lonely, tightly enough that she couldn't leave him. He wanted her to melt in his arms and become a permanent part of him.

At the same time, he wanted to push himself away from her so that she couldn't hurt him again. Because want her or not, he wasn't sure he could ever trust her. He wasn't sure he even wanted to try.

He did nothing. Nor did he speak. There was no way he could get a word past his tight, painful throat. He merely gripped her hand, feeling the gentle softness of her own, and followed Alex to the front door.

Several men in uniform joined them, as did men in suits—FBI agents.

The same maid who had offered them champagne opened the door to them. Her shock at seeing so many men, some in uniform, was apparent in her silence.

"We're here to see Mr. Forest Burke," Alex Kaffel said, holding out his badge so she could see it.

"I'm sorry," she stammered, trying to find her voice, not knowing which man she should be looking at. "Mr. Burke is in the middle of an auction and can't be disturbed."

"We have to disturb him anyway," Alex said.

He pushed his way past her and strode into the large foyer, and the maid wasn't able to stop him. In the room where the auction was being held, all noise, all motion, everything, stopped when Alex, the uniformed officers and FBI agents in dark suits stepped into the room.

Burke stared down at them from the platform where he stood behind the podium. "Officers," he addressed them, never losing his formality, "how can I help you? Surely you haven't come to place a bid. I'm not sure what an officer makes these days, but I doubt he can afford what these people are bidding.''

Before Alex could reply, Lee, still holding Erin's hand and taking her with him, stepped into the room. His cold, hard, unforgiving gaze met Burke's with the force equal to a gunshot. "I'd like to bid on that painting," he said, his voice now able to get past this throat, but sounding like nothing more than slivers of ice slicing through the air.

"You?"

The shock on Burke's face was so genuine, so revealing, so uncontrolled, that Lee wished he'd brought a camera along.

"You didn't think you'd be seeing us again, did you?" Lee challenged quietly. He pulled Erin close to him, showing Burke that the two of them were both safe from the thugs Burke had ordered to kill them.

"H-how…" Forest Burke stammered, staring from Lee to Erin and back to Lee.

"You can ask Jimmy Doreli," Lee said, "since the two of you will be in jail together."

A hushed murmur went through the room. One man in the back called out, "What's the meaning of this?"

But he turned silent when Alex Kaffel stepped forward and held up his badge. "Forest Burke?"

"Yes?" Burke said, the word sounding hardly more than a croak.

"I'm Special Agent Alex Kaffel with the FBI. You are under arrest for conspiracy to commit murder, for theft, smuggling and kidnapping. You have the right to remain silent…"

Forest Burke looked like a whipped puppy in an expensive suit, Lee realized suddenly as he stood next to Erin and listened to Burke being read his rights. Gone was the arrogance, the confidence, the coolness, the self-control. His tanned face was suddenly pale, his body slumped in defeat. There was a brief moment when he looked at Erin and Lee with cold hatred, just as he had when he'd ordered them killed. But that look slipped away with the snap of the handcuffs that Alex Kaffel put on his wrists.

"Gerald," Burke said to a man in the front row, who was as shocked as all of the others in the room, "please contact my lawyer as soon as possible."

"Yes, Mr. Burke," the man replied.

Alex pulled him toward the door. Near Lee, Burke paused. "You'll be sorry for this," he threatened. "Some day, the cat in Ms. Flemming will run out of lives."

"I'm adding your threat to that list," Alex barked.

Lee never said a word. There were so many things he would have liked to say that he didn't have time to make up his mind which was first. Like, "Have a nice stay in prison." Or, "If you ever come after Erin or me again, you won't have the law to protect you. Threaten us again, and there's no place on earth you can hide."

Then that quickly, Forest Burke was taken away.

That quickly, it was over. Erin was safe.

Lee's job was done.

Chapter 11

"Let me give you both a ride back to Chicago. Going back by helicopter is bound to be much faster than driving," Tom Weatherby said. "There's not much more you can do here. The FBI is in charge now."

Hours had passed, hours filled with waiting for a search warrant then Erin and Lee showing the police the hidden room, hours filled with a complete, thorough search of Burke's house, hours filled with calling in experts to identify the recovered stolen art.

Lee looked out Burke's open front door at Erin. She leaned up against her car, which still remained out there, her arms crossed. She looked weary as hell.

"That sounds great," Lee muttered, never taking his eyes off Erin. "Except that we need to drive Erin's car back to Chicago, too."

"I like your suit," Tom said.

Lee chuckled. "Thanks."

"Are you going to start wearing one to work?"

"Not even in your dreams," Lee replied.

"So you really pretended to be art lovers?" Tom said, his voice filled with amusement.

"Yeah," Lee muttered.

"Would you have stayed for the auction?"

"If it came to that," Lee replied with a slight shrug.

"So you're still doing things your way."

"I guess so."

"And I suppose you'll never change."

"I guess not."

A long moment of comfortable silence passed between the two men. "What about Erin?" Tom asked, joining Lee and looking out at her.

"I don't know," Lee answered honestly.

"Don't you?" Tom asked. Before Lee could even think of a reply to that question, Tom went on, "I think you know more than you think you know. Your only trouble is, you don't know what to do with what you know. And—" he paused "—if you let her walk away a second time, I'd think you were twice the fool, Lee. Just to give you fair warning, I'm going to be calling you in a few days, when you've had a chance to recover from all of this. We need to talk about your place at the department."

"I don't know if I can come back to work for good," Lee said.

"Then you're a bigger fool than I thought. Because nobody can do the job better than you can." Tom started to move toward the front door.

Lee reached out and grasped his arm, stopping him. "Not until you get rid of the two-faced leak in your office."

"Who?" Tom asked in surprise.

"Henshaw," Lee informed him. "Gordon Henshaw. He was in the office when Erin and I came to see you. He talked to me. Then later, we heard Burke call his contact for information on us. I pressed the redial. Henshaw answered.''

Tom's eyes narrowed, the only outward sign of the anger that flashed through him. "I'll take care of it today."

"Tom," Lee said, forcing himself to look into Tom's eyes, "I'm sorry."

"What for?"

"I didn't call you because I thought you were the leak."

"Some of this was probably my own fault. I should never have met you at my office where anyone could see you and Erin." He took a step away before turning back again. "I'll be calling you." Tom walked past him and out the front door without another word.

His words left Lee feeling as though there was a sudden tornado ripping through his insides. He watched Tom approach Erin. Tom said something to her, and Erin smiled at him and replied. But they were too far away for Lee to hear anything that was said. Not that he'd be able to concentrate on any of it anyway. Tom's words had left him with mixed emotions.

Lee tried to swallow past the lump in his throat. At the same time, he forced his legs to move and take him out of Burke's house forever. He was going to face Erin. To face his uncertain future—at least in regard to her.

Yes, she'd admitted so much to him in that van. She had even gone so far as to tell him she loved him. But their lives had been at stake. His own past had taught him that people say a lot of crazy things they would never otherwise say when their lives were in danger. Things they wouldn't necessarily say at any other time.

Despite what she thought, he had heard every word of it, too. And every word had lodged in his heart.

Tom climbed into a waiting car with another Special

Division officer and Lee waved before turning to face Erin. He knew he could handle being in a car with her for the hours it would take to get back to Chicago.

He hadn't left her alone through any of this. He wouldn't start now. He knew he could handle staying close to her despite the wild emotions churning around inside him at the thought of Tom calling him. He might as well accept it. He couldn't have both Erin and his job.

"I'll drive," Erin offered.

"No, I'd rather," Lee replied, climbing behind the wheel. Concentrating on driving would be much better than just sitting beside her, feeling her heat.

They passed O'Malley's bed-and-breakfast place, and Lee tried not to look at it. He could feel the intensity of Erin's gaze, and he avoided it like the plague. He worked to keep his eyes and his thoughts on the highway before them.

"You're awfully quiet," Erin observed.

"Yeah."

"Do you want to talk about it?" she asked.

"No."

He heard her sigh, but he looked straight ahead.

"I never really thanked you for keeping me safe," she began slowly. "And I suppose a thank-you isn't even sufficient, really."

"You're welcome."

"So what was Tom talking about when he said he was going to call you?" she asked. "He mentioned something about that before he left."

"It's something about the job, what I'll be doing and where I'll be doing it," he said.

"That's great," she enthused. "You probably should have been back before now."

"I wasn't ready. They offered me a desk job months ago, and I refused it."

"Oh, yes," she said, her voice dripping with sarcasm, "I remember hearing about that. You let your ego and your pride stand in the way."

"Would you just let it go!" he snapped. "It's none of your business."

But, boy, he wished it was. He wished he could share this decision with her just as he wished he could share the rest of his life with her. But he didn't know what her plans were. After making love to her last night, he'd promised himself he wouldn't let her leave again, wouldn't let her walk away from him. Now, however, in the light of day, he didn't have the foggiest idea how to keep her from doing just that.

He could tell her he loved her, but he remembered saying that before, as she stood in the foyer with her suitcase in her hand, and it hadn't stopped her then. So he didn't think it would be enough to stop her now.

"Fine," she said, turning her head away.

That was great, he thought to himself. For all he wanted her to stay, he was sure doing his best to push her away.

Still facing the window, she shifted in the bucket seat and leaned her head back. A short time later, Lee stole a glance at her to find her sleeping. He felt himself wanting to do the same and promised himself that as soon as he got home, he would. The only problem was, he wanted to do it beside Erin.

The miles slipped by. Erin slept until Lee stopped for gas at a convenience-store gas station. He could use his credit card without worry now, so he filled the tank and got them both a cup of coffee.

"Would you like me to drive for a while?" she offered again before he got back in.

"No, I'm fine, and we don't have all that much farther to go." Driving kept his mind off other things. He climbed back behind the wheel. And the rest of the way home, whatever conversation transpired between them was nothing if not short and sweet.

There wasn't much for him to carry in once they reached his house. His leg was aching more than ever, and he wanted only the comfort of a hot shower and his bed.

"How's your head?" he asked her, just inside the door.

"Fine," she replied.

"You're not seeing two of anything, are you?"

"No. But I am seeing a mess," she remarked as they stepped into the kitchen.

There was still glass everywhere, holes in the cabinets and evidence of the police investigation. Lee uttered an oath, having completely forgotten about this disaster.

"We could always call your cleaning-service friends," Erin said with a grin.

"That's sounds like a good idea. I'll do it after I take a shower and a nap," he said.

"I like the sound of that," Erin replied.

"I thought you'd be wanting to pack," Lee blurted out. It was time to stop beating around the bush about this. He had to face up to it sooner or later. Putting it off was just putting off the pain.

"Oh," she said as though she'd just remembered. "I guess," she said.

Was he mistaken or did he hear reluctance in her voice? And why was she still standing there, not rushing off to pack?

"How come you never asked me to stay?" she demanded suddenly. "How come you never said anything at all?"

Lee had the impression that if she hadn't asked it so

quickly, she might have changed her mind about asking all together.

"I said I loved you," he said honestly. "I also asked you to talk this out with me. You said there was no more to say. How come you never asked me to stay home more often? How come you never let me know just how much it was bothering you?"

"I knew what your job meant to you," Erin explained. "I know what it still means to you."

And look what happened to that job when you left, he thought ruefully. "Maybe you should have asked. You might have found you meant more to me than the job," he said, letting go of his own past. "I didn't know so much of it was bothering you. We talked about so much, but never that."

He met her gaze for the first time, and was taken aback by the tears he saw filling her eyes. The room was quiet for a long moment.

"I want to stay here, Liam. With you. I want to come home again," Erin said.

Lee stared at her for a long moment, his throat so tight he wasn't able to get a word through it. This was his dream come true, to have her back with him again. But he wouldn't accept it. Slowly, he shook his head. "I don't know," he said.

"Don't know what?" she whispered.

"I don't know if I can trust you."

"You didn't trust Kaffel, either, but you gave him a second chance and worked with him in taking down Burke. I'm asking for a second chance, too."

"Why?" Lee asked. "So you can leave me again when you start to worry too much or when you're lonely because I'm off doing my job—a job that I love? So when you go, you can take my soul with you again? I won't let you do that to me a second time. I'd rather you walk away right now, Erin. Hell, I'd rather get shot again than feel the pain of that. Because being a cop is what I am. It's all I am. That's not going to change.''

The tears were spilling down her cheeks. Lee tried to ignore them. ''Liam, if this has taught me anything, it's that there can be danger anywhere, not just in your job. Yes, I'll probably worry about you, and I'll be lonely when you're gone. But I'll be safe. We'll keep each other safe. And I'll be loved. I hope. That's what's most important....''

''You've always been loved,'' Lee said. ''And if there's one thing I've learned through all of this, it's that you always will be. By me.''

Lee was suddenly touching her, and he couldn't remember even moving. His hands on her arms, he gently turned her to face him. Cupping a gentle hand beneath her chin, he gazed warmly into those shining green eyes.

''You'll stay with me? You won't leave?'' he asked.

Slowly, she shook her head. ''I won't leave,'' she replied.

''Will you marry me?'' he asked.

''Marry you?''

''I've got a ring upstairs that I've had for nine months,'' he said.

''Really?''

Lee nodded. ''I want the whole nine yards with you, Erin. I want complete commitment. I want what Tom has—wife, home, possibly kids, family. It's what I've always wanted. With you. Who knows, maybe we'll even get a dog, a real big watchdog.''

It was enough to make her giggle despite the tears that still spilled over onto her cheeks. Lee chuckled and wiped them away gently with his thumb. "Don't cry. It tears my heart out when you cry."

"I can't help it."

Pulling her against him, he cradled her against his chest. "It doesn't matter where we are or what we have as long as we're together and you never leave me again."

"Never..." she promised.

"And if you ever decide to," he whispered into her hair, "just shoot me first. I've experienced both. Your leaving is definitely more painful and harder to live with than being shot."

"Okay," she agreed.

"Does this mean that you'll marry me?" he had to ask.

"Yes, I'll marry you."

They were both quiet for a long moment.

"You know," he whispered, "we could take a shower and a nap together. Then start cleaning this mess up tomorrow. We'll also need to see about cleaning up your dad's house. I'd hate for him or one of your brothers to pop in for a surprise visit and find it that way."

"That sounds absolutely wonderful," she replied, fitting up against him like a puzzle piece that was made just for him.

Lee woke some time later only to find Erin snuggled up against him in what was once again their bed. The pain in his leg was gone.

Despite the mess he knew was still waiting downstairs, Lee thought everything was in its proper place. He was in bed with Erin beside him, both snug under the quilt Erin had taken out of the guest bedroom, the quilt that had been on this bed before she'd left. On the nightstand stood Cupid, the symbol of their love, propped up between the lamp and the phone, his broken arrow pointed at them. True, he was damaged, but like the two of them, he had endured. Their love continued and that was what was important. He was in his rightful place. So was Lee. So was Erin.

Here.

Together.

Now. And forever.

Lee pulled her closer and held her in his warm embrace meant for all eternity.

* * * * *

1

Morgan Brigham slowly set down his coffee cup on the kitchen table and stared at the comic strip in the center of his paper. It was nestled in among approximately twenty others that were spread out across two pages. But this was the only one he made a point of reading faithfully each morning at breakfast.

This was the only one that mirrored *her* life.

He read each panel twice, as if he couldn't trust his own eyes. But he could. It was there, in black and white.

Morgan folded the paper slowly, thoughtfully, his mind not on his task. So Traci was getting engaged.

The realization gnawed at the lining of his stomach. He hadn't a clue as to why.

He had even less of a clue why he did what he did next.

Abandoning his coffee, now cool, and the newspaper, and ignoring the fact that this was going to make him late for the office, Morgan went to get a sheet of stationery from the den.

He didn't have much time.

Traci Richardson stared at the last frame she had just drawn. Debating, she glanced at the creature sprawled out on the kitchen floor.

"What do you think, Jeremiah? Too blunt?"

The dog, part bloodhound, part mutt, idly looked up

from his rawhide bone at the sound of his name. Jeremiah gave her a look she felt free to interpret as ambivalent.

"Fine help you are. What if Daniel actually reads this and puts two and two together?"

Not that there was all that much chance that the man who had proposed to her, the very prosperous and busy Dr. Daniel Thane, would actually see the comic strip she drew for a living. Not unless the strip was taped to a bicuspid he was examining. Lately Daniel had gotten so busy he'd stopped reading anything but the morning headlines of the *Times*.

Still, you never knew. "I don't want to hurt his feelings," Traci continued, using Jeremiah as a sounding board. "It's just that Traci is overwhelmed by Donald's proposal and, see, she thinks the ring is going to swallow her up." To prove her point, Traci held up the drawing for the dog to view.

This time, he didn't even bother to lift his head.

Traci stared moodily at the small velvet box on the kitchen counter. It had sat there since Daniel had asked her to marry him last Sunday. Even if Daniel never read her comic strip, he was going to suspect something eventually. The very fact that she hadn't grabbed the ring from his hand and slid it onto her finger should have told him that she had doubts about their union.

Traci sighed. Daniel was a catch by any definition. So what was her problem? She kept waiting to be struck by that sunny ray of happiness. Daniel said he wanted to take care of her, to fulfill her every wish. And he was even willing to let her think about it before she gave him her answer.

Guilt nibbled at her. She should be dancing up and down, not wavering like a weather vane in a gale.

Pronouncing the strip completed, she scribbled her signature in the corner of the last frame and then sighed.

Another week's work put to bed. She glanced at the pile
of mail on the counter. She'd been bringing it in steadily
from the mailbox since Monday, but the stack had gotten
no farther than her kitchen. Sorting letters seemed the least
heinous of all the annoying chores that faced her.

Traci paused as she noted a long envelope. Morgan
Brigham. Why would Morgan be writing to her?

Curious, she tore open the envelope and quickly scanned
the short note inside.

> Dear Traci,
> I'm putting the summerhouse up for sale. Thought
> you might want to come up and see it one more time
> before it goes up on the block. Or make a bid for it
> yourself. If memory serves, you once said you wanted
> to buy it. Either way, let me know. My number's on
> the card.
>
> > Take care,
> > Morgan
>
> P.S. Got a kick out of *Traci on the Spot* this week.

Traci folded the letter. He read her strip. She hadn't
known that. A feeling of pride silently coaxed a smile to
her lips. After a beat, though, the rest of his note seeped
into her consciousness. He was selling the house.

The summerhouse. A faded white building with brick
trim. Suddenly, memories flooded her mind. Long, lazy
afternoons that felt as if they would never end.

Morgan.

She looked at the far wall in the family room. There
was a large framed photograph of her and Morgan standing
before the summerhouse. Traci and Morgan. Morgan and
Traci. Back then, it seemed their lives had been perma-

nently intertwined. A bittersweet feeling of loss passed over her.

Traci quickly pulled the telephone over to her on the counter and tapped out the number on the keypad.

*　*　*　*　*

Look for TRACI ON THE SPOT
by Marie Ferrarella, coming to
Silhouette YOURS TRULY
in March 1997.

At last the wait is over...
In March
New York Times bestselling author

Nora Roberts

will bring us the latest from the Stanislaskis as
Natasha's now very grown-up stepdaughter,
Freddie, and Rachel's very sexy brother-in-law
Nick discover that love is worth waiting for in

WAITING FOR NICK

Silhouette Special Edition #1088

and in April
visit Natasha and Rachel again—or meet them
for the first time—in

The Stanislaski Sisters

containing TAMING NATASHA
and FALLING FOR RACHEL

Available wherever Silhouette books are sold.

NRSS

SILHOUETTE... Where Passion Lives

Order these Silhouette favorites today!
Now you can receive a discount by ordering two or more titles!

SD#05890	TWO HEARTS, SLIGHTLY USED		
	by Dixie Browning	$2.99 U.S. ☐	/$3.50 CAN. ☐
SD#05899	DARK INTENTIONS		
	by Carole Buck	$2.99 U.S. ☐	/$3.50 CAN. ☐
IM#07604	FUGITIVE FATHER		
	by Carla Cassidy	$3.50 U.S. ☐	/$3.99 CAN. ☐
IM#07673	THE LONER		
	by Linda Turner	$3.75 U.S. ☐	/$4.25 CAN. ☐
SSE#09934	THE ADVENTURER		
	by Diana Whitney	$3.50 U.S. ☐	/$3.99 CAN. ☐
SSE#09867	WHEN STARS COLLIDE		
	by Patricia Coughlin	$3.50 U.S. ☐	
SR#19079	THIS MAN AND THIS WOMAN		
	by Lucy Gordon	$2.99 U.S. ☐	/$3.50 CAN. ☐
SR#19060	FATHER IN THE MIDDLE		
	by Phyllis Halldorson	$2.99 U.S. ☐	/$3.50 CAN. ☐
YT#52001	WANTED: PERFECT PARTNER		
	by Debbie Macomber	$3.50 U.S. ☐	/$3.99 CAN. ☐
YT#52008	HUSBANDS DON'T GROW ON TREES		
	by Kasey Michaels	$3.50 U.S. ☐	/$3.99 CAN. ☐

(Limited quantities available on certain titles.)

TOTAL AMOUNT	$_____
DEDUCT: 10% DISCOUNT FOR 2+ BOOKS	$_____
POSTAGE & HANDLING	$_____
($1.00 for one book, 50¢ for each additional)	
APPLICABLE TAXES*	$_____
TOTAL PAYABLE	$_____
(check or money order—please do not send cash)	

To order, complete this form and send it, along with a check or money order for the total above, payable to Silhouette Books, to: **In the U.S.:** 3010 Walden Avenue, P.O. Box 9077, Buffalo, NY 14269-9077; **In Canada:** P.O. Box 636, Fort Erie, Ontario, L2A 5X3.

Name:_____

Address:_____ City:_____

State/Prov.:_____ Zip/Postal Code:_____

*New York residents remit applicable sales taxes.
Canadian residents remit applicable GST and provincial taxes.

Silhouette®

SBACK-SN3

FORTUNE'S Children™

Bestselling Author

MAGGIE SHAYNE

Continues the twelve-book series—FORTUNE'S CHILDREN—
in **January 1997** with Book Seven

A HUSBAND IN TIME

Jane Fortune was wary of the stranger with amnesia who
came to her—seemingly out of nowhere. She couldn't deny
the passion between them, but there was something
mysterious—almost dangerous—about this compelling
man…and Jane knew she'd better watch her step….

MEET THE FORTUNES—a family whose legacy is greater than
riches. Because where there's a will…there's a *wedding!*

Look us up on-line at: http://www.romance.net

FC-7

Harlequin and Silhouette celebrate
Black History Month with seven terrific titles,
featuring the all-new *Fever Rising*
by Maggie Ferguson
(Harlequin Intrigue #408) and
A Family Wedding by Angela Benson
(Silhouette Special Edition #1085)!

Also available are:
Looks Are Deceiving by Maggie Ferguson
Crime of Passion by Maggie Ferguson
Adam and Eva by Sandra Kitt
Unforgivable by Joyce McGill
Blood Sympathy by Reginald Hill

On sale in January at your favorite
Harlequin and Silhouette retail outlet.

In February, Silhouette Books is proud
to present the sweeping, sensual new novel
by bestselling author

CAIT LONDON

about her unforgettable family—*The Tallchiefs.*

TALLCHIEF FOR KEEPS

Everyone in Amen Flats, Wyoming, was talking about
Elspeth Tallchief. How she wasn't a thirty-three-year-old
virgin, after all. How she'd been keeping herself warm at
night all these years with a couple of secrets. And now one
of those secrets had walked right into town, sending
everyone into a frenzy. But Elspeth knew he'd come for
the *other* secret....

"Cait London is an irresistible storyteller..."

—*Romantic Times*

Don't miss TALLCHIEF FOR KEEPS by Cait London, available
at your favorite retail outlet in February from

COMING NEXT MONTH

#769 RENEGADE'S REDEMPTION—Lindsay Longford
Royal Gaines was on the edge. Why else would he agree to track down some lowlife's ex-wife and kid...for a price? But when he located innocent Elly Malloy and her adorable son, he realized they'd all been had. Now he would do anything to protect them...and redeem himself in their eyes.

#770 SURRENDER IN SILK—Susan Mallery
Seven years ago Zach Jones trained Jamie Sanders to survive in a man's world. And she'd learned well, becoming the best spy in the business. Now she wanted a normal life, wanted to feel like a *real* woman. But could the only man she'd ever loved see her as wife material?

#771 BRIDE OF THE SHEIKH—Alexandra Sellers
Minutes from becoming a newlywed, Alinor Brooke was kidnapped from the altar—by her *ex*-husband! Sheikh Kavian Durran claimed they were still married, that Alinor had ruthlessly deserted *him* years ago. But Alinor remembered differently, despite Kavian's claims. And then the truth became startlingly clear....

#772 FRAMED—Karen Leabo
Detective Kyle Branson was playing with fire. He'd grown too close to suspected murderess Jess Robinson, and now his job—his very life—was on the line. Because though he believed in Jess's innocence, he couldn't deny that her closely guarded secrets threatened them both.

#773 A CHILD OF HIS OWN—Nancy Morse
Though Dory McBride was wary of rugged drifter Ben Stone, she hired him as her handyman. There was something about his soulful expression that had her aching to heal his lonely heart. But the closer he grew to Dory and her young son, the more she suspected Ben's true motives for entering her life.

#774 DARE TO REMEMBER—Debra Cowan
Devon Landry thought she'd put her dad's death—and a broken engagement—behind her. Until she learned the images stirring in her mind were actual *memories*...of her father's murder! Lead investigator Mace Garrett knew he had his work cut out for him—especially when he learned the star witness was the woman who'd thrown him over!

invites you to meet the folks of

a brand new mini-series
by
Marilyn Tracy

ALMOST, TEXAS, a small town where suspense runs
high and passions run deep, and a hazard-free
happily-ever-after is *almost* always guaranteed!

It all begins with
ALMOST PERFECT
(February 1997)

A drifter has hired on at widow Carolyn Leary's ranch.
Pete Jackson may be handsome as sin and know his
way around horses, but the loner is just a might too
handy with a gun. What's his secret? And does
Carolyn even want to find out?

Be sure to look for other stories set in this unforgettable
town, coming later in the year—only from
Silhouette Intimate Moments.

AT